The new Ze_____the cover is a p_____The fashionable_____th a satin or ve_____rant nosegay. Us_____uried in design from the elegantly simple to the exquisitely ornate. The Zebra Regency Romance tuzzy-muzzy is made of alabaster with a silver filigree edging.

A PENCHANT FOR PASSION

"I should hope I always conduct myself with propriety, my lord," she said, her cheeks flushing.

Lucien smiled. "I doubt if you even know the meaning of the word," he murmured, his hands dropping to her narrow waist as he drew her firmly against him. "You are the biggest virago it has ever been my misfortune to encounter."

"And you, sir, are the greatest bully I have ever met," she returned. She knew she should step back, or at least demand that he end their quasi-embrace. But the ability to speak seemed to have fled along with her common sense.

"Then 'twould seem we are well matched," he murmured huskily. His lips came down on hers in a kiss of searing demand.

The feel of his mouth against her own shocked Elly, a shock that quickly escalated into delight as desire swept through her. "Lucien . . ." She whispered his name against his lips, her arms twining about his neck to hold him closer still . . .

DISCOVER THE MAGIC OF REGENCY ROMANCES

A Spirited Bluestocking
Joan Overfield

ZEBRA BOOKS
KENSINGTON PUBLISHING CORP.

This book is dedicated to
Tatiana Virginia Eldore.
A new life, a new beginning.

ZEBRA BOOKS

are published by

Kensington Publishing Corp.
475 Park Avenue South
New York, NY 10016

First printing: April, 1992

Printed in the United States of America

Prologue

He was back again. Mrs. Magney watched from the shadows, her dark brows beetling in disapproval as the tawny-haired man crept down the hallway towards the south turret. He'd been here many times this past year, always appearing at moon's rise and leaving at dawn's light. It seemed to her he had been coming more oft of late, and she had to admit 'twas comforting to share her long watch with another, even though he was unaware of her.

Her thin lips moved in a silent smile to think of the start she would give him were she to step out of the darkness and make her presence known. Like as not the poor lad would leap clear out of his skin and run screeching from the house; people would stare at him afeared, and ask him if he'd seen a ghost. A dry chuckle rose from her at what his answer would be.

The man stopped and whirled around, a pistol clutched in his gloved hand. "Who is it?" he called out, lifting the lighted torch he held in his other hand a little higher. "Who is there?"

Mrs. Magney shrank back slightly, and the flickering circle of light swept past her dark corner. The man waited a moment longer and then shook his head.

"You've been at this ghost business too long, my boy," she heard him mutter. "You're even starting to spook yourself."

She waited until his footfalls died away before

5

emerging from her hiding place. Change was in the air; she could sense it, and she knew full well what that meant: people. People coming into her nice clean house and making a mess as they always did. Mayhap she would give this new lot the benefit of the doubt, she thought, nervously fingering her chamberlain's keys. Having a master or a mistress to do for might be nice for a small while, provided her orderly house wasn't disturbed.

Yes. She gave a brisk nod. That is what she would do. She would keep hidden for a wee bit, and if she liked them she'd let them stay. But if she didn't like them . . . Her ebony-flecked eyes took on a malicious sparkle, and she vanished into the dark, endless shadows of the deserted house.

Chapter One

London, 1813

"What do you mean he said no?" Lord Lucien Wendon, marquess of Seabrook demanded, his dark brown eyes flashing with fury as he glared at his solicitor. "My God, has he any idea of the condition that pile of stones is in?"

"I . . . that is to say, I believe he does, my lord," Mr. Sailing stammered, nervously dabbing his upper lip with his handkerchief. "Both their solicitor, Mr. Ballert, and myself were quite blunt as to the condition of Seagate, but it didn't seem to have the slightest impact. Indeed, she said that after having spent the last two years living in a tent even a tumbled-down Gothic ruin would seem as a mansion to her."

"Her?" Lucien leapt on the telling word, his dark eyebrows gathering in a threatening scowl. "Do you mean to say that you never even saw Denning? That you discussed this with his wife?"

Mr. Sailing looked affronted. "I should say not, my lord!"

"Good."

"She is his sister."

"His . . ." Lucien's voice trailed off, and he erupted into a spate of strong language that had the poor solicitor quailing in fear. He wasn't usually so short-tempered with those in his employ, but given the seriousness of the situation he felt his anger was more than justified. Devil take it, he cursed silently; he had to have that house.

"Double it," he ordered tersely, rising from his desk to stalk over to the window.

"My lord?" Mr. Sailing looked confused.

Lucien swung around to glare at him. "My offer on Seagate," he said. "I want you to double it."

"Double it!" The solicitor looked as if he would swoon. "But — but my lord, that is lunacy! The house is one step above a stable! Granted the land has some value, but —"

"Are you presuming to question my orders?" Lucien interrupted, his voice soft with menace. "Because if you are, I might remind you there are other solicitors in London. I trust you take my meaning?"

Mr. Sailing's plump cheeks paled at the veiled threat. "Indeed, my lord," he said fervently, "and I can assure you that I will do everything within my power to assure that your offer is given the utmost consideration."

"I do not wish it 'considered,'" Lucien retorted coldly. "I want it accepted; the sooner, the better."

Mr. Sailing licked his lips anxiously. "That . . . that could be a problem, your lordship."

Lucien stiffened at the trepidation in the solicitor's voice. "What do you mean?" he asked, more curious than annoyed.

"Well, it is Miss Denning," Mr. Sailing said, relieved his employer's fearsome temper now seemed under control.

"What of her?" Lucien demanded, brushing the matter aside with an impatient wave of his hand. "Denning is the heir; concentrate on him, and the devil with his sister."

"But that is precisely the problem, my lord!" Sailing wailed. "Mr. Denning may well be the heir as you have indicated, but 'tis plain as a pikestaff that 'tis

8

Miss Denning who rules the roost! And just as well, if you want my opinion."

"Oh?" Lucien was surprised by the other man's candor.

Mr. Sailing nodded. "I did speak with him upon my arrival," he confessed in a confiding manner, "and rather rough going I found it, too. To quote my late father, the lad is so heavenly minded he's no earthly good! Every other word out of his mouth was Latin, and all he could speak of was his precious plants! Had Miss Denning not been there to make some sense of his speech I would have thought him quite queer in his upper stories."

Lucien rubbed his chin as he considered what he had just learned. "An apeleader, is she?" he asked, his sharp mind turning to thoughts of Miss Denning and the best way of handling her.

"And a bluestocking," Mr. Sailing supplied eagerly. "She was throwing Shakespeare and Milton at my head when she wasn't spouting Latin at her brother."

"What does she look like? Is she pretty?" Lucien demanded, the beginnings of a plan forming in his mind.

Mr. Sailing's shrug was more eloquent than words. "Attractive might be a better description. Pale eyes, light brown hair, and a rather fine figure, although she is too thin to be considered in the fashionable mode. But she does have a delightful smile," he added with an eagerness that in no way fooled Lucien.

"And where are they residing?"

"Belgravia," Sailing supplied. "They are currently staying with their aunt, a Mrs. Thomas Shaftson, wife of the MP for Dorestone. I am sure you have not heard of him, but—"

"A Whig, and an intimate of Wilberforce," Lucien provided, displaying the knowledge he was usually careful to keep well hidden. At the solicitor's look of amazement he shrugged his broad shoulders. "He had occasion to contact me at the House of Lords," he

9

said by way of explanation, remembering the rather earnest politician who had petitioned him on behalf of a constituent.

"Ah." Sailing looked relieved. "Well then, perhaps it might be advisable if we were to approach Mr. Shaftson," he said. "As a politician he will see the generosity of your offer, and I am sure we may rely upon him to advise his niece properly."

"It is obvious you know little of the Whigs," Lucien returned, a slight smile on his well-shaped lips. "But if it will ease your mind, by all means contact the man. I am sure it will do no harm, and in the meanwhile, I believe I shall call upon the Dennings myself."

"A personal appeal," Sailing said, more relieved by the second that his rather difficult employer had seen fit to take charge of matters himself. "I daresay it will prove most efficacious."

Lucien's smile grew more pronounced. "Oh, I certainly hope so, Sailing," he drawled. "I certainly hope so."

"Eureka!" Mr. Henry Denning dashed into the small book-lined sitting room, his dark blue eyes bright with excitement. "I have found it, Elly! I have found it!"

"I am well aware of what 'eureka' means, Henry," Miss Elinore Denning returned, carefully setting her quill in its stand before raising her eyes to study her brother's flushed countenance. "Now, kindly be so good as to tell me what it is you have found. The rest of our baggage, I hope?"

"As if I should give a jot for a bunch of old shirts and the like," Henry's indignant sniff put an end to Elly's faint hopes. "No, this is what I found, *rosa arvensis*," and he laid a half-opened flower on the center of her desk.

She picked up the fragile blossom, her annoyance fading at the sight of the delicate pink petals beaded with dew. Her eyes closed in pleasure as she lifted the flower to her nose and inhaled its sweet fragrance.

" 'That which we call a rose by any other name would smell as sweet,' " she quoted, carefully laying the rose back on her desk. Although not a botanist like her brother and their late father, she did love plants, and treating them with the utmost care was almost second nature to her.

"Eh?" Henry retrieved his precious specimen. "What was that you was saying, Elly?"

"Shakespeare, Henry." Elly shook her head at him in tolerant exasperation. "I was quoting Shakespeare."

Henry looked puzzled for a moment and then snapped his fingers. "Oh, that play-writing fellow you're always going on about," he said, giving his sister a beatific smile. "Well, mayhap if we are lucky you shall meet him while we are in London. You did say something about going to one of his plays, didn't you?"

"*Othello,*" she replied, not bothering to explain that it would be highly unlikely for the playwright to put in an appearance at this particular performance. "Now, if you are done interrupting me, I really must get back to work. There is a great deal to be done if we hope to have Seagate opened by the end of the month."

Henry's handsome features gathered themselves into a frown of Byronic proportions. "I still don't see why you are going to all this bother," he grumbled in faintly accusing tones. "We shall only be selling it in a few months when we return to Africa."

Elly glanced down at her ledger, her eyes refusing to meet his as she fiddled with her papers. "It is as I have already explained," she began, her tone sharp, "Cousin Bevil allowed the house to fall into a shocking state of disrepair, and we shall have to work very hard if we hope to find a buyer for it. No one would give us so much as a brass farthing for it the way it is now!"

"Lord Seabrook offered us three thousand

pounds," Henry pointed out in one of his rare flashes of acuity.

Elly's gray-blue eyes narrowed at the hated name. Although she had yet to meet the marquess of Seabrook, she already regarded him as her personal nemesis. "How many times must I tell you that whereas one must never buy a pig in a poke, neither should one be so foolish as to *sell* one!" she replied tartly, her full lips thinning into a determined line. "If his lordship offered us three thousand for Seagate, then we can safely assume it is worth twice that. Leave the dickering to me, we both know 'tis my special providence."

"That is so," Henry agreed, thinking of the numerous times when Elly had successfully wrangled with Hottentots and Bedouin chieftains for the necessities of everyday life. In the next moment, however, he was frowning again. "But I still do not see why we had to leave Cape Town and return home in order to settle the matter. What of my work?"

"You may work on your collection here as well as in Africa, Henry, dearest," she said through clenched teeth, struggling to hold on to her patience. "And think of the libraries and the company of other botanists you will enjoy while we are here. Your work can not help but benefit from such contact."

Henry allowed himself to think of it and presently drifted away, images of himself addressing the Oxford Botanical Society filling his mind. The moment the door closed behind him Elly collapsed against the back of her chair, feeling like the most villainous sister to ever draw breath.

Poor Henry, she thought, pushing her papers to one side as she propped her chin on her hands and stared out the window. How was she ever to tell him that they weren't returning to Africa? He might regard this as no more than a temporary visit, but as far as she was concerned, it was permanent. After spending the majority of her life following first her father

12

and then her brother to virtually every corner of the globe, she had had enough. She wanted a home, and for her Seagate was that home.

From the moment she'd opened the solicitor's letter in Cape Town she'd been unable to think of anything else. She'd prodded, threatened, cajoled, and pleaded to get Henry to abandon his field work and return to England, and nothing, she vowed, was going to stop her from claiming the home she regarded as hers. Well, she amended ruefully, Henry's, if one was going to be a stickler for details, but the point was still the same. Seagate was *hers,* and the sooner the grasping Lord Seabrook accepted that fact, the better off they would all be.

After completing her chores Elly presented herself to her aunt's sitting room, where she found the older woman poring over the latest copy of *La Belle Assemblée.* "Ah, there you are, my dear," she said, lifting her cheek for Elly's kiss. "All done?"

"Finally, thank heavens," Elly muttered, dutifully kissing her aunt's cheek. "I had no idea setting up a household could be so arduous! In Africa all we ever needed was a cook, a houseboy, and the occasional snake catcher."

"Ugh!" Mrs. Flavia Shaftson shuddered delicately. "My poor lamb! When I think of the horrors you must have suffered, I vow I could box my brother's ears! What could he have been thinking of to drag a delicately bred girl to such places?"

"It wasn't so very bad," Elly felt duty-bound to defend her late parent. "And really, I have seen far more of the world than most women of my class could ever hope to."

"Which is precisely my point, my dear." Her aunt gave her hand a maternal pat. "Women of our class aren't supposed to see the world. Now, come and tell me what you think of this gown. It is just the thing for

13

you to wear when you make your bows."

Having already lost this particular argument, Elly bent to examine the print indicated by her aunt's slender finger. Fashioned out of watered silk, the gown was a pleasing shade of light blue, with a rounded neckline and tiny puff sleeves that would leave her arms and shoulders bare. It was unadorned except for the double row of flounces above the hem, and Elly sent a grateful prayer winging heavenward. She'd been terrified she would be forced to make her entry into society beribboned and festooned like a ship of the line.

"And I thought perhaps a small cap of soft blue velvet with a single white plume might be just the thing for a lady of your advanced years," Flavia continued, indicating another illustration. "Not so aging as a turban, but more suitable than a deb's curls."

Elly bit back an anguished protest. If she could be said to be vain about anything it was her hair, and the thought of covering her golden-brown tresses with the frivolous head dress quite cast her into the sulks. Still, she supposed it would be best if she bowed to her aunt's superior knowledge of the subject. For all her flightiness, the older lady was always dressed in the first stare of fashion.

"Very well, Aunt," Elly swallowed her objections. "It sounds quite lovely. Thank you."

"You are more than welcome, my dear," Flavia gave her a sweet smile. "But it is more delight than chore for me, I assure you. I have always adored clothes and frivolous things, and I was quite looking forward to having a daughter to take shopping and the like. Unfortunately the good Lord saw fit to bless me with three strapping sons instead." She sighed at the thought of her three boys, the youngest of whom already stood six feet although he had yet to turn sixteen.

Thinking of Flavia's hulking sons made Elly remember her brother, and she gave her aunt a worried

14

look. "What about Henry?" she asked worriedly. "He will be needing a new wardrobe as well, for his clothes are in even a more deplorable condition than my own."

Flavia laid a thoughtful finger on her lips as she considered the matter. "Ordinarily I would have Thomas take him about, but with Parliament in session the poor man has scarce a moment to call his own. And I dare not ask Roderick to advise him," she added, referring to her eldest son recently sent down from Oxford. "Since he has set himself up as a Corinthian, neither his clothes nor his conversation are fit for polite company!" She was quiet another moment and then shrugged her shoulders.

"Well, I must own to being *point non plus!* We shall simply have to study the journals and put our trust in them. Fortunately the lad is an Adonis, and will show anything to its best advantage. Such fine eyes, and his glossy black curls are sure to set the debs to swooning! Lords Byron and Seabrook had best look to their laurels, you mark my words."

Elly's amusement at her aunt's effusive praise of her brother's physical perfection vanished at the mention of the marquess. "Seabrook?" she repeated, a sulky pout forming on her lips. "What has he to do with anything? Never say he is a dandy?" The thought was quite pleasing, as it fit her image of a rich and petulant lord who had nothing better to do than turn a covetous eye towards his neighbor's estate.

"Heavens no!" Flavia was clearly scandalized at the very thought. "Seabrook is one of the most elegant men in the whole of England, as well as being very handsome and highly eligible!"

"Then why did you link him with Byron?" Elly was quite vexed to hear her enemy described in such glowing terms.

"I was being clever," her aunt explained, her cheeks pinking with embarrassment. "It happened when you were out of the country so you would not have heard

15

of it, but it was quite the talk of the town for weeks afterwards."

"Heard of what?"

Flavia cast a furtive glance about her as if fearing French spies were lurking behind the drapes and then leaned towards Elly. "It was almost two years ago," she began in a confiding whisper. "He had been in mourning after his mother's death and had only just returned to the city. He was introduced to a deb, a Miss Haverley if memory serves, and the girl went quite mad for him. She began sending him flowers and notes, and even went so far as to dedicate a poem to him which she called 'The Modern Adonis.' Well, to make a short story of it, there was a dreadful scandal, and Lord Seabrook was forced to flee to the country to escape the taddle!"

"Is that all?" This seemed rather tame fare to Elly, who had been hoping for something truly shocking.

"All?" Flavia stared at her in disbelief. "The poor man could scarce poke his nose out of the door! Every time he ventured out the ladies would surround him, and the gazettes printed the most cruel caricatures! His friends all roasted him about it, and even Byron joined in the fun by indicating he would challenge Seabrook to a duel over the title of Adonis."

Elly felt an unwilling twinge of sympathy for Seabrook, which she quickly pushed aside. If the marquess was overly sensitive to effusive poetry, she supposed she could dash off a few lines that would send him packing. Perhaps a parody of one of Shakespeare's sonnets . . . Her lips curled in an speculative smile.

"That is it!" Flavia's sudden cry made Elly wonder if her aunt possessed preternatural abilities. "The very thing! We shall ask Seabrook to take Henry under his wing!"

"What?"

"He is a Tory, but Thomas assures me he is most understanding," Flavia continued as if she hadn't

16

heard Elly's strangled outburst. "And even Roderick admits that the marquess is a bang-up fellow. You could not hope for a better pattern card."

"But . . . but Aunt Flavia, what about the marquess's attempts to steal — to purchase — Seagate?" Elly protested, horrified at the very thought of exposing poor Henry to a man of Seabrook's stamp. She would rather have him ape the worst tulip of the *ton* than that . . . that person.

"Oh posh!" Flavia cast her an impatient look. "If Henry wishes to sell Seabrook the house, he will, and if he doesn't, he won't. That doesn't mean the two of them can not be friends."

Elly could think of several reasons why they could not be bosom beaus, the primary of which was that her brother was as easily led as a lamb. A wolf like Seabrook would soon have him devoured whole . . . after first fleecing him of his inheritance, she mentally added with growing annoyance.

"I still do not think it would do," she said firmly, using her most commanding tones. "We have never even met the marquess, and it would be too forward by half to ask such a thing of him. I will not have him take us for a bunch of encroaching Cits."

Flavia looked much-struck by this. "I suppose you are right," she said at last. "Seabrook is known for being stiff-rumped at times, and as you say, you would not wish him to take you into dislike."

"I do not care if he loathes us," Elly corrected, her chin coming up with pride. "But I will not have him looking down his nose and treating us like country bumpkins!"

"Oh, I am sure he would not do *that*," Flavia said quickly, although her expression was doubtful. "But if you don't wish Seabrook to assist you, who else is there?"

Elly shrugged. "How am I to know? But if worse comes to worse, I shall simply handle the matter myself. I have been dressing him for the greater part of his life, after all, and in any event Henry never notices what he is wearing."

Flavia nodded her head in sympathy. "Men," she said with a sigh. "My Thomas was the very same way when first we met." And she launched into a glowing description of how she had first met her beloved husband.

As this was a tale Elly had heard many times since her return to London some two weeks ago, she listened only half-attentively, her mind on Seabrook and how she would deal with him. The offers to sell Seagate had begun arriving almost from the moment they'd stepped ashore, but she'd managed to keep them hidden from Henry. Just as she thought she had succeeded, the marquess's man of business appeared on her aunt's doorstep, and before she could stop him he was making his offer to Henry.

Despite her sneering words to the contrary, Elly knew three thousand pounds was more than a generous offer for a house that even her own solicitor had described as "a ruin." For a moment she greatly feared Henry would accept, and managed to distract him by encouraging him to talk of his work. She added further fuel to the fire by sending him off to the garden to find a rose, and in his absence firmly rejected the marquess's offer. She'd like to think that was the last of it, but she was far too wise in the ways of the world to believe that.

Seabrook would not give up so easily, and this time she had the feeling he would come himself. Doubtlessly he thought them a flock of pigeons to be plucked, and she decided she would foster that image. Let him think they had been culled, she thought, her aquamarine eyes taking on a cold sparkle. It would make her victory all the sweeter in the end. And she would be victorious. She had crossed the veldts of Africa, the steaming jungles of the equator, and even the trackless sands of the desert; all before her eighteenth birthday. If a spoiled English lord with the looks of a

18

Greek hero thought to make a May game of her, he was about to learn differently.

Two days later Elly was closeted in her study going over one of her lists when there was a knock at the door, and Clemment, the Shaftson's elegant butler bowed his way into the room. "I beg your pardon, Miss Denning," he began in his wooden tones, "but the marquess of Seabrook has arrived and is asking to speak with your brother."

Elly glanced up in surprise, making no effort to hide her smug smile from Clemment's discerning eye. His lordship had to be even more desperate than she'd realized, she gloated, all but rubbing her hands together in glee. Good. Had their situations been reversed, she'd have left him stewing in his own juices for at least a week before renewing her petition.

"Thank you, Clemment," she replied coolly, eyeing the butler with interest. "Have you informed my brother as to his lordship's arrival? I am sure he will want to know."

Clemment's impassive features did not betray themselves by so much as a flicker. "He is in the library, miss," he intoned stoically. "That is why I thought it best to notify you of the marquess's presence. If you like, I can inform his lordship that Mr. Denning is," he paused delicately, "indisposed."

Elly grinned at the major domo's wonderful sense of discretion. "Indisposed" was as good a word as any to describe her brother's predilection for burying himself in his studies, she supposed. "That might be for the best, Clemment," she replied, glancing at the clock on the mantelpiece and calculating how long it would take her to change into a suitable gown. "Please inform Lord Seabrook that I shall be with him shortly. Oh, Clemment?"

"Yes, miss?"

"Has my aunt returned as yet?"

"No, miss, but I expect her momentarily. I am sure it will be quite all right."

"Very good, Clemment, thank you," Elly said, certain she could count upon the rigidly proper butler to keep her from committing a social solecism. Since her return to England she had been amazed at the restrictions placed on her by the dictates of Society, but she had quickly come to the conclusion that there was little she could do about it. If she hoped to take her place in the rather insular world of the *ton* she knew she would have no choice but to adhere to their rules; however silly she might find them.

After making a few notations on her lists she slipped quickly up to her room, where she began searching her wardrobe for just the right dress in which to make her entrance. She rejected her newer purchases as being too frivolous, and finally settled on one of her older black frocks. Perfect, she decided, studying the dress with satisfaction. If this did not convince the haughty lord that she was a country mouse with no knowledge of the world, then she would eat the wretched thing.

In the parlor, Lucien was waiting with increasing impatience. The news Denning had taken to his bed and he would have to settle for the sister was a set back, but he was determined that he would not allow it to upset the outcome. He'd purposefully waited two days before approaching the Dennings' so as to avoid appearing too anxious. He'd already decided that the best way of obtaining his objective would be to act completely indifferent about Seagate. He would act as if he couldn't care less about the wreck, and then, when he had her quaking in her slippers for fear of having lost out on the sale, he would coolly double his offer. With luck, he would have the matter resolved within the hour.

As he paced the confines of the lavishly-decorated

parlor, he caught a glimpse of himself in the gilded mirror above the mantel, and paused to glance at his reflection. In honor of the occasion he'd donned his new cutaway coat of maroon velvet, and his cravat was tied in a subdued arrangement his valet insisted upon calling "the Seabrook." He'd abandoned his breeches for a pair of nankins, and he'd had his Hessians polished twice before he was satisfied with their glossy shine. Studying himself he decided he looked a perfect tulip, and the realization brought a cold smile to his lips. Good, he thought cynically, let her think him a delicate dandy who could be easily culled. That would put her off her guard and make it that much easier to manipulate her to do his bidding.

He was so intent with his plans for wresting Seagate from its owners, that he wasn't aware the door had opened behind him. Elly stood in the doorway, the cool smile on her lips becoming a smirk at the sight of the handsome man standing in front of the mirror. Arrogant coxcomb, she thought, quickly schooling her features to the proper expression. She would have him packing outside of the hour. She cleared her throat loudly, and watched in satisfaction as he gave a start of surprise.

"Lord Seabrook," she gushed, infusing her voice with as much girlish awe as she could muster. "It is an honor to make your acquaintance! I-I am Miss Denning." And she lowered her eyes, all maidenly blushes and stammers.

Lucien swung around, quickly masking his embarrassment at having been caught staring in the mirror. "Ah, Miss Denning," he said, stepping forward to suavely offer her his hand. "May I say what a pleasure it is to make your acquaintance? Although I hope you will forgive me for calling upon you in such a havy-cavy manner?"

"Oh, indeed not, dear Adon—that is to say, Lord Seabrook," Elly fluttered her lashes for all she was worth. "I am more than happy to meet the

21

man of whom I have heard so much!"

Lucien's eyebrows raised at her near use of the word "Adonis." Doubtlessly she was thinking to disarm him by making reference to that old scandal, but little did she know that the entire fiasco had been a carefully orchestrated ploy so that he could leave town on a mission without raising suspicions.

"I am sorry to hear your brother is unwell," he said, moving judiciously away from her. "I trust it is nothing serious?"

"Oh, just a touch of *Stachys betonica,*" she said, naming one of her brother's favorite flowers and praying the marquess's Latin was as loose as his ethics. "It will pass with time. But pray, will you not be seated? My aunt will soon be returning, and I know she will be wanting to meet our nearest neighbor."

Lucien took the chair she offered, and tried to think of something to say. He was aware that somewhere, somehow, his plans had gone awry, but for the life of him he could not say just how this event had come about. Although he had a strong suspicion his erstwhile hostess had a great deal to do with it. Just what the devil was going on? he wondered, his eyes resting on Miss Denning's heart-shaped face.

On the surface she appeared to be exactly what he had been expecting; a plain country spinster with more breeding than sense. Certainly she looked the part. The ill-fitting black gown she was wearing was almost a decade out of fashion, and made her look far older than her actual years, which he knew to be twenty-four. Her hair, which was a glorious blend of light brown shot through with gold was pretty enough, although it was difficult to tell as she wore it scraped back in a painfully neat bun. Her eyes could also be considered an asset, being well formed and the color of the sea at mid-day; but as she persisted in either casting them down or rolling them at him like the parlor maid in a French farce, he found them more annoying than attractive.

22

Another thing which annoyed him was that she had lied to him. Botany had been one of the few branches of learning at which he'd excelled, and he knew damned well that *Stachys betonica* was a common flowering plant, and not some rare tropical disease.

While he had been studying her, Elly had also been looking her fill of him. Granted her wide-eyed perusal was part of her act as a flustered spinster, but the greater share of it had been vulgar curiosity, and, she admitted with a heavy sigh, admiration. As Aunt Flavia had said, he was a very handsome man.

His carefully-cropped hair was almost the same shade as her own, and it provided a startling contrast to his dark eyebrows and velvet brown eyes. His nose was straight and a touch arrogant, but she rather liked his strong, square chin, and the vertical cleft that divided it. She could see strength and character in that chin, as well as in the shape of his chiseled lips. This was no elegant dandy to be easily brushed aside, she realized apprehensively. This was a man, and a dangerous man at that. She cleared her throat nervously.

"Lord Seabrook, I—"

"Miss Denning—"

They both broke off, looking at each other uncertainly. When he indicated with a wave of his hand that she should go first, she tried again. "Lord Seabrook, I was wondering if you would answer a question for me?"

"If I can," Lucien agreed warily. "What is it?"

Elly cleared her throat again, wondering if she should wait until a more auspicious occasion before asking him why he wanted Seagate. And he *did* want it; she could see it in the depths of his dark eyes. "Well," she began, gathering her courage as she spoke, "I would like to know about Seagate."

"What about it?" His wariness increased ten-fold.

"What does it look like, to begin with?" Elly said, somewhat taken aback by his gruffness. "I've never seen so much as a painting of it, and I must own to

23

being curious about it. It is my ancestral home, after all."

"No, it is *my* ancestral home," he shot back, his lips thinning with annoyance. "It was the country seat of my family for generations until my great-grandfather saw fit to sell it to your great-uncle. That is why I want it back."

Well, now she had the truth, she realized, and wondered why she was still not satisfied. She lifted her chin and regarded him coolly. "Your interest in the matter has been duly noted, my lord," she informed him sweetly. "As, I hope, has my brother's resolve not to sell."

Those dark eyebrows she had earlier admired lifted in a haughty arch. "Your brother's?" he questioned in his most derisive tones. "Or your own? According to my solicitor he seemed far more interested in his plants than in his estate. And for your information, Miss Denning, I speak fluent Latin. Do tell your brother for me that I hope he recovers from his case of wood betony. I have heard it can be fatal if not properly treated."

Elly's cheeks burned scarlet at his hit. "You are rude, sir!" she snapped, too angry to formulate a proper set down.

"And you are a hellcat," he inclined his head in cool mockery. "Tell your brother I will give him six thousand pounds for Seagate, and not one farthing more."

"Six . . ." Such largesse was enough to rock even Elly's iron determination, but only temporarily. She rose to her feet, her hands clenched at her sides. *"Our* home," she said, stressing the word with a cutting smile, "is not for sale. Not for six thousand pounds, not for six hundred thousand pounds! You may think your title and your wealth entitle you to whatever you want, my lord, but you are wrong. Seagate shall never be yours."

Lucien also rose to his feet, his eyes never leaving

hers. "Are you by chance challenging me, Miss Denning?" he asked softly.

She tossed back her head defiantly. "And if I am?" she goaded.

The smile he gave her was as cold and cutting as a blade of ice. "Then I accept, Miss Denning," he replied in a deadly tone. "It will be interesting to see which of us shall emerge victorious." And with that, he turned and walked out of the parlor, leaving an angry Elly to glare after him.

Chapter Two

After leaving Miss Denning's Lucien went directly to his club, where he proceeded to drown his anger in a glass of claret. He didn't partake of strong spirits as a rule, but given his present temper he felt it was the only gentlemanly thing to do. Had he given in to his impulses and done what he really wanted to do, he would have shaken Miss Denning until her prim bun came tumbling down.

Of all the stubborn, willful, obstreperous females, he fumed, lifting his glass to his lips. He pitied her unfortunate brother; it was obvious the poor lad was kept firmly under the cat's paw. First thing tomorrow he would find some way of circumventing the little minx and would make his offer to Denning face-to-face. Not that it would do him much good, he decided bitterly. He doubted the timid scholar so much as wiped his nose without his formidable sister's express permission.

"Ah, Seabrook, I thought I would find you here," Lord Alexander Twyford drawled, his gray eyes sharp with curiosity as he took the chair facing Lucien. "I trust all is well with you?"

"Then you would trust wrong," Lucien grumbled, shooting the viscount a dark look. "Things are in a damned coil!"

Alex looked surprised. "Indeed?" he murmured sympathetically. "What is the impediment then, if I may make so bold? I thought the matter was all but resolved?"

Lucien's response was decidedly profane as he poured some of the claret into a glass and handed it to the viscount. "The impediment," be began heatedly, "is a shrew of a bluestocking who has taken leave to inform *me* that she won't sell back my own house; not even for six hundred thousand pounds!"

Alex sipped his claret thoughtfully before setting his glass down. "You are referring, I take it, to Miss Denning?" he asked, studying Lucien's angry face. At his curt nod he gave an indifferent shrug. "Then I do not see that you should have a problem. It is Mr. Denning who is the heir, is it not?"

"That is what *I* thought," Lucien muttered, partaking of another sip. "But to get to him one must first get past her, and that is not so easy as it would seem. She guards him with the devotion of a eunuch guarding the sultan's harem; I could not so much as get a peek at him!"

"I see," Alex's gray eyes grew troubled. "Well then, the first question to be considered is whether or not her brother shares her passionate attachment to Seagate. Does he?"

"She says he does," Lucien replied, recalling the brief but heated exchange. "But I take leave to doubt her. The lad is a noted scholar devoted to his field-work. Why the devil should he want a tumbled-down house on the outskirts of Brighton?"

"Why indeed?" Alex drawled, rubbing his square chin with his strong hand. "What is your next move to be? I can not imagine your surrendering the field after one skirmish."

Lucien's jaw hardened and his dark eyes flashed with fury. "Never," he vowed grimly. "I am returning to the Shaftsons' tomorrow, and this time I shall meet with Denning even if it means walking over Miss Denning to do it. I must have that house!"

"Agreed," Alex said, his handsome countenance

growing somber. "What contingency plans have you in the event Denning should refuse your offer?"

Lucien hesitated, his dark eyes unable to meet Twyford's ice-gray gaze. "It is somewhat unconventional," he admitted cautiously, uncertain how much he should reveal, "but I believe it shall prove effective. It has in the past."

There was another silence as Alex gave a nod of understanding. "I see," he said at last, giving Lucien a thoughtful look. "Well then, so long as a plan is effective, what more can one ask of it? You will begin immediately, I take it?"

"The moment it proves necessary," Lucien replied, sending him a grim smile. "You must be sure to visit me at Seagate the next time you find yourself in Brighton."

A rare smile touched the viscount's mouth. "Confident, are you?"

"I prefer to think of it as determined."

"I see." Twyford rose to his feet and stared down at Lucien. "Just mind you don't grow too complacent. I am sure I need not tell you what proceeds a fall. Good day to you, Seabrook, and best of luck haggling with Denning. I have the feeling you may have need of it."

The door had scarcely closed behind Seabrook before Elly was giving full vent to her anger. "Odious, puffed-up toad!" she charged heatedly, pacing up and down the confines of the drawing room. "Just let him *try* turning us out of our home! I shall pour burning pitch on his head if he but attempts it!"

In the next moment her temper cooled, and the more practical side of her nature asserted itself. Ideally, it would be best if she could keep Henry ignorant of Seabrook's new offer, but after contemplating various stratagems she discarded that notion as impossible to implement. Her nemesis was nothing if not determined, and unless she was prepared to lock

28

Henry in the attic like a mad relation, there was nothing she could do to keep Seabrook from contacting him. Her only option, therefore, was to inform Henry of the offer herself, but to do it in such a way that he would be certain to refuse.

She was contemplating this dilemma when the door opened and Mrs. Shaftson came scurrying in. At the sight of her niece standing in the center of the room she skittered to a halt, turning her head this way and that as she glanced about. "But where is Seabrook?" she demanded, her brow wrinkling with confusion. "Clemment informed me he had called."

"He did, Aunt, but I am happy to report he has taken himself off," Elly informed her with an angry toss of her head.

"What? But he couldn't have been here above five minutes!" Mrs. Shaftson exclaimed, shooting Elly an accusing look. "You didn't say anything to upset his lordship . . . did you?"

"Me!" Elly's temper flared to life once again. "What about him? Do you know what that . . . that dandy had the audacity to say? He all but *ordered* us to sell Seagate to him!"

Mrs. Shaftson clutched a hand to her bosom, her eyes closing as she sank to the overstuffed chair. "Oh, Elinore, never tell me you have argued with the marquess," she moaned in faint accents. "You can not have been so foolish!"

"And what is so foolish about defending one's home?" Elly demanded, flushing at her aunt's scolding words. "Lord Seabrook was the height of arrogance, and so I took leave to tell him!"

Flavia uttered a shriek and clapped both hands over her ears. "No more, I implore you. I do not think my poor heart can take it! We are ruined."

The piteous words brought Elly up short, and she cast her aunt a suspicious glance. "How do you mean 'ruined'?" she asked cautiously. "What could Seabrook do to us?"

Flavia's hands dropped as she stared at Elly in astonishment. "What could he do?" she echoed weakly. "Upon my word, Elinore, there is no end to what he could do if he were to put his mind to it! He is an intimate of the prince, and the Patronesses at Almack's positively dote on him; a wrong word from him is tantamount to social extinction! Oh, we are ruined!"

"I wish you would stop saying that," Elly grumbled, a faint twinge of remorse pricking her conscience. She was very grateful for the kindness her aunt had shown her and Henry, and she disliked the notion that her actions should cause the other woman any distress.

"Why not? 'Tis the truth!" Mrs. Shaftson retorted, pulling a handkerchief from her sleeve and applying it to her eyes. "Oh, this could not have happened at a worse time! Thomas's cousin's gel is to make her bows next year, and I was so hoping to get her a voucher. Now . . ." She buried her face in the lace-edged hankie.

Elly's sense of guilt increased ten-fold, but she buried it beneath a show of anger. "Do you mean to say Seabrook would have you barred from Almack's merely because he is hipped with me?" she asked, enraged by such casual cruelty.

"Of course, and who is to blame him?" Flavia said, blowing her nose vigorously. "Seagate is his ancestral home, and it is only natural he should wish to see it in the hands of its rightful owners."

"It is in the hands of its rightful owners," Elly returned hotly, annoyed by her aunt's defection to the enemy's camp. "And that is where it shall remain, regardless of Seabrook's threats."

"But what of Almack's?" Flavia wailed, looking as if she would swoon. "You can not be so callous as to deny Caroline a proper entry to Society!"

Elly muttered an unladylike sentiment beneath her breath before surrendering to the inevitable. It was one thing to risk the marquess's temper on her own, but quite another to expose the rest of her family to his vindictive nature. Whether she liked it or not, she knew she had no choice but to make amends.

"Oh, very well," she grumbled, flinging herself on to the settee. "I shall write the wretch a very pretty letter of apology. But that is all," she added as her aunt erupted into effusive gratitude. "I won't allow Henry to sign over our home merely to provide Thomas's cousin with a voucher!"

"As if I would expect such a thing," Flavia sent her a reproving frown. "When will you send the note?"

"This very afternoon," Elly promised, swallowing her pride with a resigned sigh. "Now, if you will excuse me, I must go and speak with Henry. He still doesn't know about Seabrook's visit."

"What shall you tell him?" Flavia was already thinking ahead to next year when she would introduce her pretty cousin-in-law to the *ton*. The chit was as well dowered as she was lovely, and Flavia saw no reason why they shouldn't hold out for a viscount at the very least.

"The truth," Elly replied, although at that moment she wasn't precisely certain what that truth would be.

"Sell Seagate?" Henry exclaimed in disbelief, gazing at Elly as if she'd taken leave of her senses. "Good heavens, El, how can you even suggest such a thing? I thought you had set your jaw against the very notion."

"And so I have," Elly demurred, mentally crossing her fingers. She'd spent the last two hours devising her strategy, and she knew she would have to tread lightly if she was to make it succeed. "But six thousand pounds is nothing to sneeze at, and as his lordship informed me, Seagate *is* his home."

Henry frowned at this piece of intelligence. "It is far more our home than his, if it comes to that," he grumbled, casting a longing look at the papers and journals littering the surface of his desk. He'd been busily transcribing his father's notes when Elly came bursting into the library with the news that she expected him to sell the house. He disliked having his work disrupted for so trivial a thing, and wondered querulously why she did not attend to the matter herself rather than fobbing it off on him.

"Undoubtedly," she agreed, monitoring his expression through half-lowered eyes. "But as I say, six thousand pounds is a considerable sum, and I thought you should know of it. His lordship shall probably be expecting an immediate answer."

Henry's frown blossomed into a scowl. "Am I a tradesman to await his leisure?" he complained, vexed by this disruption of his orderly life. "You have already declined his insulting offer in my stead, what is there left to discuss? This Seabrook is too forward by half, if you ask me. Who does he think he is to turn us out of our home without so much as a by-your-leave?"

The use of "our" home gladdened Elly's heart. She had wagered everything on her brother's dislike of being forced into making a decision, and knew he would doubtlessly take out his displeasure on the source of his irritation. Poor Seabrook hadn't a chance in Hades that Henry would now accept the offer, she decided, lowering her gray-blue eyes to hide the flash of victory.

"He is the Marquess of Seabrook, Henry," she said instead, her voice as demure as she could make it. "And according to Aunt, a most powerful man. It may not do to cross him."

Henry's loud snort made it obvious what he thought of such flummery. He raked an impatient hand through his ebony curls and began pacing the room, his usually orderly mind filled with anger and confusion. Only yesterday he had been approached by a publisher who had offered him considerable compensation to set down the details of his and his father's sojourns, but he did not see how he should ever have the time to write with a tiresome lord pestering him every five minutes. He stopped pacing and whirled around to shoot Elly an exasperated look. "What do you think we should do to keep Seabrook from claiming our home?" he demanded, thrusting the problem back in her lap.

"Well," she pretended to give his question careful thought, as if she hadn't already worked out every detail in her mind, "the first thing I would do would be to establish immediate residency at Seagate. His lordship won't find it so easy to dispossess us once we are actually living there."

Henry rubbed his chin thoughtfully, deciding he rather liked the sound of that. "That is so," he agreed in his ponderous way, "for they do say that possession is eleven points of the law."

"And of course, away from the distractions of the city you would be better able to continue your studies," she said, laying her trump card on the table with the cool cunning of a cardsharp. "But naturally the decision is yours, Henry dearest."

"Then that is what we shall do," he declared with uncustomary decisiveness, pleased with the clever way he'd resolved everything. "Besides," he added, glancing towards Elly for approbation, "I have been thinking, and I've decided we shall have need of a country house when we retire; might as well keep this one. We can always rent it out when we're out of the country."

"Henry, you are a genius!" Elly clasped her hands together in delight, although, of course, she had no intention of letting the house out to anyone. "That is positively inspired! And over the period of twenty or thirty years we shall certainly realize a great deal more profit than six thousand pounds."

"A paltry amount." Henry dismissed the marquess's offer with a wave of a well-shaped hand. "I think you were right about him from the start, El. The man is obviously a Johnny Sharp who meant to pluck our pockets as if we were a bunch of country flats.

33

You were wise to give him his *congé*."

Elly squirmed uncomfortably, her heady sense of victory giving way to a reluctant shame. Despite her dislike of Seabrook her sense of fair play would not allow his honor to be impugned so unfairly. "I shouldn't go so far as to call him a Johnny Sharp," she mumbled, looking everywhere but at her brother. "He was merely out to win the best price for himself."

"Ha!" Having decided the man was but one step removed from a cutpurse, Henry wasn't about to be dissuaded. "He was out to take advantage of us, just as you warned me he would. You said when he offered us three thousand that Seagate was doubtlessly worth double the amount. Now he has offered us that. What does that tell you?"

His acumen amazed Elly. She was too accustomed to thinking him just like their father; his head filled with nothing but botany or some other weighty matter. It was reassuring to know he'd inherited some of their mother's stolid practicality as well.

As always, the thought of her beloved mother brought a sharp pain to her heart. When she was sixteen they had been in some godforsaken village in Africa, and her mother contracted the fever and died within a matter of days. There was nothing Elly could do but bathe her fevered body and hold her hand until it was over. Her father and brother had been out in the bush at the time, and she had been left all alone; thousands of miles from anyone who spoke her language, and so terrified, so damned terrified. . . .

". . . leave?" Henry concluded, shooting her a questioning look.

Elly's cheeks flushed with color as she realized she hadn't heard a single word he had said, save the last. She seized upon it eagerly, guessing what she thought he may have asked.

"That is surely up to you," she said quietly, praying she wasn't making a cake of herself. "We must stay at least until Aunt Flavia's party, but once that is over I

34

see no reason why we shouldn't leave right away. Shall we say a week? That will give me sufficient time to hire an adequate staff."

Henry pouted. He would have much preferred leaving immediately, but he supposed it could not be helped. "Oh, very well," he said with ill grace. "But not one second above that, else his lordship may move in ahead of us and barricade the doors."

"He can't, Henry, the house is legally ours . . . yours." She had corrected the slip at once. "But should he call, you will give him your answer, will you not?"

His square chin came up and his indigo-blue eyes flashed with manly resolve. "I shall throw him out the door," he announced proudly. "He shall soon see that we Dennings are not to be turned out of our home by anyone, even a marquess."

Elly's lips curved in a crafty smirk that she made no attempt to hide. "Very well, Henry," she murmured dulcetly. "I am sure you know what is best."

Aunt Flavia took the news of Elly and Henry's impending retreat to the country with a silent sigh of relief. Dear as they were to her heart, she found a niece who would boldly challenge a marquess to be a decided burden, and she could not wait to be shed of them. She allowed none of her true feelings to show but acted as the perfect hostess; spending the next two days guiding an enthusiastic Elly to all the sights of the bustling city. Henry, of course, stayed locked in his study, too busy with his books and papers to accompany them. When she mentioned Henry's studious habits to Elly, the troublesome girl merely shrugged her slender shoulders.

"It is his way, Aunt," Elly said, trying not to gape about her as her aunt's coachman tooled them about Hyde Park. "Papa was much the same way if you will but recall."

"Yes, but your papa did not look like an Adonis," Flavia grumbled, nodding her head as an acquaintance passed them bound in the opposite direction. "Henry could have his pick of the ladies if he but raised his handsome nose out of those demmed books! 'Tis a most unnatural preoccupation if you want my opinion of it."

"I daresay you are right, ma'am," Elly agreed, secretly amused by her aunt's ill humor. It was obvious that having despaired of ever making her niece an eligible match, Flavia was now turning her matchmaking skills on her nephew.

"Of course I am!" Flavia said, shooting her a fulminating look. "Henry is as handsome as can be, and even though he has no title, nor a great fortune to speak of, he would still be considered an eligible *parti* by all but the highest sticklers. When you are in Brighton you must take care to see that he does not molder amongst his wretched tomes."

Elly had the sudden image of herself bear-leading a scowling Henry to the various routs and balls that constituted society in the famous resort city. He would be perfectly miserable, she knew; and if she pushed him too hard he might grow so disgusted he would insist upon leaving England altogether. After all she had endured to get to this point, she wasn't about to allow that particular calamity to befall them, and vowed she would not unduly press her brother.

Not that she intended that they should become hermits, she amended quickly. In fact, she was rather looking forward to the social whirl. She would buy herself an elegant turban and start a *salon,* she decided with mounting eagerness. She would invite the most learned people in Brighton to attend, and become famous as a bluestocking. Why, she might even set down her down adventures as Henry was doing, and—

"Oh heavens, 'tis Seabrook!" Flavia's anguished cry shattered Elly's reverie, and she glanced up to see the marquess, astride a magnificent gray, bearing down on them.

"Oh dear, oh dear, this is dreadful!" Flavia muttered, well aware that they were surrounded by the *crème de la crème* of society. She whirled on Elly, her eyes wide with pleading. "You are not to quarrel with him, do you hear?" she instructed frantically. "No matter the provocation you are not to say so much as a disrespectful word! And under no circumstances are you to mention Seagate!"

"Yes, Aunt," Elly replied dutifully, wondering with private amusement what her poor aunt thought she meant to do. Besides, the matter of Seagate had already been resolved yesterday when Henry politely but firmly rejected Seabrook's offer. She was only surprised that the marquess should be seeking her out now, for according to Henry he had seemed to take the refusal as final.

Before she could discern his motives Seabrook was upon them, sweeping his tall beaver hat from his head as he gave them both a deep bow. "Mrs. Shaftson, Miss Denning," he murmured, his voice coolly polite. "I trust you ladies are enjoying our pleasant weather?"

"Oh my, yes, your lordship!" Flavia gushed, giving Elly one last speaking glance. "Indeed, I was just remarking to Elinore that I have never known a more pleasant April. Is that not so, dearest?"

"Yes, Aunt Flavia," Elly answered, sending the marquess a serene smile. "And I must say it is a welcome change from the heat and dust of Africa, where Henry and I spent last April."

"Yes, I believe he mentioned that fact when we spoke," Lucien said, studying his adversary through narrowed eyes. She was wearing a demure carriage dress of yellow cambric, a straw bonnet tied with yellow ribbons perched on her golden-brown curls, and she looked very much the proper miss.

"He also mentioned that you and he would soon be

retiring to your home in Brighton," he said, hiding his anger behind his most tantalizing smile. "That will make us neighbors, you know."

His pleasant tones as well as his toadying smile set Elly's back up at once, but with Aunt Flavia quaking at her side there was little she could do. "Really?" she enquired politely, her eyes filled with the challenge she dared not voice. "How nice."

"Indeed." The defiance in her remarkably colored eyes pleased Lucien. It would make taking her down a peg or so all the sweeter. "As a matter of fact, we shall probably be seeing a great deal of each other as I mean to spend the greater part of the Season there."

"You won't be staying in London, my lord?" Flavia asked quickly, anxious to avoid the scene she was certain was imminent.

He controlled his impatience long enough to send her a cool smile. "Unfortunately, Mrs. Shaftson, I fear not. My duties at home command my immediate attention, and I shall be leaving the city within the month."

What was the wretch up to now? Elly wondered, her eyes narrowing in suspicion. He'd said nothing to Henry about his plans, else her brother would have told her. Well, if he thought to continue harassing them once they were in the country, she would soon disabuse him of *that* particular notion! She raised her chin and gave him a smile that was patently insincere.

"In that case, my lord, you must make sure to join Henry and myself for tea," she said, deciding that since he had been the first to broach the matter she wasn't breaking her word to Flavia. "We shall be happy to receive you as a guest in *our* home."

Touché, Lucien conceded mentally, keeping his smile determinedly pinned in place. "That is very kind of you, Miss Denning," he said with every show of pleasure. "I have always longed to see the inside of Seagate: if only to see if the rumors are really true."

"And what rumors might those be, Lord Seabrook?" Elly answered with false graciousness.

He glanced about him and then leaned down from his saddle, his voice low and confident. "Why the rumors about the ghost, of course," he said, his velvet-brown eyes meeting her startled gaze. "Do you mean you didn't know? Seagate is haunted."

Chapter Three

"*Haunted?*" Elly and Flavia echoed, exchanging startled glances.

"Yes," Lucien nodded, pleased by their response. "By the ghost of a drowned smuggler cruelly murdered by members of his own crew. 'Tis said he walks the halls of Seagate, water streaming from his lifeless form as he seeks out the men who murdered him."

Elly stared at him for a full moment and then gave a light laugh. "What utter nonsense!" she exclaimed, slanting him a challenging look. "Never say *you* believe in such moonshine?"

"I?" His dark eyebrows arched in a superior manner that immediately set Elly's teeth on edge. "Certainly not, Miss Denning. I was but thinking of you. I thought all you ladies adore believing in spirits and the like."

Elly's brows came together in an angry scowl at knowing he should think her such a peagoose. "Not this lady," she responded with alacrity. "Ghosts are naught but the products of over-fanciful imaginations, and I refuse to be taken in by such fustian!"

"Ah," Lucien nodded, having received more or less the answer he expected. "But then you are a very intellectual lady; are you not? I might have known you would not share your less-educated sisters' opinion of ghosts and witches."

"Well, I *do* believe in them, my lord, so kindly do not say another word!" Flavia said, shivering despite the warmth of the soft spring air. "As it is, I know I shan't be able to close my eyes for the next week for thinking about it!"

"Then don't think about it!" Elly exclaimed, thoroughly annoyed at Seabrook for spouting such errant nonsense. "I know I shall not." She shot the marquess a challenging look as if daring him to comment.

He did not disappoint her. "Then you are as wise as you are lovely," he murmured suavely, his brown eyes mocking. "How comforting to know that you shall sleep undisturbed by a restless spirit walking the night in search of vengeance."

Elly ignored her aunt's shriek of horror and continued gazing at him. "As I wasn't the one to murder the poor fellow I don't see that I should have anything to fear from him even if he did exist," she told him, wishing he would drop the tiresome subject. "More like 'tis the men who caused his death who would have to keep a sharp eye over their shoulders."

"An astute observation, Miss Denning," he said, raising his hat to her in another salute. "And just the kind of calm reasoning I might have expected from such a blue — from such an intellectual."

Elly noted his deliberate slip of the tongue, but chose to ignore it. She was not the least bit ashamed of her intellect, and if her preening neighbor thought her a bluestocking, then she couldn't be more delighted. Certainly she preferred that to having him think her a hysterical widgeon who believed his prattle.

Deciding he had sown enough seeds for one afternoon Lucien dug his spurs into his horse, causing the animal to dance with indignation. He controlled the restive movements with a deft flick of his strong hands. "I pray you ladies will excuse me, but I am afraid my mount is in need of exercise," he said, giving the two women another smile.

"Mrs. Shaftson, my secretary will be sending you my acceptance for your party next Thursday. Mr. Denning was kind enough to invite me, and as I am most anxious to become better acquainted with my new neighbors I have accepted. I trust this will not upset your numbers?"

"Heavens, not at all, my lord!" Flavia denied quickly; thrilled at the prospect of having bagged such a prize for her party. "The more the merrier, as they say!"

He nodded. "Until then, ladies," he said and then whirled his horse around and departed, leaving the two women staring after him; their hearts filled with two very different sets of emotions.

"Really, Henry, how can you have been such a gudgeon?" Elly scolded, her hands on her hips as she glared at her brother. "Whatever possessed you to invite that . . . that man to our party?"

Henry glanced up from his copy of Tournefort's *A Voyage into the Levant,* which he was using as the model for his own work. "Why should I not?" he asked, resigning himself to another interruption. "Aunt did say I might ask whomever I chose."

"But Seabrook?" Elly shook her head in exasperation, scarce believing her brother should be so easily gulled. "I thought you called him a Johnny Sharp!"

Henry pushed his hair back from his forehead and frowned thoughtfully. "As to that, I believe you may have been overly hasty in your assessment," he said, conveniently forgetting it was himself who levelled those particular charges. "He really is a rather decent sort once you get to know him. He took my refusal just as a gentleman should, even offered to show me about the countryside once we are settled.

He is something of an amateur botanist, you know."

"I know," Elly mumbled, blushing as she recalled the way he had correctly identified *Stachys betonica*. "But that still doesn't explain why you saw fit to include him in Aunt's party. Such things are simply not done in London. Now poor Aunt is having to dash about and find a lady of equal rank to Seabrook in order to make out the numbers. It was very rude of you, Henry."

Henry's frown increased at the scolding tones in his sister's voice. "Well, it would have been ruder still not to invite Seabrook once I'd told him about the party!" he snapped, his eyes flashing with indignation.

"You told Seabrook about Aunt's party?"

He nodded. "He asked when we would be leaving for Brighton, and when I mentioned it wouldn't be until after that boring party you wanted, he hinted . . . very broadly . . . that he shouldn't mind attending. What else was I to do?"

Elly had to concede the point, thinking Seabrook's hint had to be very broad indeed for Henry to have caught it. She was only surprised that her brother was even aware of what his social responsibilities were in such a case. As a rule, Henry didn't have any more notion how to go on in Polite Society than did a Red Indian. Her poor mother's lectures on the niceties of civilized behavior had always seemed to go right over his head.

"Besides," Henry continued, warming to his theme, "I should think you would want to get in the marquess's good graces. He knows everyone, and I daresay he would even be willing to help you find a household staff if you were to ask him. I told him you were having a rather hard time hiring servants."

Elly bristled to think her failings had been discussed with her nemesis. Henry might be willing to forgive his high-handed manners, but she was not.

43

"That is very thoughtful of his lordship," she said in stiff tones, "but I have no need of his assistance. I shall have our home fully staffed long before we ever leave London, I assure you."

"Good. Then may I return to my studies?" He gave her a long-suffering look that made her smile.

"Certainly," she said, resisting the impulse to ruffle his hair as she had often seen her mother do. "Don't forget to dress for dinner," she warned him with a waggle of her finger. "Aunt has invited some of her oldest friends to meet us, and it will not do for you to come in looking like a ragpicker."

"Hmph," came the response as Henry lost himself in his book. "Goodbye, El."

Some four hours later Elly dressed in one of her new gowns of peach and blue silk and made her way to the drawing room where her aunt and uncle were waiting to receive their guests. At the sight of her standing in the doorway, her uncle broke into a pleased smile and motioned her forward.

"Good evening, my dear, you are looking very fetching," Thomas Shaftson said, giving her hand a comforting squeeze. "How are you feeling? Has the prospect of your first London dinner set you to quaking in your boots?"

"Not at all, sir," she assured him, unfurling her fan in the languid gesture she had learned from her aunt. "You forget I have travelled into darkest Africa, and I have learned to endure most anything. At least here I needn't fear that having been served with nuncheon, I shall now be served up as dinner!"

Thomas grinned at her. "I shouldn't be so certain of that if I were you," he drawled. "There's many a young deb who has suddenly found herself being feasted upon by the good ladies of the *ton*. Have a care, my dear, lest you should find yourself being dished up with *sauce anglaise* at the next society tea."

"Thomas!" Flavia brought her fan down on her husband's arm. "What a perfectly dreadful thing to say! You will scare poor Elinore to death with such talk."

"Never fear, Aunt, I am made of more sturdier stuff than that," Elly said with a soothing laugh. "Not that I have anything to fear from wagging tongues; Uncle's warning was for a *young* deb, after all. I much doubt that an aging bluestocking such as myself will elicit much interest in a city so accustomed to oddities as London."

Such frank honesty brought a flush to Flavia's cheeks, and she turned to her husband with a set smile pinned to her lips. "And how was your day, dearest?" she asked with bright determination. "More debate on that tiresome war, I suppose?"

"No more than usual." Thomas accepted the change of subject with his customary aplomb. "There is some concern about the conduct of the campaign in Spain, and more talk of negotiating a settlement with the Americans. I am hopeful cooler heads will prevail in this case, although I much doubt it. The Tories would rather fight than bargain, 'twould seem."

Elly listened with avid interest, anxious to learn all she could of her nation's political woes. After having spent the better part of her life thousands of miles from her home she knew her knowledge of such matters was sadly lacking, and she was anxious to correct this deficiency at once.

"What of the Regent?" she asked, after her uncle had finished talking about the Prime Minister's latest speech. "Surely he must have some opinion of the Combination Acts?"

"Prinny?" Thomas stared at her in amazement. "Good lord, I should say not! I doubt if he has even heard of them."

"But I thought you said they were enacted to keep

45

down the riots in the north," she said, looking puzzled. "I would think such a thing should concern His Royal Highness very much!"

Thomas shook his head at such naïveté. "The prince," he began carefully, "has little or no interest in such things. He leaves his advisers and ministers to run the country, and busies himself with other matters."

"What other matters?" Elly was torn between disapproval and curiosity.

"His pavilion at Brighton for one," Thomas continued, always ready to run down the prince as befitted a staunch Whig. "He has all but bankrupted England with that monstrosity of his, and there is even talk he means to add to it! It is folly and caprice of the worst sort, and—"

"Thomas, please, not another speech I beg of you," Flavia interrupted with a wifely scowl. "Our guests will soon be here, and I'd as lief not have them find you declaiming in the parlor!" She turned next to Elly. "Elinore, dearest, why don't you run along and see what is keeping that brother of yours? I do hope he hasn't gone off in one of those brown studies of his. My friends are so looking forward to meeting him . . . and you too, of course."

"Of course," Elly accepted her dismissal with a smile and went off to find Henry. Much to her relief she found him in his rooms, where he was submitting to his valet's ministration's with a martyred expression on his face. She stood in the doorway watching for several seconds before stepping forward to greet him.

"Why, Henry, how very handsome you look!" she said, smiling with sisterly pride. "That jacket is just the thing to bring out the color of your eyes."

Henry's blue eyes flashed with indignation. "That settles it!" he announced between clenched teeth, tearing off the cravat the valet had only that moment tied. "I'm not stepping a foot out of this room!"

"Mr. Henry!" Reynolds, the valet let out a strangled cry, his delicate hands fluttering to his throat. "You have *ruined* my Waterfall after I was hours creating it!"

Henry subsided at once, for he was by nature the most even tempered of persons. "Sorry," he apologized curtly, shooting his sister a dark look. "But I shan't go down there if it means I must dress like a . . . a . . . damned caper merchant."

"Nonsense, you look the picture of elegant restraint," Elly assured him, trying not to laugh at his sulky pout. When her words had no discernible effect she added, "And the very image of a famous scholar."

Henry brightened at that. "Do you think so?" he asked anxiously, ignoring Jipperson's scolding protests as he bent forward to study his reflection. "I was afraid I looked like a blasted dandy."

Actually, Elly thought he looked more like the hero of one of Lord Byron's more romantic epics, but she was far too savvy to say such a thing. Henry's jacket was of plum velvet, with a notched collar and wide lapels that emphasized his broad chest. His black hair fell over his tanned forehead in an artful arrangement of curls even a girl might envy, and his blue eyes glittered like the Indian Ocean in his handsome face. She remembered what her aunt had said about the other dandies looking to their laurels and decided she was right. Not even Seabrook could outshine her brother tonight.

As if privy to her thoughts Henry said. "Don't think this jacket is too old-fashioned, do you? It doesn't look at all like the jacket the marquess was wearing when he called the other day."

At first Elly was too stunned to speak. Henry *never* paid any attention to such mundane things as

47

clothes. Why, he had once worn his shirt inside out for an entire day, and when she'd pointed this out to him he had simply shrugged and said he'd wear it right side out on the morrow!

"Seabrook said his tailor's name was Weston," Henry continued, not seeming to notice his sister's stunned silence. "Said he'd give me his card if I liked. What do you think?"

"All the gentlemen go to Weston," Jipperson said with an approving nod. "I am quite sure he should be more than happy to dress you, sir."

"Yes," Elly echoed weakly, feeling rather like a mother whose child had just taken his first steps. "You might want to call on him before we leave London."

"And boots," Henry added, looking thoughtful. "Mean to start riding while we're in the country, and I'll need a decent pair of boots. Seabrook said I ought to visit a man named Hobbs. That's where he buys his boots."

"I see." She swallowed a particularly large lump in her throat. "His lordship appears to have been most accommodating."

Henry sent her a stern look over his shoulder. "I told you you'd misjudged him," he said.

Elly thought about that for a long moment. "Do you know, Henry, I do believe you are right," she admitted, looking thoughtful. "Only 'misjudged' is not the word I would use."

"And what word would you use?" he asked curiously.

Elly's full lips thinned in anger. "Underestimated."

"So you're the gel what was raised in a tent," Lady Ablethorpe said, regarding Elly through her quizzing glass. "Can't say you look all that exotic to me. Speak English and wear your drawers just as a

48

young lady ought to . . . even if you are too dark to be pleasing," she added with a suspicious sniff.

Elly choked on the mouthful of sherry she had just taken, and fought the temptation to empty the rest of the wine over the elderly woman's hideous wig. The hag had literally pounced upon her the moment Aunt Flavia had performed the introductions, and there was naught Elly could do but grit her teeth and answer the dowager's increasingly obnoxious questions.

"I *am* English, your ladyship," Elly managed, in a voice that was tight with the effort of control. "And I was not raised in a tent."

" 'Course you was," Lady Ablethorpe retorted, her bushy eyebrows drawing themselves into a haughty scowl. "Your good aunt told me all about it; also said you was blue as a Scotsman's knees. Say something in Greek!"

The command made Elly's eyes grow stormy as she recalled an epithet she'd heard their Greek boatman shout at a passing French frigate. She had no notion what it might mean, but it had sounded delightfully insulting, and for one moment she was strongly tempted to utter it. Discretion prevailed however, and she gave Lady Ablethorpe a sugary smile.

"Non compos mentis," she said, deciding the elderly countess was unlikely to recognize Greek from Latin.

"Ah," Lady Ablethorpe gave a smug nod. "You see? Flavia was right; you are a dashed bluestocking. And if she was right about that, stands to reason she is right about t'other."

"I bow to your ladyship's superior logic," Elly said, mentally throwing her hands into the air. "I was raised in a tent, and am but one step above a monkey."

"Oh, Grandmother, there you are," a soft, femi-

49

nine voice cut into the silence following Elly's sarcastic rejoinder, as a sweet-faced blonde took a seat beside the countess. "Mrs. Shaftson has asked me to fetch you. She is in the dining room and desires your help in arranging the guests' namecards."

"Of course she does," Lady Ablethorpe gave a loud sniff. "Flavia never did know her Honorables from her lordships," and she hauled her emaciated frame from her chair and toddled out of the room, leaving Elly alone with the newcomer.

"I do hope Grandmother hasn't upset you," the girl murmured with a comforting smile. "I fear she is getting up in years, and isn't always aware of what she is saying."

"That is very kind of you, Miss . . . er . . . Lady Ablethorpe," Elly replied, struggling to recall the proper form of address for the daughter of an earl. "I have been asked far worse questions in my four and twenty years of life, I assure you."

Lady Miranda Ablethorpe smiled again. "But in not so public a place, I should think," she said gently, "and it would please me if you would call me Lady Miranda. I am hoping you and I shall become fast friends, you see. We have much in common."

"Oh, were you raised in a tent as well?" Elly asked, then flushed in embarrassment.

To her surprise the younger girl gave a merry laugh. "Almost," she said, her deep blue eyes dancing with amusement. "My father is General William Barrett, and prior to my mother's death she and I both followed the drum. Such adventuring makes Society seem sadly flat at times, don't you think?"

"Oh no!" Elly replied quickly, warming at once to her new-found friend. "I find it endlessly fascinating! I am quite longing to become a hostess and have my own dinner parties the moment Henry and I are settled in our home."

Lady Miranda looked rather surprised. "But I understood your brother to say your stay in England was only temporary, until his book was finished at the very latest."

"You have spoken to Henry?" Elly's eyes sought out her brother and found him huddled on a chair in the corner, a look of acute suffering on his face as he listened in stoic silence to the pretty brunette who was chattering at him.

Lady Miranda's eyes followed Elly's gaze. "Yes, at least I was . . . until Sally Mackleroy cut me out. She seems most taken with your brother's appearance."

"Henry has that effect upon the ladies," Elly said, turning back to the younger girl with a smile. "Fortunately he never seems to notice."

Lady Miranda's creamy cheeks turned a gentle shade of rose. "He does seem rather studious," she said, fiddling with one of the velvet bows adorning her violet silk gown. "And he seems to know everything there is to know about flowers and plants. They . . . they are something of a hobby of mine."

The shy confession made Elly blink in amazement. First Seabrook and now Lady Miranda, she thought, a rueful smile tugging at her lips. Good heavens, was society overrun with amateur botanists? If so, perhaps she and Henry might not have such a hard time of it after all. Although not so passionately consumed with botany as was her brother, she did know more than a little on the subject, and did not think she should have any trouble holding her own even with the most learned of scholars.

Perhaps she might even start up her own Botanical Society, she thought, her excitement mounting. It was just the thing to draw Henry out, and perhaps even, with a bit of luck, to introduce him to the kind of lady who might make him a decent wife. It had occurred to her that having a wife and family would tie Henry down far more than she could ever do,

51

and she was anxious to begin matchmaking at once. She eyed Lady Miranda speculatively.

"Do you ever visit Brighton, my lady?" she asked, studying the other girl through half-lowered lashes.

"Why, yes we do," Lady Miranda replied, looking puzzled. "Grandmother keeps a house on the Royal Crescent, and we visit whenever the Regent is in residence."

"Indeed?" Elly was hard put not to rub her hands together in satisfaction. "How wonderful! Perhaps I might prevail upon you and your grandmother to visit us when you are next in town? I should like it above all things."

A smile of pure happiness lighted the other girl's face. "Why, that would be delightful!" she exclaimed, her small hands clasping in delight. "I have always longed to visit Seagate."

"Then by all means you must come." Elly rose as the dinner bell sounded and gave Lady Miranda another smile. "Do you know, my lady, I do believe you are right and we shall become the best of friends. As you say, we have much in common!"

Chapter Four

The days leading up to the dinner party flew past for Elly. With her aunt's blessings she accompanied Lady Miranda to various social functions, and by observing the other girl's well-bred behavior, she was able to learn much about how to go on in the Polite World. Lady Miranda also introduced her to the lending library, an institution that had her wide-eyed with delight.

"Do you mean I can just go into one of these places and they will lend me a book?" she asked, scarce believing such a wondrous thing could be true.

"For a small fee, and providing the book is available," Lady Miranda clarified with a gentle smile. "You will find the most popular books go rather quickly, and you will have to be fast to get your name on the list else you will have to wait forever. I noted there is already a considerable wait for *Pride and Prejudice,* but you needn't worry. I have a copy of my own I should be happy to lend you."

Such generosity left Elly speechless with gratitude. She reciprocated by offering the other girl a copy of Pulteney's *Progress of Botany in England,* which she intended pilfering from her father's collection the moment Henry's back was turned.

On the day before the party Lady Miranda—or Miranda, as she had requested Elly call her—invited her to tea at her elegant town house. There Elly met several of Miranda's closest friends; young ladies much like herself who were intelligent and accomplished, and not the least bit ashamed to display these facts to the world.

"We are even thinking of forming our own club, not unlike Boodle's or White's," Miss Lydia Averleigh, a dimpled blonde who had recently inherited a fortune confided, her light brown eyes dancing with laughter. "It will give us a place to go when we tire of the superficiality of the social whirl."

"Yes, but unfortunately we can't decide what to call it," added a Miss Jessica Kingsley, Miss Averleigh's closest friend. "I rather favor Spinster's Haven, but Miranda feels it lacks delicacy. What do you think?"

"I fear I would have to agree," Elly replied, smiling at the brunette's breezy matter-of-factness. "It is somewhat lacking in subtlety. And what if one of you should marry? Would she then be considered ineligible for membership?"

"My point exactly, Miss Denning," Miss Elisa Worthing agreed, her gray eyes owlish behind her spectacles. "That is why I feel it should be called The Learned Ladies of London Club. It has more of a feeling of *je ne sais quoi* to it, don't you agree?"

Jessica shook her head decisively. "Too pretentious, to say nothing of being an awful alliteration." Here she grinned at her own joke. "But never fear, we shall think of something. Meanwhile we have more important matters to discuss." She turned inquisitive green eyes on Elly.

"What is your opinion of the work of Mr. Wilberforce in Parliament? Do you not feel it is hypocritical that he should wish to see slavery abolished in the colonies even as he opposes unions which would benefit the working poor?"

This sparked a lively debate, and Elly was surprised to learn that the other ladies, especially Lydia and Jessica, were so passionately interested in politics. She mentioned this as they were driving back to Aunt Flavia's, and Miranda gave an affectionate laugh.

"Yes, it is their *raison d'être*. If they were men I daresay they would stand for Parliament, but as it is, their only hope is to marry a budding politician and become his hostess. Or I should say, it is Lydia's only hope. Jessica has already confided to me that she is a dedicated spinster and means never to marry."

"That is how I feel," Elly said eagerly, delighted to find another female who shared her rather unorthodox ambition. "I fear I am much too independent and set in my ways to make any man a good wife. Besides, who would look after Henry?"

Her rhetorical question brought a distressed look to Miranda's face. "Is it so unlikely he should marry?" she asked, not quite meeting Elly's gaze. "That is, he is so very young yet; surely he can not be considered a confirmed bachelor at his age?"

"He is eight and twenty. At that age a female would be considered at her last prayers." Elly retorted, tongue-in-cheek. Then she remembered her plans for Miranda and Henry, and began hastily repairing whatever damage she may have inflicted.

"But you are right, of course. Henry is just at the age where he ought to be considering matrimony. In fact, it is my fondest wish that he do so."

Miranda's eyes flashed to Elly's face. "Then . . . then you would not object to his marrying?" she asked shyly.

"Heavens, no! I should be delighted," Elly was quick to assure her. "I have been rather lonely since my mother's death, and the presence of another lady would be more than welcome."

Miranda said no more of the matter, but Elly made a mental note to begin mentioning her to Henry at once. The poor boy was so hopelessly dense it would take considerable effort on her part even to make him aware of the pretty blonde's existence. She would also have to set the house to rights even sooner than she'd originally planned. Henry could hardly expect his high-born bride to live in a Gothic ruin!

After Miranda dropped her off Elly went to her study to go over the list of that afternoon's appointments. Another institution Miranda had introduced her to was the Employment Office, which had greatly simplified her search for a household staff. Today they were sending her two more applicants, one for the post of butler and the other for that of housekeeper; the two positions she had yet to fill. As these were the most important posts in any household, she was anxious to acquire the most qualified persons available. So far she had yet to interview a single candidate who satisfied her exacting requirements.

While she was waiting for the first appointment to arrive she went over the packing lists; a task which kept her happily occupied until there was a discreet tap at the door. One of the maids stepped inside and dropped a hasty curtsey. "Beg your pardon, miss, but Mr. Clemment said I was to tell you that the marquess of Seabrook has arrived and is asking to speak with you. He is in the Drawing Room, if you please."

The hated name brought a scowl to Elly's face. Since accepting Henry's decision he'd been an almost daily visitor to the house, spending as much time with Henry as she was spending with Miranda. In fact, she was surprised he was asking for her rather than her brother. She gave the maid a speculative look.

"You are quite sure it is me whom he asked to see?"

The maid nodded briskly. "Oh yes, miss, he asked for you special like.

"I see," Elly's brows drew together in a suspicious frown. "Where is my brother?"

"Out, miss. He and Mr. Jipperson was going to the tailor's."

That was another thing, Elly thought with mounting ire. Since meeting Seabrook her brother had become positively obsessed with his appearance; yesterday she'd even discovered him reading a copy of *Le Beau Monde!* Clearly the marquess was having a detrimental effect on poor Henry, and as his sister it was her job to protect him from such evil influences.

A quick glance at the clock on the mantel showed she still had fifteen minutes until the first applicant was to arrive, and she reached a swift decision. If she meant to protect Henry she would have to learn what the devil Seabrook was up to, and clearly she could not obtain that information cowering in her rooms. Besides, she wouldn't want to give the wretch the impression she was afraid of him. Her chin came up proudly. Now that the battle was well and truly joined, it was time she entered the fray.

What the deuce was keeping the girl? Lucien fumed, studying his gold pocket watch with an annoyed frown. It had been well over ten minutes since his arrival, and Miss Denning had yet to make an appearance. He would have accused her of using the old feminine ploy of keeping him dangling in order to whet his appetite, but he doubted she was interested in such machinations. Doubtlessly he was being forced to cool his heels out of sheer perversity, and the knowledge made his lips tighten with anger.

Since he'd failed in his original objective of buying Seagate outright, he was forced to fall back on his secondary plan of ingratiating himself with the Dennings so that he might run tame in the old house without eliciting undue suspicion. He'd succeeded with Henry, but he doubted his sister should prove half so compliant. The two of them had been at dagger's drawn almost from the moment they'd clapped eyes on one another, and he knew he would have to work long and hard to overcome her animosity. He smiled grimly. It was a good thing he enjoyed a challenge.

"Good afternoon, my lord." Her soft voice interrupted his thoughts, and he turned around as she came striding into the room. "Clemment said you wished to see me?"

"Miss Denning." He bowed suavely, taking in her appearance through knowledgeable eyes. She'd changed greatly from the first time he'd seen her, and he approved of her stylish gown and sophisticated coiffure. "I trust you are well today?"

Such a banal opening gambit brought a mocking smile to Elly's lips. "Oh, I am feeling very well, thank you, my lord. And as you are looking in the pink, I can see that you are also enjoying the best of health."

Hellcat! Lucien struggled to hold his temper, and then gave her a cool smile. "Yes, I am," he said, keeping his voice even with a determined effort. "How kind of you to ask."

Round one to you, Elly thought, conceding his reply with a smile. She had already made the mistake of dismissing the marquess as a fashionable fribble, and she wasn't about to repeat the error. "Pray will you not be seated, my lord?" she enquired sweetly, indicating the striped settee beside

58

the fireplace. "Then perhaps you could tell me the purpose of your visit. Is there something I can do for you?"

"Actually, there is something I can do for you," he said, handing her the wrapped parcel he had been holding. "I found this in my attic, and thought you might want it. It is a sketch of Seagate."

Elly gave him a surprised look and began tearing off the wrappings. When she had the framed picture free she held it up, turning it towards the sunlight streaming through the mullioned windows. "Oh, it is beautiful!" she exclaimed, studying the exquisitely-crafted drawing with delight. "Thank you!"

"You are welcome," he replied, pleased to see his gift so well received. "I thought you would enjoy it."

"Oh, yes," she said, forgetting her distrust in her pleasure. "It looks just as I always dreamed it would. I can not wait to see it for myself."

"It doesn't look like this now," he warned, feeling an annoying stab of regret for puncturing her happiness. "This was drawn almost sixty years ago when the property still belonged to my family. I fear it is not nearly so elegant these days."

"Oh, but it looks just like a home," she murmured, tracing the graceful lines of a turret with a loving finger. "It must be so lovely to see when the sun is rising and the sea is at rest."

"It is," Lucien said softly, smiling in memory. "When the sun hits it just right it glows like gold tinged with pink, and if you are out on the south terrace it feels as if you are wrapped in sunlight."

The poetic description brought Elly's head up in surprise. "But I understood you to say you have never been in Seagate," she said, studying him with marked suspicion. "Are you now saying you have?"

59

Lucien mentally cursed his slip of the tongue. "Not *in* the house, no," he answered quickly, inventing the tale as he went along. "But as a young boy I often used to sneak on to the south turret and play when no one was about. I recall your cousin caught me once and gave me a devil of a shaking."

"Did you see the ghost?" Elly asked, her gray-blue eyes twinkling in delight at the thought of a younger version of the marquess being confronted by her irate relation.

Lucien hesitated, and then gave a casual shrug. "Alas, no. I was quite disappointed too, if I remember correctly."

"Poor boy," Elly sympathized with a smile. "Perhaps your luck will change when you come to tea."

"Perhaps," he agreed, bracing himself for the storm he knew was about to descend. "But, speaking of Seagate, there is something else I should like to discuss with you."

"What about it?" She was instantly wary. "Henry has told you we shall not sell, and that is all there is to it."

"I am aware of that." Lucien's voice grew chilly. "Henry and I have already discussed the matter, and I accept his decision to retain ownership of Seagate. That is not what I meant."

"Then what did you mean?"

"Henry mentioned you were having some difficulty in obtaining the proper staff," he said slowly, choosing his words with the utmost care. Learning of her domestic problems had given him a wonderful idea, and he knew if he wanted it to work he would have to proceed with the greatest delicacy. "I thought perhaps I might be able to help you in the matter."

Even though she knew Henry had spoken with Seabrook, Elly felt her cheeks coloring with embar-

60

rassment. "It is very kind of you to offer, my lord," she said stiffly, "but I can assure you I have everything well in hand. In fact, I must beg your pardon as I have an appointment arriving at any moment, and I must go and meet her."

Lucien drew a steadying breath; knowing this was the most dangerous part of his plan. One wrong move on his part could upset everything. "You are referring, I gather, to a Mrs. Delfrey?"

Elly stared at him in amazement. "How do you know that?"

"Because I have taken leave to inform her not to bother coming as the position of housekeeper has already been filled. I did the same with Mr. Ferrall and the post as butler."

"What?"

"You heard me."

For a moment sheer disbelief made it impossible for Elly to speak, and then her temper exploded. "Of all the arrogant . . . overbearing . . . toplofty . . ." Words failed and she simply glared at him. "How dare you presume to do such a thing!" she raged. "Just who the devil do you think you are?"

"Your brother's friend," he replied without a flicker of emotion. "And as difficult as you may find this, your own friend as well. I was only thinking of your welfare."

"My welfare?" She tossed her head back, her eyes glittering as she met his gaze. "Do you really expect me to believe that?"

Had a man challenged his word in such a contemptuous manner, Lucien would have demanded immediate satisfaction. As it was, he forced himself to count to ten before answering. "I expect you to believe the truth," he told her through clenched teeth. "Henry was quite concerned that you were pushing yourself too hard and asked me for my assistance. As I know most of the people in the area, I was more than happy to comply."

Much as she would have liked to continue the argument, Elly knew he was telling the truth. "I do not see why he should concern himself," she muttered, her eyes shifting away from his. "I have always seen to the running of the house."

"I am aware of that," Lucien answered evenly. "But Henry mentioned you were dangerously ill shortly before your departure, and he is afraid you may suffer a relapse. Believe it or not, Miss Denning, your brother loves you, and he only wants what is best for you."

Elly ducked her head, feeling like the worst villainess alive. During her bout of fever Henry hadn't left her side, and when she'd finally regained her senses she'd seen tears of relief in his eyes. "I know he loves me," she said, still reluctant to meet the marquess's eyes. "And I appreciate your assistance. But what shall I do for a butler and housekeeper? I can hardly be expected to run Seagate without them."

"Of course not," Lucien replied, amazed it had proven so easy. "And with that in mind I have engaged the services of Mr. and Mrs. Stanley; they were employed in those capacities while your cousin was still alive, and they were more than happy to return to their previous positions. They should be waiting for you when you arrive."

"I see," Elly said, disliking being handed the *fait accompli* but not seeing that there was anything she could do about it. "In that case, my lord, you have my thanks. This greatly relieves my mind. I must own I was growing desperate." She stole a quick peek at his face.

He was smiling at her. "You are welcome, Miss Denning," he said with a polite bow. "And now it is I who must beg your leave. I am meeting some old friends, and I fear I shall be shockingly late if I don't leave this instant."

"Of course, my lord." Elly was more than delighted to be rid of him. "And . . . and thank you once again for the sketch. I can't wait to show it to Henry."

"I am glad it pleased you" was all he said, still smiling. "Speaking of Henry, he informs me there is to be dancing tomorrow evening. May I hope you will save me a dance?"

His request made Elly start with surprise. "Certainly, my lord, I should be more than happy to do so," she said, uttering a silent prayer of thanks that she had undertaken to learn the latest dances on the tedious voyage from Cape Town.

"Very good." He took her hand in his and carried it to his lips. "Until tomorrow, then, Miss Denning," he said, depositing a brief kiss on her warm flesh. "I shall be looking forward to it."

Less than an hour into the dinner party Elly was certain she had made the worst mistake of her life. While in the depths of Africa, shivering from fear and loneliness, she'd often amused herself by imagining a scene just like this, a beautiful ballroom filled with elegantly-dressed people. In those daydreams she'd pictured herself as the center of all attention, laughing and flirting with a crowd of admirers. But all of her fantasizing hadn't prepared her for the noisy, overheated, overbearing reality of one hundred people crammed into a room designed to hold fifty.

"Are you all right, my dear?" Thomas Shaftson enquired anxiously, bending closer to give Elly's hand a comforting squeeze. "You are dreadfully pale."

"I am fine, Uncle Thomas, thank you," Elly an-

63

swered, forcing back her choking sense of panic long enough to send him a grateful smile. "It is just . . . I hadn't thought there would be quite so many people here."

"Yes, Flavia always did like a good crush," he agreed, casting an amused glance about the ballroom. "And since you and Henry have been the object of so much speculation, a good turnout was more or less guaranteed."

"Indeed," Elly's sense of humor stirred to life. "I can not remember the last time I was the object of so many sets of eyes. I am beginning to feel rather like one of the exhibits at the Royal Menagerie."

Her uncle gave a delighted chuckle. "I know what you mean. But chin up; our hour in purgatory is almost at an end and then you shall be free to move about as you wish."

Elly said nothing, although she privately thought "purgatory" was far too mild a description of a formal reception line. She stole a quick glance at Henry, relieved to see he was bearing up so well. Rather than scowling and pouting as she had feared he would do, he was all smiles and conversation, charming the circle of young ladies surrounding him. He was looking even more handsome than usual in his faultlessly-cut jacket of black velvet and cream evening breeches, his blue eyes matching the sapphire winking from the folds of his snowy cravat.

She was wearing the simple blue gown she and her aunt had originally selected, although she'd decided against the small cap. Mary had removed the white plume and fashioned a charming aigrette from it, making Elly feel every bit as stylish as the other ladies gliding languidly about the room. In honor of the occasion her uncle had allowed her to wear the family pearls, and they hung from her neck and ears in creamy perfection.

"Well, this is a surprise," her uncle said suddenly, raising his quizzing glass to his eye. "Flavia mentioned she'd invited him, but I never dreamed he would actually attend."

"Who?" Elly glanced about expectantly; half hoping for a glimpse of the Royal Dukes or perhaps even Prinny himself. Instead she saw Lord Seabrook, accompanied by a tall blond man making his way towards them.

"Lord Twyford," Mr. Shaftson said, running a nervous hand through his thinning hair. "He is considered to be one of the most powerful men in Parliament."

"He is?" Elly gave the approaching man a searching look. Dressed in much the same fashion as the other men present he didn't look so very powerful to her. In fact, compared to Seabrook's aura of arrogant control he seemed more dandified than dangerous.

"Don't let appearances deceive you." Mr. Shaftson correctly interpreted her skeptical expression. "The man is highly connected with the Home Office, and 'tis said he has the ear of the Prime Minister himself. I wonder what he is doing here."

Before Elly could offer any speculations the two men were upon them, and her uncle was performing the necessary introductions.

"Miss Denning, Mr. Denning." The viscount acknowledged them with his most charming smile. "It is a pleasure to meet you. I have read several of your father's tracts with great interest, and only wish I might have had the honor of meeting him. The man was clearly a genius."

"Thank you, my lord." Henry accepted the praise with a pleased smile. "It is kind of you to say so."

"Not at all," Twyford returned, his gray eyes warm. "I was particularly interested in his work involving medicinal plants native to the Nile region.

Seabrook has mentioned you are compiling a book based on his last expedition; is that so?"

Henry brightened at once, always more than happy to discuss his life's work. "Indeed it is, my lord," he said eagerly. "I mean to work on it while we are in the country."

"Then I shall look forward to its release with the greatest pleasure," Twyford turned to Elly, smiling again. "And what of you, Miss Denning?" he enquired suavely. "How do you mean to occupy your time while your brother is scribbling away?"

"Oh, I shall think of something, my lord," she returned, annoyed by his hint that she would be enjoying herself while poor Henry labored away in his airless study.

"I am hoping Miss Denning will allow me to show her something of the area once she and her brother have settled in," Lucien inserted, reading his opponent's displeasure in the flash of her blue and gray eyes. "Brighton is a beautiful town filled with charm, and I can not wait to give her the Grand Tour."

A sarcastic rejoinder came readily to mind, but in deference to her aunt and uncle Elly managed to control herself. "That sounds delightful, Lord Seabrook, thank you," she said with a stiff smile. "It is kind of you to offer."

Lucien gave her a sharp look, but with the crowd of late arrivals queuing up behind him there was little he could say. He and Alex remained another few moments and then took their leave, after extracting a promise from Miss Denning that she would save each of them a dance.

"Well? What do you think?" Lucien demanded the moment they were out of earshot.

"As you say, a shrew of the first water," Alex replied, nodding to an acquaintance. "And I quite agree with your estimation that she shall prove our greatest obstacle. The lady is a tigress in bluestocking's clothing."

Lucien's eyes slid back to Elly, taking in her appearance with a thoughtful frown. "A tigress, indeed," he murmured, reluctantly admiring her feminine slenderness. "It shall be a pleasure to trim her claws."

"Just be careful you don't get ripped to pieces in the process. Miss Denning looks as if she could give a good accounting of herself should the need arise."

Lucien's mouth quirked in a wry smile. "I shall keep that in mind," he drawled, amused by Twyford's teasing warning. "But may I remind you that I am not totally without defenses? When pressed I too can prove my mettle."

"I am sure you can," Alex replied, his eyes gleaming with laughter. "Although I much doubt a deadly proficiency with pistols and swords will do you much good in this case. Which reminds me, is all in readiness?"

"Almost." A wolfish smile spread across Lucien's face. "There are still a few details to be worked out, but I think I can promise you that Miss Denning will receive a welcome to Seagate she shall not be soon forgetting."

Chapter Five

The journey to Seagate was accomplished in less than a day, no easy feat considering Henry kept insisting the coachman stop every few miles so that he could gather samples of the local flora. Finally after what seemed an eternity to Elly they were pulling up in front of the ancient house, and after one glance at its massive walls and crumbling turrets she fell irrevocably in love.

"Oh, Henry, look at it," she sighed, the hood of her cape falling back as she tipped her head to gaze up at the structure. "Isn't it beautiful?"

Henry said nothing, his expression troubled as he studied the stone and brick edifice that cast its ominous shadow across the cobblestoned courtyard. In the gathering darkness the latticed windows glowed like malevolent yellow eyes, and he had the uneasy sensation that he was being watched and weighed by an unseen presence. He swallowed uncomfortably and drew his cloak closer about him.

"Don't know that I would go quite as far as that," he mumbled, not wishing to put a damper on Elly's enthusiasm. "But it certainly is . . . er . . . impressive. I wonder how many rooms there are."

"Twenty-five, not including the servant's quarters," Elly answered promptly; having already committed the information to memory. "And once the south wing is repaired, we shall have even more rooms to use."

Henry cast a nervous glance at the section of house she had indicated, and for a brief moment he found himself wishing he'd accepted Seabrook's last offer. This wasn't at all what he'd been expecting since his sister had first mentioned the "country house" he'd inherited.

Elly finally noticed her brother's uneasy silence, and cast him a questioning look. "Well?" she demanded, giving him a prod with her elbow. "Are we going to stand out here all night, or are we going to go inside? 'Tis cold."

Henry shivered, his heart sinking as he realized he had no choice but to enter the brooding structure. Swallowing his trepidation, he grasped her by the elbow and guided her up the stone steps and into the old house.

Mrs. Magney shifted restlessly, uncomfortable with the presence of so many people. She would have preferred waiting until the soothing darkness of night before appearing, but as the housekeeper she felt it only proper that she be there to greet her new master and mistress as they entered the Grand Hall. And it wasn't as if they could see her. Her dark eyes gleamed with amusement as she clung to the familiar shadows.

The sight of these two people pleased her. A young couple would mean children, and it seemed an eternity since she had last beheld a babe. She liked the looks of her new mistress; the lass had a competent air about her, and Mrs. Magney knew she could trust her to take good care of the house. The master also met with Mrs. Magney's approval, for he was as handsome as the devil and would doubtlessly give Seagate many children. Yes, she decided with a smug nod, things were looking up at last. She gave her new employers a final look, and then vanished with a rattle of her keys.

"Welcome to Seagate, Miss Denning, Mr. Denning," the butler, Mr. Stanley intoned, bowing deeply as he greeted Elly and Henry. "I trust the two of you had a pleasant journey?"

"Quite pleasant, thank you, Stanley," Elly replied, with a conflicting set of emotions studying the gray-haired man. On the one hand she was pleased to see he seemed so well suited for his position, but on the other she couldn't help but be piqued that Seabrook had done such an excellent job in hiring him. It would have been far more satisfying to arrive and find all in chaos, she thought, feeling a prick of remorse that she could be so small minded.

"That is good to hear, miss," Stanley replied, unbending so far as to smile at her. "If it pleases you, I have instructed Cook to serve dinner an hour after your arrival. I am sure you and Mr. Denning will wish to freshen yourselves after your long journey."

Elly glanced down at her travel-stained cloak. "Yes, that would be lovely," she murmured, amused by Stanley's diplomacy. "And perhaps tomorrow Mrs. Stanley could show me about the house?" She smiled at the thin woman whose chain of keys betrayed her identity.

"As you say, Miss Denning," Mrs. Stanley bustled forward to give her an approving nod. "In the meanwhile, let me escort you to your rooms. I'm sure you'll be wanting to get out of them dirty clothes and into a warm bath; now, won't you?"

Elly agreed that a bath sounded just the thing, and after promising Henry she'd meet him in the drawing room for a pre-dinner glass of sherry she allowed the older woman to guide her to her rooms. Her maid, Mary had arrived ahead of her, and was already unpacking the trunks as Elly and Mrs. Stanley entered the room.

"I hope these meet with your approval, Miss Denning," the housekeeper said, casting a critical eye about the burgundy and blue sitting room. "It is one of the better suites in the house, and it has by far the best view." She opened the heavy velvet drapes, and Elly found herself gazing down at the restless sea.

"Oh, how very lovely!" she cried, although it was difficult to see anything in the fading light. "I shall leave my window open at night, and go to sleep lulled by the sound of the waves."

"Oh, I shouldn't do that, miss," Mrs. Stanley advised with a frown. "The night air is most unhealthy, and the salt from the spray would turn these drapes to rags in no time at all. You'd not believe the chore I've had keeping everything from rotting clean away!"

Elly, who'd spent more years than she cared to remember fighting the corroding influences of heat and humidity sympathized with the housekeeper at once, and promised to leave the windows firmly closed. After the other woman departed she quickly removed her soiled clothing, slipping into the tub of steaming water with a contented sigh. She would have preferred lingering in the scented bath, but she knew Henry would be waiting for her and climbed reluctantly out to be dressed by a scolding Mary.

"You ought to be taking your dinner on a tray," she said, binding Elly's hair back in an attractive coronet of braids. "Ladies of quality are supposed to be delicate. It's what society expects of 'em, and it's what the gentlemen prefer as well. You'd not want them to think you *robust*," she added, her tone darkly disapproving.

For some reason Elly thought of the marquess of Seabrook, and she wondered if this was the sort of insipid behavior he expected of the poor unfortunate girl he would make his bride. Probably, she decided, her lips curving in a smile. Given that, it was small

71

wonder the two of them struck such sparks off each other. Delicate was not a word that could ever be truthfully applied to her, and she thanked God it was so.

Once her appearance met Mary's exacting specifications Elly went off in search of Henry. After a few false starts and wrong turns she finally located the drawing room and hurried inside. She discovered her brother perched on the edge of a gold brocade settee; his back as stiff as a rod and his hands clenched tightly on his lap.

"Henry, what on earth ails you?" she demanded, giving him an incredulous look as she took the chair facing him. "You look for all the world like a nervous suitor calling on his beloved's father!"

Henry flushed at her analogy, and shot her an aggrieved look. "Nothing is wrong," he denied, tensely running a finger under his collar. "It is just . . . er . . . didn't you say something about this place being haunted?"

Elly gaped at him for a moment and then burst out laughing. She knew she was being unkind, but she couldn't help but find amusement in the situation. That it should be Henry—practical, staid Henry—who succumbed to Seagate's infamous resident struck her as especially hilarious, and she was unable to stop herself. She wondered what Seabrook would have to say about this.

Henry's eyes flashed with embarrassment. "It's not funny, blast it," he muttered, rising to his feet to pace about the room. "This house gives me the horrors, and I have half a mind to sell it to Seabrook the very next time I see him!"

Elly's amusement faded at his angry words. "You can't be serious," she said weakly, seeing her carefully-laid plans collapsing before her eyes. "You would never do such a thing!"

"No, I suppose I would not," Henry conceded, frowning as he resumed his seat. "But dash it all, El,

I don't like this place. There's something about it. . . ." His voice trailed off as he glanced uncertainly about him.

"It is very old," Elly agreed carefully, praying that she wouldn't overplay the scene. "And I must own it does have a certain . . . Gothic air about it. But you really do not believe in ghosts, do you?"

"Well . . ."

"Of course you don't." She gave his hand a quick pat. "You are a man of science and learning; naturally you would not be taken in by all that ghostly mumbo jumbo. That would be more likely to happen to me."

Henry's expression grew thoughtful. "That is so," he said, his shoulders relaxing slightly. "You always did have an overactive imagination, El."

"Very true." She was more than willing to sacrifice her pride in the interest of preserving her home. "Remember the time we were in Egypt and I insisted I had seen an ancient priestess?"

"Yes, you screeched like a scalded cat and wouldn't go in that tomb no matter how Papa threatened you," he said, a grin of brotherly indulgence spreading across his face. "And then there was that time in the jungle when you thought a tiger had invaded the camp while we were gone, and you made our bearers check your tent before you'd go inside."

"A typically feminine response I now blush to recall," she said, wisely not mentioning the scratch marks on a tree that had first alerted her to the animal's presence. She also refrained from reminding him that not two days later the cook had shot a huge tiger not ten yards from their camp.

"Yes, now that I think of it I ain't the least bit surprised that you should think the house is haunted," Henry said, happily transferring his uneasiness to his sister. "But just as I told you, it's only because the house is so old. It'll be all right, El;

don't worry." This time it was he who gave her hand a condescending pat.

Elly swallowed the natural inclination to box his ears, and managed to look grateful instead. "I daresay you are right, Henry," she said with a tight smile. "It is just my silly nerves."

"This won't work."

"Of course it will, Alex, now stop grumbling and help me move this stone."

Twyford glared at Seabrook one last time and then put his broad shoulder to the large boulder that blocked access to the hidden tunnel. "Of all the stupid . . . adolescent . . . pranks," he grunted as he gave the rock a determined shove. "This is undoubtedly the most absurd thing I have ever heard of! Do you have any idea how ridiculous you look?"

"So long as it does the trick I don't give a tinker's curse what I look like," Lucien answered, muttering a curse as he threw his own weight against the rock. "And I do not see why you're complaining. At least you're not the one rigged out in this dammed costume!"

Alex refrained from comment, although the look he flashed his friend spoke volumes. It was approaching midnight, and the last thing he wanted was to be out in this chilling mist with a man who glowed eerily in the darkness. It is a good thing I'm not the superstitious sort, he thought, heaving a sigh of relief as the stone finally shifted. Otherwise the sight of Seabrook would have been enough to send him into the vapors.

"Pass me that torch, will you?" Lucien held out a hand as he peered into the dark passageway. "It is black as the hubs of hell in here."

Alex complied and then followed Seabrook into the narrow stone tunnel that led into the house. "I still don't see why you insist upon this charade," he grumbled, trying not to notice the frantic squealing noises about his booted feet as they made their way through the passageway. "Why can't we mount our watch on the cliffs? The view is every bit as good."

"But not as safe," Lucien answered grimly. "Besides, the house has a secret tunnel that leads from the cellars to the cove. When that long boat lands on the beach, it is imperative that we move quickly *and* undetected. We need the house."

Alex conceded the point, although he was still far from satisfied. "What will we do if it doesn't work?" he asked, his mind as usual focusing on all aspects of the situation. "You seemed adamantly opposed to placing them in custody when I first suggested it. Have you changed your mind?"

"No," Lucien said quickly, his jaw tightening at the thought of young Denning, whom he was growing to like, suffering under the indignity of house arrest. The poor lad would probably wither and die under such circumstances; to say nothing of how his hell-cat of a sister would react. They'd probably have to keep her bound and gagged, and even then he wouldn't put it past her to make an escape attempt. He grinned, envisioning the redoubtable Miss Denning tying the bedsheets together and climbing out a convenient window. It would be just like her. . . .

"Ouch!"

The cry of pain was followed by a flow of blistering curses, and he turned to see Alex rubbing his forehead. "Are you all right?"

"Damned low ceiling," Alex replied, still looking far from pleased. "Your ancestors must have been dwarfs!"

"No, merely Catholics who were slow to see the light," he replied, resuming his journey towards the main house. "The first set of tunnels and secret passages was built during the reign of Queen Elizabeth."

"The first set?" Alex asked, intrigued despite him-

75

self.

"There are at least two separate series of tunnels, to say nothing of hidden rooms and staircases."

"Good God, what reasons could your relations have had for such secrecy? Surely they weren't all political rebels?"

"No." Lucien frowned as he thought of his family's convoluted past. "The second set of secret tunnels was built in the last century by a great-great-uncle who was reputed to be hideously deformed."

"Reputed?"

"No one, not even his servants, saw him for the last fifteen years of his life," Lucien explained. "He had rooms built in back of rooms so that he could come and go without ever being seen. That was why he had the tunnel leading to the beach dug; by using it, he was able to slip in and out of the house unobserved. His house in London was said to be the same, although there is no way to be certain. It burned to the ground shortly after his death."

Alex gave a low whistle. "How extraordinary," he said, looking thoughtful. "I can see then why you have such confidence in this scheme of yours. You should be able to pop in and out of the house virtually undetected, almost as if you were a ghost. You have my compliments, Seabrook."

"Thank you." Lucien paused at the moss-covered door barring entrance to the main house. "Now watch carefully; this is what must be done to go any further. Whatever you do, don't mix up the sequence."

"What will happen if I do?" Alex asked, watching intently as Lucien pressed three bricks in the pattern of a triangle.

"The stone will roll over the passage, sealing you in here forever."

"Ah." Alex tried not to shudder at the thought of being entombed alive. "Cautious men, your ancestors."

"They survived," Lucien answered, stepping back as the door swung open. "This way. I had Mrs. Stanley place her in the east wing. It has a hidden room built off the main bedroom."

"And you are certain that no one else knows about this intriguing network of tunnels and hidden rooms?" Alex pressed, his hand closing about the pistol he had tucked in his pocket. "Can't say as I relish the prospect of encountering an enemy in this Cretan maze."

"No one knows," Lucien assured him coldly. "Denning's relations may have succeeded in buying my ancestral home, but they didn't buy my family's secrets."

"In that case, lead on," Alex said with a sudden smile. "I find I am growing increasingly interested in seeing you perform your ghostly magic. Only mind you're not *too* convincing. I fear I am not quite as brave as you, and I wouldn't want to disgrace myself by swooning. Besides, it wouldn't do if you were to conjure up a real ghost, hmm?" And he laughed at his own joke.

Lucien smiled sickly, the memory of a ghostly laugh bringing goose bumps to his flesh. In the next moment he was shaking his head in disgust. Of course there are no such things as ghosts, he told himself sternly; they were only figments of the imagination, or the result of clever machinations. No one knew that better than he.

At first Elly took the low moaning she was hearing for the creaking boards of a ship, and imagined she was back at sea. Wretched boat, she thought, pulling the sheets over her ears and snuggling deeper into her pillow. She only hoped the vessel made it back to England before breaking apart. The rusty rattle of a chain was next heard, adding to her sleepy impression that she was at sea. Such noises were commonplace aboard ship, and she simply ignored them. She was so tired. . . .

"Leave this place. . . ."

The husky whisper penetrated the comforting mists of sleep, bringing Elly's eyes flying open in alarm. She lay stiffly on the bed, her heart pounding in her chest as she tried to discern what could be responsible for the paralyzing fear washing over her. Then the voice came again.

"Get out!"

She sat bolt upright, clutching the sheets to her chest as she glanced wildly about the room. "Who is it?" she called, willing her voice not to shake as she searched the velvet shadows for any sign of the intruder. "Who is there?"

"Leave . . . will you live . . . leave now," the voice moaned again, the sound coming from almost directly in front of her.

She squinted, trying to see her tormentor. "Henry Aloysius Denning, if this is your idea of a joke, then you are sadly mistaken!" she protested, desperately mustering the remnants of her courage. "If you don't stop this nonsense at once I vow I shall . . ." Her voice trailed off in horror as a shape emerged out of the darkness.

He was tall. Or at least, she thought with a brittle calm, he must have been tall in life. His features were mercifully indistinguishable, although she could see the shadows of his eyes and mouth as he drew closer. He was an unearthly green-white, and as he pointed a hand at her she could see that he was emitting a strange glow.

She opened her mouth, but no sound would come. It was every nightmare she had ever had come to life, and the worst of it was knowing that it was real, that this was actually happening. She tried again, and this time the sound that erupted from her throat was a piercing scream of pure terror.

* * *

"Are you quite sure you are all right, El?" Henry asked for the tenth time in less than half an hour. "We can send for a doctor if you would like one."

"No, Henry, I am f-fine," Elly replied, her voice trembling despite her resolve that it should not. "You can go to bed now if you wish."

"What? And leave you alone to face another nightmare? I should say not!" He seemed incensed that she should think him so lacking in filial responsibility. "I am staying here until you are asleep."

Then he will doubtlessly remain for the rest of the night, Elly thought, sighing as she leaned her head against the pillows. It seemed unlikely she would get so much as a wink of sleep before daylight.

Her screams had brought the household running, and when the servants and Henry had come bursting into her room they'd discovered her cowering under the bedclothes. That she had behaved in such a missish fashion was a source of great embarrassment for her, but there was no way she could have continued gazing at the apparition and still maintained her sanity.

"Well, if you won't have the doctor in, won't you at least have a sip of this?" Mrs. Stanley implored, stepping forward to press a glass into Elly's hands.

"What is it?" She gave the contents a suspicious sniff.

"Warm milk laced with a wee bit of laudanum," the housekeeper responded, nervously twisting the cord that fastened her nightrobe. " 'Tis just what you need to help you sleep."

Elly hesitated, but in the end she capitulated to the older woman's urging. As a rule she avoided the dangerous mixture of opium and alcohol, but this was an emergency. She raised the potation to her lips for a cautious sip.

"That's it," Mrs. Stanley urged, placing a maternal arm around Elly's shoulder. "Mind you drink every drop."

Elly dutifully did as she was told, draining the glass of its contents before handing it back to the hovering housekeeper. "Thank you," she said, forcing a wobbly smile to her lips. "I'm sure I shall be fine now."

Mrs. Stanley seemed far from convinced, but she and the other servants eventually filed out of the room, leaving Elly alone with Henry. "Are you certain you're all right?" he asked, once the door had closed behind them. "You're rather pale."

"I'm fine," she repeated, touched by his obvious concern. "I told you it was just a . . . a bad dream."

"Can't say I can remember you ever having one of those before, except right after Mama died," Henry said, his blue eyes sharp as they rested on her face. "What was it about?"

She squirmed uncomfortably, plucking at the quilted satin coverlet. Since the moment Henry had come bursting into her room, a poker held in his upraised arm, she clung to the fiction that her screams were the result of a vivid nightmare. She didn't know why precisely, but she did not want her brother to know she had seen the ghost. It seemed so . . . silly, so typically feminine, that she decided she'd rather face the specter again than endure her brother's teasing. And perhaps it was just a dream, she told herself hopefully. Everyone knew there were no such things as ghosts.

"I . . . I can't remember," she muttered, flushing at the lie she was forced to utter. "It was just one of those silly dreams. I must have had too much fish at dinner; it often upsets my system."

"Mmm." The look he flashed her was frankly skeptical. "Are you sure your bad dreams weren't caused by something else, say our conversation about the ghost? Perhaps you dreamed of him."

His acuity stunned her, but she was quick to grasp his explanation. "Yes, perhaps I did," she said slowly, giving him a thoughtful look. "We *did* discuss him at some length, did we not? And as you pointed out I have always been cursed with a vivid imagination. It is not surprising my fancies followed me in my sleep. I am sorry if I disturbed you."

"You didn't disturb me," he assured her, smiling as he covered her chilled hand with his own. "Although I must say you did give me a devil of a fright when you started screeching like that. For a moment I thought . . ." He stopped and shook his head. "Well, if you're certain you're all right, I believe I shall be retiring now. I saw a chaise longue in your sitting room; if you like I could—"

"Henry, go to bed," Elly pointed an admonishing finger at the door. "For the last and final time, I am perfectly fine. The laudanum Mrs. Stanley gave me is beginning to take effect, and I shall doubtlessly sleep until morning. Good night."

Henry took the hint, chuckling as he bent to brush a kiss across her cheek. "Good night, El," he said, drawing back to give her a tender smile. "Sleep well."

"I will," she promised, keeping a smile pinned to her lips until he was safely out of the door. The moment she was alone she collapsed against the pillows, a very unladylike word forming on her lips.

"I don't believe in ghosts," she said, clutching her bedsheets to her chest and fighting to keep her eyes open. "I . . . do . . . not . . . believe . . . in . . . ghosts . . ." Her voice trailed off and died as she surrendered to the powerful drug, falling into a deep and blessedly peaceful sleep.

Chapter Six

Elly was up early the next morning, bleary-eyed and misty-headed from the laudanum. She found Henry lingering over his breakfast, and after pouring herself a restorative cup of tea she sent him a teasing look. "No need to ask how you are feeling," she drawled, raising her cup to her lips. "You look bright as a newly-minted guinea. I trust you slept well?"

"Like a babe," he assured her, his blue eyes shining as he studied her. "And what of you? Any more bad dreams?"

Elly hastily lowered her eyes to her plate. "No, no bad dreams," she said in a falsely-bright tone. In the clear light of a soft spring morning the very notion of a ghost seemed so ludicrous, and she was grateful she'd withheld the truth from him.

"What are your plans for the morning?" he asked as they shared the companionable meal. "Will you go riding?"

"Later, perhaps," she replied, thinking of the many tasks that lay ahead. "I'm to meet Mrs. Stanley after breakfast and we shall tour the house together, and then this afternoon I thought to have a look about Brighton. What about you? You don't mean to cloister yourself in the library, do you?" She sent him a reproving look.

"No." He greeted her mild reproach with a grin. "As a matter of fact, I'd also planned to explore the town. They have quite a Botanical Society here, and Lord Seabrook has given me a letter of introduction. Was that not kind of him?"

"Very kind," Elly muttered, her appetite deserting her at the mention of the troublesome marquess. She'd hoped by removing Henry to Brighton she would free him of the haughty lord's influence, but apparently it wouldn't be as easy as she'd thought.

"The prince is also very fond of botany," Henry continued, blissfully unaware of his sister's dark thought's concerning his friend. "He has an excellent conservatory at the pavilion, and his lordship has promised to secure an invitation for us. I am to have tea with him when he comes down next Thursday."

Elly's cup clattered as she set it down in its saucer. *"Next* Thursday!" she exclaimed, shooting him an indignant look. "Do you mean to say that wretch shall be plaguing us already?"

"Oughtn't call Seabrook a wretch, El," he replied, his tone censorious. "The man's a marquess, after all, and a dashed fine fellow once you get to know him."

"I am sure he is," she retorted, torn between her dislike of Seabrook and her desire to meet the prince. As neither she nor Henry could claim noble birth, it was unlikely they should ever be invited to the pavilion on their own, and if her plans for him were to succeed, it was imperative that they move in the proper circles. Much as it vexed her, she knew she had no choice but to accept the marquess's patronage.

"Well, he certainly is." Henry was scowling at her. "He's been a very good friend to me, and I'll not have you snubbing him. Besides, the pair of you have a great deal in common."

"What could I possibly have in common with that . . . with Lord Seabrook?" she demanded, amending her speech out of courtesy for her brother's feelings.

"To begin with, neither of you is willing to give so much as an inch," he said bluntly, folding his arms across his chest. "You're both as proud and as stubborn as the very devil, and 'tis no wonder to me that the two of you have been at dagger's drawn since the first. You're also well educated and intelligent, and even like the same literature. He is almost as fond of that Shakespeare fellow as you are."

"Seabrook likes Shakespeare?" Elly was vaguely surprised. She would have thought the marquess much too busy chasing lightskirts to bother himself with intellectual pursuits.

Henry nodded. "Even has a Shakespearean garden at his house here in the country, which he has invited us to see. Not that *you* would be interested, I am sure."

Elly had the good grace to be ashamed by her poor manners. "I am sure it is lovely," she muttered, her cheeks pinking with embarrassment. "Did his lordship say when the prince would be coming to Brighton? I should think he would wish to remain in London for the Season."

"I'm not sure, but I think it must be quite soon. I overheard Seabrook talking to Lord Twyford, and he mentioned something about 'the preparations' for the prince's arrival. Does it matter?"

"No, I was just wondering," Elly answered, her lively mind turning to what the prince's arrival could mean. She knew society revolved around His Royal Highness, and if he came to Brighton then the rest of the *ton* was sure to follow. Perhaps Miranda might even come down, she mused, brightening at the thought of her friend.

"Well, if that is all then I believe I shall be off," Henry announced, laying his napkin beside his plate. "The sun is out, and I want to have a look about before it disappears again. Will you wish me to escort you when you go out?"

His request took Elly by surprise, for Henry seldom concerned himself with such niceties. "Why, yes, Henry, I will," she said, shooting him a pleased smile. "It is very kind of you to ask."

He shrugged somewhat uncomfortably. "Seabrook said I shouldn't let you go about so much on your own," he said, not quite meeting her eyes. "Said it was probably why you was such a hoyden. I'll see you at luncheon, then," and he was gone before his furious sister could sputter a reply.

After dining Elly went in search of the housekeeper. She located her in a small room just off the kitchens, and entered after a perfunctory knock on the door. "Good morning, Mrs. Stanley," she said, advancing on the older woman with a smile. "I trust you were able to get back to sleep after last night's alarm?"

To her surprise the elderly housekeeper gave a squeal of fright, leaping from her desk and whirling around to face Elly with a look of wide-eyed panic on her face. "My patience, me!" she cried, laying both her palms against her chest. "What a fright you have given me, miss!"

"I'm sorry, I didn't mean to startle you." Elly's apology was automatic as she gazed worriedly at Mrs. Stanley. "Didn't you hear me knocking?"

"My mind must have been awandering," the housekeeper replied, straightening her starched cap with a nervous tug. "Things have all been at sixes and sevens since Lord Seabrook brought us back, and what with Mrs. Magney plaguing the new girls it seems I'm two steps behind before I even get started! But enough about me, what was it you was wanting, Miss Denning?"

"Yesterday you mentioned showing me the house," Elly replied, wondering who Mrs. Magney might be. "But naturally if this is an inconvenient time I could—"

"Oh no!" Mrs. Stanley interrupted, flashing her a nervous smile. " 'Twould be my pleasure to take you about the place. Where would you like to start?"

Elly was quiet a moment. "The south wing, I

think," she said at last. "The solicitor said it was in the most need of repair, and I should like to have a look at it before deciding what we should do."

Mrs. Stanley grew pale. "The south wing?" she quavered.

"Yes," Elly gave her a puzzled look. "Is there some impediment?"

The housekeeper gave another start. "Oh no! It is just . . . well, the house was empty a good year afore they was able to locate your brother, and heaven only knows what sort of vermin and the like may have moved in to make their homes. I meant to have a rat catcher in, but there's not been enough time."

"Oh, mice," Elly dismissed the threat with a light laugh. "Don't worry, Mrs. Stanley, I'm not so weak as to be put off by a few rodents. Why, once in Africa I found a half-grown lion cub in my garden! I shan't swoon, I promise you."

"It was not the mice I was thinking of," Mrs. Stanley muttered beneath her breath before pinning a polite smile on her face. "Very well, Miss Denning," she said, covering her trepidations with a look of brisk efficiency, "the south wing it shall be. Would you like to start in the cellars or the attics?"

"The attics," Elly replied, deciding to ignore the housekeeper's odd behavior for the moment. "No need to disturb the rats just yet. Lead the way, Mrs. Stanley."

The housekeeper complied, and less than five minutes later Elly found herself standing in the decayed ruins of what had once been an elegant drawing room. Beneath her feet the carpet had faded to an unrecognizable shade somewhere between gray and pink, and stains, the origins of which she did not even wish to contemplate, littered the tattered shreds that remained. Moldering velvet drapes hung crookedly on broken rods, and layers of dust covered the few pieces of furniture that remained.

"Good heavens!" Elly exclaimed, poking at a rotting tapestry with the tip of her finger. "What has happened here? I have seen Arab villages in better condition!"

"Nothing has happened, miss, and that is the problem," Mrs. Stanley replied, her nose wrinkling at the smell of mold and mildew that hung in the air. "A grand house like this needs constant upkeep, and your late cousin, if you'll forgive me for speaking ill of the dead, had neither the blunt nor the inclination to look after the place. He'd as lief have the whole house tumble down about his ear as spend a farthing to keep it up."

"So I see." Elly sighed, casting a discouraged look about the squalid room as the enormity of the situation struck her. "Are all the rooms as bad as this?"

"Worse," Mrs. Stanley said, noting her young mistress's downcast expression with a pang of guilt. "The roof's mostly gone, and as for the chimneys, well, it would take a miracle if any of them was to be salvaged."

Elly was silent a long moment, fighting the urge to burst into bitter tears. All her life she had dreamed of the day she would have a house to call her own, and achieving her goal only to find the house of her dreams in ruins was a crushing disappointment. Tears shimmered in her blue-gray eyes, but before they could fall her customary sense of determination stirred to life and she turned to the housekeeper with a set smile.

"I shall discuss this with my brother," she said briskly. "In the meanwhile, I want the entire wing scrubbed from top to bottom. Perhaps it won't look so bad once it's been cleaned and properly aired."

"Perhaps," Mrs. Stanley echoed, although it was obvious she did not share Elly's optimism. "Will you want to be seeing the rest of the house?"

"We might as well," Elly answered, her heart lifting somewhat. "After viewing *this* place, I'm sure it will look as a palace to me."

They spent the rest of the morning touring the ancient dwelling, and Elly was appalled to see signs of her cousin's neglect in nearly every room. One room had the wallpaper peeled away, while another stood in obvious need of painting, and another still had suffered severe water damage from a leaky drainage pipe. There were broken windows everywhere, and in the grand ballroom the once exquisite parquet floor had been ravaged by wood rot and termites. By the time they reached the front parlor, her shoulders were sagging with defeat.

"Now I know why our solicitor was so insistent we accept Lord Seabrook's offer," she muttered, gratefully accepting the cup of tea Mrs. Stanley offered her. "This place is a disaster! The only wonder is why the marquess should want it at all."

"Seagate is his lordship's ancestral home," the older woman reminded her primly. "Why, when your cousin was still alive there wasn't a month that went by but an offer wasn't made. And of course, when the marchioness was so ill his lordship was more determined than ever, but Mr. Bevil would not hear of selling. I think he liked holding what a lord coveted, if you'll pardon my being so blunt."

"Not at all," Elly said, wondering for a horrified moment if her own reason for wishing to hold on to Seagate was equally reprehensible. To be sure, she did desire a home above all things, but did it *have* to be Seagate? How much of her determination to keep the house was lofty idealism, and how much pure spite?

"Well, it's only natural, if you want my opinion," Mrs. Stanley continued, not seeming to notice her employer's preoccupation. "The Seabrooks built this house not long after the Battle of Bosworth Field, and they held it through war and siege until the marquess's great-grandfather had the new manor house built and sold this one to Mr. Bevil's grandfather."

"The house dates back to the Yorks?" Elly set her

cup down and began glancing around her with renewed interest.

"Oh, yes, miss." The pride was obvious in Mrs.
Stanley's voice. "This is a very old house, and it is
filled with history. Why, the stories I could tell
you . . ." She stopped abruptly, flushing as she recalled the marquess's explicit instructions.

"What stories?" Elly asked eagerly, leaning forward
in her chair. "Don't stop now, ma'am, when you have
me at the very edge of my chair!"

"Oh . . . you know, tales of honor and that sort of
thing," the housekeeper stammered, regretting her
earlier outburst. "And a few tales of bloodshed and
evil-doing thrown in in the bargain. I'm sure you've
heard the like before."

"Yes, but I didn't happen to be residing in the place
in question," Elly replied, annoyed by the older woman's reticence. Then a sudden thought occurred to her.
"Has this anything to do with the ghost?"

"Which ghost, miss?"

The calm response to her query made Elly blink in
surprise. "Well, the smuggler, of course," she said,
gazing at Mrs. Stanley with a confused expression.
"How many ghosts are there, for heaven's sake?"

"Not to say as there are any, Miss Denning," Mrs.
Stanley answered quickly, relieved to have the conversation on a less dangerous subject. "But a house like
this has many legends, and I was only curious what
you may have heard. You're referring to Old Jenks, I
reckon."

"Old Jenks?" Elly echoed, thinking that a rather
paltry name for a ghost.

Mrs. Stanley nodded, lifting her cup to her lips for
a noisy sip. "He drowned in our cove, you know, and
'tis said he walks these very halls searching for the
men what betrayed him."

"Well, why should he walk here?" Elly wanted to
know, her heart beginning to pound in memory of the
glowing hand pointing at her. "One would think

89

ghosts — if there were such things — would want to remain closer to the scenes of their . . . er . . . demises."

"Perhaps," Mrs. Stanley agreed with an indifferent shrug. "But as it happened, Old Jenks had a very good reason for wanting to haunt this place."

Elly waited expectantly, but there was no further explanation forthcoming. "Well?" she prodded, her eyes bright with interest, "I pray you don't stop now!"

Mrs. Stanley leaned forward, her voice pitched so low Elly could scarce hear her. "Because Mr. Bevil's own father was the leader of the smugglers, and 'twas he who ordered Jenks's death."

Elly sat back, intrigued at the thought she might be descended from a line of murderous smugglers. "My heavens," she said somewhat weakly, "why would he do such a thing?"

Mrs. Stanley felt another pang of guilt. Although the story she was telling Miss Denning was perfectly true, she still could not help but feel like a villain for leading the poor girl on. Still, she did not see that she had any choice in the matter. She and Edgar had both given Lord Seabrook their word.

" 'Tis said Jenks was stealing cargo," she said, her dark eyes flicking away from Miss Denning's inquisitive expression. "And when William Denning learned of it, he ordered Jenks killed as a lesson to the others."

Elly felt the chill of horror creeping over her. When Lord Seabrook had first mentioned the ghost in the warm sunlight of Hyde Park, it had been easy to dismiss his words as errant nonsense. But after last night . . . Her hands crept up to chafe her arms.

"Well," she said in a falsely-bright tone, "if what you are saying is true, then I can understand why Mr. Jenks should see fit to honor us with his presence. I only hope he doesn't take to bothering poor Henry. Unless the man was interested in botany, I doubt they should have much to say to one another!"

Rather than smiling at her wry observation, Mrs, Stanley gave her a startled look. "You don't believe in ghosts, miss?"

Elly summoned up a cheerful smile. "Heavens, no."

"But . . ." The housekeeper moistened her lips with her tongue. "But if you was to actually *see* a ghost—"

"Then I should begin to doubt my sanity and take immediately to my bed," Elly finished in a firm voice. "As I have oft said of late, ghosts are nothing more than superstitious moonshine."

"But—"

"That is quite enough on the subject, Mrs. Stanley," Elly interrupted, raising her cup of tepid tea to her lips and praying the housekeeper wouldn't notice how her hand was trembling. "Now I should like to discuss the household staff and what their duties are. We shall begin with the cook. . . ."

"You are certainly looking hale and hearty for a dead man," Alex commented as he faced Lucien across the breakfast table. "Allow me to congratulate you on your resurrection."

Lucien shot his friend a sour look. "Very funny, Twyford," he muttered, motioning for the butler to freshen his cup of coffee. "If you find the situation so amusing then you are more than welcome to take over this evening's performance. That costume is damned uncomfortable!"

"That is exceedingly kind of you, Seabrook, but I fear I must decline."

"Coward."

Alex smiled at Lucien's grumbled comment. "Perhaps," he drawled, his eyes bright with amusement. "But as it happens I have decided to return to London earlier than expected."

Lucien glanced up in surprise. "You are going to Whitehall?"

Alex shot the hovering servants a speaking look,

and Lucien dismissed them with a wave of his hand. Once they were alone Alex resumed the conversation.

"I plan to seek an audience with the Foreign Secretary and report my findings," he said without preamble. "After last night I agree with you that Seagate is vital to our mission's success, and I must inform the viscount of my decision."

"That is good to hear," Lucien replied, feeling somewhat reassured. "I was beginning to think that—"

"There is just one problem."

Lucien's relief vanished at his friend's implacable tone. "And what might that be?" he asked warily.

Alex rose to his feet and began pacing the elegant confines of the morning room. "I know you are reluctant to place your neighbors under the king's guard," he said, gazing out at the misty green fields, "and I admire your sensibilities. Unfortunately I fear we may not have any choice in the matter."

Lucien straightened in his chair, eyeing his friend with mounting trepidation. "What do you mean?"

Alex swung around to face him, his gray eyes hard. "The prince's life is at stake," he reminded Lucien coldly. "With such risks we can not allow for even the smallest margin of error. If Seagate is necessary to secure His Highness's safety—and I believe that it is— then we will do whatever we must to obtain the house."

"But that isn't fair, damn it!" Lucien surged to his feet, his dark eyes blazing as he confronted Twyford. "The Dennings have done nothing to warrant arrest! Granted they are proving a bit of an obstacle, but I do not see—"

"May I remind you that we are at war, and that in war the innocent are often among the first casualties?" Alex said softly, studying Lucien with cool dispassion. "It is regrettable, but it is nonetheless the truth. They shall be taken into custody as soon as it can be arranged."

Lucien was silent a long moment as he considered what Alex had told him. "When will you and the prince be returning to Brighton?"

"At the end of the month, as well you know," Alex was frowning at him. "His Highness's regiment is to give a parade, and—"

"That would give me three weeks," Lucien cut into Alex's reply, his mind spinning with plans.

"Yes, but I do not see why that should change anything," Alex replied, his frown deepening. "Our contacts in France have indicated they are already preparing a stockade for the prince; I trust you do not wish to see it utilized?"

"Of course not!" Lucien was incensed that he should ask such a thing.

"Then what the devil are you talking about?" Alex demanded, obviously frustrated.

Lucien sighed, thrusting a hand through his light brown hair as he turned away. "I want those three weeks," he said, his expression hard. "My plan will work, Twyford. I know it will."

Alex opened his mouth to disagree, but abruptly he closed it again. "Very well," he said, studying Lucien coolly. "But I can not give you the entire three weeks. In the event you are unsuccessful in driving out the Dennings, we shall need time to secure the premises. A fortnight is all I can grant you."

Lucien inclined his head gratefully. "Thank you, Alex. I promise you that I shall—"

"But," Alex interrupted, "should you fail, you will personally deliver the Dennings into my custody, is that understood? Two weeks, Seabrook; take care you use them well."

Chapter Seven

It was after luncheon before Elly and Henry set out to explore Brighton. Aware this would be the first time she would be meeting many of her neighbors Elly agonized over her appearance, lingering over her toilet until a frustrated Henry threatened to leave without her.

"I don't see why you're being so silly about this," he grumbled a short time later as they were rolling down the road towards Brighton. "When we was in Cape Town you never gave a second thought to how you looked."

"When we were in Cape Town there was never anyone about to notice my appearance except monkeys and snakes," she returned, anxiously inspecting her reflection in the small mirror she'd extracted from her reticule. "Besides, you are a fine one to talk. Unless I am much mistaken, aren't those a new pair of buff nankins you're wearing? And you have your cravat tied in a mathematical, I note."

Rather than taking umbrage at her challenging words, Henry preened like a deb. "Do you like it?" he asked, transferring the spirited team's reins from one hand to another with astonishing ease. "When we were still in London Seabrook sent his man over to instruct my valet on how to tie a proper cravat. He said it wouldn't do for me to be taken for a quiz."

Seabrook again. Elly's brows gathered in a quick frown, although she wisely withheld any comment. Besides, if she was to be totally honest with herself she would have to admit that since meeting the marquess, her brother's appearance had improved beyond all recognition. Only look at him, dressed in a blue coat of Bath superfine, with a tall, beaver hat set rakishly on his head. Quite a departure for a man who used to go about dressed in his father's cast-off clothing, she thought, flicking him a look of sisterly amusement from the corners of her eyes.

Seagate was located some two miles outside of Brighton, and so it took them almost half an hour to reach the center of the famous resort town. As the London season was underway most of the town's more fashionable citizens had left for the city, but it was still far from deserted. An interesting collection of curricles and coaches could be seen on the elegant streets, and Elly was pleased to find herself and Henry the object of obvious speculation. When she'd decided they'd been on display long enough she instructed Henry to pull up in front of a series of small shops.

"Ain't going to the modiste's are you?" he asked, scowling suspiciously as he helped her down from the highly-sprung phaeton.

"No, I'm not," she replied calmly, hiding a grin at his typically male aversion to dress shops. "But now that you mention it, I would like to stop in at the draper's shop and have a look at their stock. There's not a chair at Seagate worth sitting on, and I'm afraid most of the drapes will have to be replaced as well."

"You might want to start with the library," he suggested, falling into step beside her as they made their way down the cobblestoned street. "It is in dreadful condition."

"The whole house is in a dreadful condition," she

95

answered, some of her pleasure in the outing vanishing at the memory of the devastated south wing. "Cousin Bevil ought to be horsewhipped for what he did; or rather, for what he didn't do!"

Henry gave an uncommunicative grunt and Elly fell silent, turning her attention to the gaily-decorated shop windows. One particular window caught her eye, and she tugged Henry to a halt.

"Let's go in here."

"A book shop?" Henry ducked his head to study the colorful array of prints and books displayed in the shop's bowed window. "All right," he agreed reluctantly, "but only for a minute, mind. I don't intend spending the whole afternoon twiddling my thumbs while you moon over some silly book."

They went inside, Henry hurrying towards the scientific journals while Elly drifted over to a stack of slender, neatly-bound volumes of poetry. She was examining one of the books when she felt a frisson of awareness prickling down her spine, and she glanced up to find an auburn-haired man regarding her with intense, emerald green eyes. When he saw he had her attention he made his way to her side.

"Byron, I see," he said, indicating the book in her hand with a charming smile. "I might have guessed; all the prettiest ladies are mad for our brooding peer."

Elly bristled at his too-familiar tone. "I beg your pardon, sir," she said frostily, tilting back her head to meet his bold gaze. "I do not believe we have met."

"And so we have not." He accepted her rebuff with a good-natured bow. "Allow me to introduce myself; I am Marcus Claredon, my father is Squire Claredon of Ashurst Hall. And you are . . . ?" his voice trailed off expectantly.

"Miss Elinore Denning," Elly supplied reluctantly, seeing no other course but to follow his suit. "My brother, Henry, and I have recently moved to Brighton from—"

"Say no more, Miss Denning," he interrupted, his green eyes taking on a lively sparkle. "All the countryside has heard of you . . . and your esteemed brother," he added, his eyes flicking to the corner where Henry was avidly studying the newest copy of *Britannica Botanica*.

Elly, who had been about to give the forward stranger a set down, gave him a startled look instead. "They have?" she asked, finding the notion both pleasing and somewhat alarming.

"Of course," Mr. Claredon's grin widened. "We here in the country are not so jaded as our London counterparts, and we find the doings of our neighbors to be a source of endless fascination."

Despite her determination to remain aloof, Elly was unable to hold back a small smile at his teasing words. "Indeed?" she asked, gazing up into his handsome features. "And pray, what has either Henry or myself done to be of such er . . . endless fascination?"

"Why, inheriting Seagate, of course," he replied, feigning surprise at her question. "And managing to put Seabrook's nose out of joint in the bargain. Not an easy task, I assure you."

"Henry inherited Seagate," Elly pointed out, pedantic as always, although she found Mr. Claredon's cavalier attitude towards the marquess much to her liking. He was the first person she'd met who did not regard her private bane with some degree of awe. Even Jessica Kingsley, who had little use for any man, had always referred to Lord Seabrook in terms of the greatest respect.

"Yes, and you are his sister," Mr. Claredon returned, still smiling. "Now tell me, what do you think of Seagate? Is it haunted as everyone claims?"

For one moment Elly was strongly tempted to reveal last night's events, sensing a certain kinship with the handsome stranger. But at the last minute her innate sense of reservation stayed her tongue, and she shook her head instead. "Not that I have noticed, Mr. Claredon," she said with cool politeness. "No doubt it is all a hum."

"What is all a hum?" Henry asked, drifting over to join them as he finally noticed his sister was conversing with a strange man. "Don't believe I have had the pleasure, sir," he said, extending his hand to the other man in a smooth gesture that had Elly gaping in astonishment. "I am Mr. Henry Denning."

"Marcus Claredon." Mr. Claredon accepted Henry's hand politely. "And as I told your charming sister, my father is Squire Claredon. Perhaps you have heard of him?"

"Can't say as I have," Henry replied truthfully, if not altogether politely. "What is his direction? I shall have to call upon him once we are settled in."

"Ashurst Hall, just outside of Hove," came the reply as Mr. Claredon made to take his leave. "I shall tell my father you will be calling on him, sir. I am sure he will be looking forward to it, as he was a great admirer of your father's. Now if you will excuse me, I really must be off; it was nice meeting you. Miss Denning, Mr. Denning." He doffed his hat to each of them in turn before hurrying out the door.

"Henry Denning, what was that all about?" Elly rounded on her brother, her cheeks flushing with embarrassment. "You were very rude to Mr. Claredon!"

"Rot," Henry returned inelegantly, grasping her firmly by the elbow and all but dragging her out of the shop. "The fellow was too forward by half, El, and well you know it; you ought not to have been talking to him at all. People will think you fast."

Elly's jaw dropped in shock. "Since when have

you ever given a snap for the social conventions?" she demanded, scarce believing what she had heard.

"Don't be a gudgeon," he grumbled, sounding suspiciously like another male of her acquaintance. "I hope I may care enough not to let my sister flirt with every Johnny Sharp who approaches her. As your brother I am responsible for your behavior, and —"

Elly pulled her arm free and shot him a furious look. "You have been talking to Seabrook, haven't you?" she accused, planting both hands on her hips. "He has put you up to this!"

"Of course I have spoken with his lordship." If Elly was unaware of the attention they were attracting, Henry was not, and he grabbed her arm again and began dragging her toward the phaeton. "Now kindly stop screeching; you sound like a fishwife."

The comment kept Elly determinedly silent as they made their way back to Seagate. She couldn't remember the last time she'd been so furious with her brother, and the force of her emotions left her fighting back tears. She and Henry had grown up all alone, with only each other to depend upon, and she hated being estranged from him.

This was all Seabrook's fault, she decided, transferring her anger to the marquess's broad shoulders. How dared he interfere between her brother and herself? They had gotten along famously until his lordship had seen fit to poke his aristocratic nose into their personal affairs, and so she meant to tell him at the earliest opportunity. But even as she was making this silent vow, she found herself acknowledging that Seabrook was not wholly to blame.

She and Henry *had* gotten along, but only so long as he did what she told him to do. It wasn't that she meant to be managing, she told herself anxiously, it was just that she had promised their mother she would look after him. Henry was a dear, but like their late father he was too engrossed in his studies

99

to be able to function in the mundane world. She'd always been the one to arrange the order of their lives, which, she supposed, was why she was so upset now. After years of being the one in command, it was decidedly unsettling to find the tables suddenly turned on her.

"Elly?" Henry shot her a nervous look as they drew within sight of Seagate. "You ain't mad at me . . . are you?"

She softened at the hesitancy in his tone. "No, Henry, I'm not mad," she said, sending him a wistful smile as she lightly touched his arm. "And much as it pains me to admit it, you were right; I shouldn't have spoken to Mr. Claredon. If it helps, I was just as taken aback by his forwardness as you were."

Henry gave a solemn nod. "Seabrook warned me Brighton was thick with fortune hunters," he said. "He told me to keep my eyes open for overly-familiar men as they were likely to be up to no good."

"Indeed? And what about overly-familiar ladies?" she asked, feeling somewhat aggrieved. "Did his lordship warn you about them as well?"

"As a matter of fact, he did," Henry surprised her with his admission. "But I told him I wasn't as big a flat as all that. I can tell a lightskirt from a lady of quality the same as any man."

"I see," Elly replied weakly, wondering if she really knew her brother at all. He had depths to him she hadn't even suspected . . . until now.

"I'll call at Ashurst next week," Henry concluded as they drove into the stableyard. "If this Claredon fellow is who he claims to be, then I suppose it wouldn't hurt to ask him to tea. If that is what you wish?" Here he gave her a questioning look.

"That would be fine, Henry," she murmured, feeling more bemused than ever. "Whatever you decide."

"Good." He gave a decisive nod. "El, I think I am going to like living here in the country. It is nothing at all like I expected it would be. Do you know what I mean?"

"Yes, Henry," Elly gave a heartfelt sigh as she accepted the groom's hand in climbing down from the phaeton. "I know precisely what you mean."

It was approaching midnight as Lucien made his way slowly down the shadowy corridor. He'd meant to be in place long before now; but a last-minute crisis involving his other contact had kept him hopping, and it was after eleven o'clock before he'd been able to leave the house. He'd have to write Alex about Flanders, he decided, ducking his head as he rounded a particularly narrow curve. He was beginning to have doubts as to the young man's veracity.

Ten minutes after entering the secret tunnel he was in the small chamber on the other side of Miss Denning's room. A quick peck through the monk's hole showed her curled up in the canopied bed, a flickering candle set on the table beside it. The sight of the meager light set out by its flame brought a frown to his face.

His disguise, while more than adequate in a darkened room, did have its limitations, and in the flickering candlelight there was every danger it might be revealed for what it was. For safety's sake, he would have to remain hidden . . . for tonight at least. Giving the hunched figure on the bed a baleful look, he raised the chain he'd left on the floor and gave it a loud rattle.

"Leave this place," he moaned in a hoarse voice.

At the sound of the wail and the clanging chain Elly bolted up in bed; bedsheets clutched protectively to her as she searched the shadows for any sign of the ghostly visitor. Her first thought was that she was grateful she'd left the candle burning at her bedside, although she'd felt like a fool at the time for doing so. Its dancing light scarcely pierced the Stygian darkness beyond the bed, but it was better than nothing and she took comfort in its golden presence.

"Who is there?" she demanded in a querulous tone, raising the candle and holding it directly in front of her. "I must warn you, whoever you are, that I do not find this prank in the least bit amusing."

Lucien bit back an oath at her brave words. Blast it, why couldn't the chit scream and swoon like a proper female, he thought impatiently. He gave his chain an irritated rattle.

"Leave. . . ."

The sound seemed to be coming from near the fireplace, and although it took every ounce of courage she possessed, Elly climbed out of the bed and advanced warily towards the darkened corner. "I have no intention of leaving," she said, feeling slightly foolish for arguing with a wall. "Why don't *you* leave?"

Hell. She was practically right on top of the mechanism that would trigger the secret door, Lucien realized, scrambling back into the shadows. All she had to do was touch the third acorn carved into the mantel and . . . He made one last, desperate try.

"You will die. . . ."

"Oh, pooh," Elly was more irritated than alarmed by the disembodied voice. She'd had very little sleep the night before, and she was in no mood to humor Seagate's nocturnal resident. "See here," she began in the tones she'd used to intimidate Arab shopkeepers and officious ship's stewards, "I am very sorry that you don't want me here, but there is nothing you can do to make me leave. Now do be quiet, and let me sleep," and with that she turned and stalked back to the bed.

Lucien watched her go with a mixture of fury and

102

grudging admiration. Much as it enraged him to have her be so recalcitrant, he couldn't help but respect her courage. When he'd tested his costume on one of the smugglers sniffing around the cave's entrance, the terrified man had screeched like a scalded cat, knocking over his own men in his mad dash to safety. Miss Denning simply rang a peal over his head and told him to be quiet. Well, his jaw hardened beneath his mask, much as he might admire her spirit he could not allow her to jeopardize his mission.

He raised his chain and was about to moan again when he felt a presence beside him in the darkness. Without questioning his instincts he dropped the chain to the floor, pulling a pistol from his pocket as he whirled to face his enemy. There was no one there. For a moment he simply stared into the endless blackness of the corridor, refusing to believe the evidence of his own eyes.

Damn it, someone *has* to be there, he thought savagely, his grip tightening on the pistol. He'd felt the presence too strongly to dismiss the incident as mere imagination. Removing the torch from its mounting in the stone wall he began a methodical search of the tunnels, but he could find no physical evidence of another living soul.

Another living soul, the phrase echoed in his mind along with the memory of a rusty laugh and the faint rattling of keys. Is it possible? he wondered uneasily, and in the next moment he was giving his head an impatient shake.

Idiot, he castigated himself silently, as he began making his way towards the main passage. Of course there was no one in the tunnel with him. He was tired, that was all, and his mind was but playing tricks on him. What he needed was a good night's sleep, and then he would be much more himself again.

Yes, he decided, a feeling of profound relief chasing out the remnants of fear he would not acknowledge; that is what I shall do. He would leave for now, letting Miss Denning think she'd won, and then when her guard was down he'd pay her another visit in his ghostly guise. In the meanwhile, he would begin calling on her and her brother in the day-time. Now that they'd actually had to live in Seagate, he was certain he would find them more of a mind to sell.

Pleased with the way he'd worked things through, Lucien secured the entrance to the small chamber and began making his way towards the main tunnel. He was so lost in his own plots and machinations that he was totally unaware of the disapproving eyes that watched him from the black depths of the endless shadows. . . .

Elly spent the next two days making endless lists of supplies and helping the staff set the huge house to rights. At first Mrs. Stanley and the other maids seemed reluctant to accept her help, but given the magnitude of the job that lay before them, they soon gave in, assigning her the less arduous tasks of dusting and polishing. She was happily engaged in polishing a Sheraton sideboard discovered in one of the storerooms when one of the maids came in to announce a visitor.

"The marquess of Seabrook!" she howled, dropping her rag to the floor. "The devil take that man, he is supposed to be in London!"

"Oh, no. Miss Denning," the wide-eyed maid assured her solemnly, "he is in the parlor and askin' for Mr. Henry."

"Have you informed my brother of his visitor?" she asked, resigning herself to putting in a brief appearance.

"Yes, miss. He told the footman to inform his lordship he'd be with him as soon as he finished the chapter he was studyin'."

Elly muttered an imprecation beneath her breath as she scrambled somewhat awkwardly to her feet. If Henry was reading, they would be lucky to pry him loose before dinner; which meant the task of entertaining their visitor fell to her. She glanced down at the varnish-stained apron covering her, and realized she would have to change. Tempting as it was to go to Seabrook as she was, she knew she could not. She was mistress of Seagate now, and it was only proper that she greet him in clothes befitting the lady of the manor.

Some twenty minutes later she walked into the parlor, noting its altered appearance with a smug sense of pride. The maroon drapes, while still faded and in need of mending had been freshly cleaned, and sunlight streamed through mullioned windows that had been scrubbed until they sparkled. The cream and rose carpets had also been cleaned, and if the rosewood furniture set before the freshly painted fireplace was old, then at least it was unsoiled; a definite improvement from the first time she had seen it.

At the sound of the door opening Seabrook had turned around, his dark brown eyes taking in Elly's appearance with cool approval. "Good afternoon, Miss Denning," he said suavely, stepping forward to take her hand. "My apologies for dropping in on you so unexpectedly. I trust I haven't inconvenienced you?"

"Not at all, my lord," Elly lied politely, indicating he should take one of the chairs set before the fire. "Although I must own to some surprise; I believe my brother mentioned you weren't expected until later this week?" Her light brown eyebrows arched in cool enquiry.

Lucien settled back in the over-stuffed chair, crossing one foot over the other as he sent her a lazy smile. "I had some estate business which needed attending," he replied, ignoring the challenging light in her aquamarine eyes. "And truth to tell, I was looking for an excuse to leave the city. After eighteen years the delights of a season tend to pall rather quickly."

"Eighteen years? I had no notion you were as old as that!" The exclamation burst from Elly's lips before she could stop them, and she clapped a hand over her mouth in horror of what she had said.

Mercifully, he seemed more amused than insulted by her outburst. "Oh, I am quite the Methuselah," he drawled, his dark eyes gleaming as he took in her mortified expression. "Any day now and I shall take to powdering my hair and sewing brass buttons on my jacket."

"And boring all about you with tales of what the world was like when you were a lad," she finished, relieved he was taking her gauche remark so amicably. "My apologies, sir, for that ill-bred remark. What I *meant* to say is that I am surprised to learn you are such a seasoned veteran of the Marriage Mart."

He grinned at her embarrassed expression. "Think nothing of it, ma'am, for you are not the first person to speculate on my single state. My relations are forever twigging me on the subject; reminding me oh-so-subtly that 'tis time I was marrying and seeing to the succession."

The idea of Seabrook beset by hectoring relatives demanding he take a bride made Elly's eyes dance with mischief. "Really?" she drawled, her full lips curving in a teasing smile. "And here I thought it was only we poor females who suffered such indignities."

"A common feminine misconception," he assured

her, thinking she was rather a taking little thing when she smiled. He particularly approved of the stylishly-cut gown of heather cambric she was wearing. The purplish-blue hue emphasized her delicate coloring, while the simple lines of the gown showed her slender form to its best advantage. One would never suppose by looking at her that she possessed the courage to brazenly order a ghost from her room.

Thinking of the ghost made him remember the purpose behind his call, and he stirred restlessly in his chair. "Is Henry about?" he asked coolly. "I was hoping for a brief word with him."

Elly noted the subtle change in his demeanor, and wondered what had brought it on. "I fear Henry is in the library," she began apologetically, "which means he shall be incommunicado for the rest of the afternoon. Is there anything I can do to be of assistance?"

Lucien bit back an impatient curse; he'd been fearing something like this from the moment she had appeared. "No, thank you, ma'am," he said politely, deciding that since she was proving so biddable, he had nothing to lose by discreetly questioning her. "I had a question to ask of him, but it is nothing that can not wait." He glanced about the room as if noticing it for the first time.

"In the meanwhile, pray accept my congratulations for the changes you have already made. I daresay the old place hasn't looked half so well in years."

"Thank you, my lord," Elly beamed at his words, "although it is Mrs. Stanley who is most deserving of your praise. She and the other servants have worked like Trojans these past few days."

He gave her a close look, noting the small smear of varnish that adorned her small chin. Without pausing to consider his actions he leaned forward, lightly touching the brown smear with the tip of his finger. "It is not just the servants who have been working so hard," he said, smiling down at her stunned expression. "You have been doing your share too, it would seem."

She flushed at his touch. "Pesky varnish," she muttered, scrubbing distractedly at her chin as he drew back. "It won't come out no matter how hard I scrub."

"Try turpentine, I think you will find it far more effective than lilac soap," he suggested, remembering the soft, floral scent that had clung to her warm skin as he had bent over her.

The arrival of the tea saved Elly the necessity of answering the marquess, and the next several minutes were given over to the pleasant ritual. After she had seen to her guest's needs, Elly poured herself a cup of tea and settled back in her chair to enjoy the brief respite.

"How are you and Henry settling?" Lucien asked, his eyes intent on her face. "Have you met many of your neighbors?"

Elly shook her head. "I am afraid not," she said with a regretful sigh. "Both Henry and I have been quite busy since our arrival, and there has been very little time for socializing. Although we did meet a Mr. Marcus Claredon on our trip to Brighton," she added, recalling their overly-friendly neighbor with a vague smile.

"Claredon? The squire's son?" Lucien asked, recalling a red-haired dandy with a penchant for gaming and lightskirts. "Where did you meet him?"

"At a book shop," she replied, relieved that apparently the man had told them the truth. "He introduced himself to Henry and me, and Henry promised to call on him once we are settled."

"Did he?" Lucien decided he would drop a flea in young Henry's ear about the inadvisability of associating with men of Claredon's stamp, and then he pushed the matter from his mind. At the moment he had a more immediate goal.

"Tell me, Miss Denning, what is your opinion of Brighton? A lovely city, is it not?" he asked, assuming a polite mien.

"From the little I saw of it, yes," Elly said, surprised by her guest's genial behavior. If anyone had told her that she and the marquess could pass a quarter-hour in conversation without coming to blows she would have thought that person quite mad, and yet here they were. Perhaps Henry was right, she mused, ready as always to own up to a mistake. Lord Seabrook really was quite nice once you got to know him.

"You've not seen much of it?" he pressed, a plan forming in his mind. He'd known from the start that Miss Denning was the key to obtaining Seagate, but he'd allowed his personal dislike of her to get in the way of his mission. Now he was being handed a golden opportunity to place himself in her good graces, and he was determined to grab it with both hands. If nothing else, he would at least be able to learn why she was so hell-bent to hang on to the ancient house.

"Not as much as I would like," Elly admitted with a sigh. "Henry and I went into town that first day, but since then there simply hasn't been enough time. Perhaps next week we shall go in for another peek."

"Nonsense, Miss Denning," he said, smoothly slipping into the opening she had provided. "Have you not forgotten you have already agreed to let me take you about? And there is no time like the present, as they say. I should be happy to act as your escort."

Elly colored in confusion, praying he didn't think she had angled for his invitation. "That is very kind of you, my lord," she said swiftly. "But I would not wish to impose upon your kindness. I —"

"Oh, it is no imposition, I assure you," he interrupted with a warm smile. "I am a native of the place, you know, and I can show you many sights our visitors seldom see. When would you like to go? Today?"

Elly considered his offer for a moment before rejecting it with a shake of her head. "I am afraid not," she said with genuine regret. "It is much too late, and in any case there is still much left to be done. Perhaps tomorrow . . . ?"

"Tomorrow would be fine," he said, quickly amending his plans to haunt her that night. "At what time would you like to leave?"

"After luncheon?" she suggested, puzzled by his eagerness to accommodate her.

"That would be fine," he set his cup down and rose to his feet. Much as he would like to remain, there was still a great deal he had to do, including conferring with the Stanleys. It was almost time to begin the next phase of the operation. "Shall we say two o'clock then?"

"Two o'clock would be fine, my lord," Elly demurred, scarce believing her good fortune. Two nights of blissfully uninterrupted sleep, and now the marquess was actually going out of his way to be nice to her. Things were definitely improving.

Chapter Eight

There was more good news awaiting Elly as she came down to breakfast the following morning. The post had been delivered, and among the various gazettes and journals was a letter from Lady Miranda. Smiling in delight, she broke the wax circlet sealing the missive, unfolding the delicate sheets of paper with a mounting sense of anticipation.

"Oh, how wonderful!" she cried after reading the first few lines.

"What's wonderful?" Henry asked, glancing up from the gazette he had been perusing.

"It is a letter from Lady Miranda Ablethorpe," Elly explained, her smile widening as she continued reading. "Her grandmother has broken her ankle."

Henry's eyebrows arched in astonishment. "And you think that wonderful?" he exclaimed, looking thoroughly disapproving. "I say, El, that's not very nice of you. I know the old tartar set your back up, but that is no reason for you to rejoice at her—"

"I am not rejoicing!" Elly interrupted indignantly. "Of course I'm very sorry her ladyship has been injured; broken bones can be extremely dangerous at her age."

"Then why did you say it was wonderful?" he demanded.

"Because it means she and Lady Miranda shall be

coming to Brighton," Elly explained, too delighted at the thought of Miranda's impending arrival to remain angry. "Apparently the dowager doesn't think it proper for an earl's daughter to go about escorted only by paid companions, and she is insisting they retire to Brighton for the rest of the Season. Oh! And Miss Kingsley and Miss Averleigh shall be accompanying them!"

"Who are Miss Kingsley and Miss Averleigh?" Henry asked, struggling to place faces with the names.

"They are friends of Lady Miranda," she said, her cheeks pinking with pleasure. "I met them while we were in London, and I found them delightful. You will like them as well, Henry, for they are quite well read and intelligent."

"Mmm," was the only response as Henry lowered his eyes to his gazette.

Elly continued reading Miranda's letter, chuckling at some of her friend's more pithy remarks. Lord Seabrook's name seemed to leap off the paper at one point, and her eyes widened as she read on.

Speaking of his lordship, it seems he and Lord Twyford left London the very same day as you and your brother. Such a pity; one could positively hear the hearts of the little debs breaking when he failed to appear at Lady P's ball. To quote dear Jessica, she hadn't seen so many long faces 'since Lord Byron took up with that dreadful Caroline Lamb'!

She lowered the letter to the table, her brows gathering as she recalled her conversation with Lord Seabrook. From what he'd said she'd formed the opinion he had but arrived in Brighton that day, although it was possible she had misunderstood him. There was also every possibility that he'd accompanied Lord Twyford to his estates before returning to Brighton. Still . . .

"Henry?"

"Hmm?" The paper rustled as he turned a page.

"Do you know when Lord Seabrook left London?"

Henry glanced up in surprise. "How on earth should I know?" he asked, clearly irritated by her question. "You was the one who told me he was here yesterday, remember? I wasn't expecting him for days yet. Why?" He shot her a suspicious scowl.

"No reason," she replied, deciding the matter wasn't worth further speculation. "I was merely curious."

Henry muttered something beneath his breath and picked up his gazette again, clearly disinclined to continue the conversation. Elly finished Miranda's letter and then turned her attention to the latest copy of *La Belle Assemblée,* which her aunt had thoughtfully had forwarded to her. But even as she studied the exquisite drawings she found her thoughts turning to the marquess and the mystery of his sudden appearance on the scene.

Or was it a mystery? She'd always considered herself to be a rational sort of female and not the type to engage in hysterical speculation, but the events of the past few days had left her more shaken than she cared to admit. Perhaps there was nothing untoward in the earl's arrival, but she was resolved to find out. She already had one mystery in her life, and far as she was concerned, one was quite enough.

"What time is Seabrook calling for you?" Henry's question cut into Elly's troubled thoughts, and she glanced up to find her brother gazing at her with an enquiring expression.

"Two o'clock," she replied, wondering how he had learned of the proposed outing. He had worked through dinner last night, and this was the first she

113

had seen of him since yesterday afternoon.

"I shall be ready, then," Henry said before burying his nose in the paper again.

Elly stared at him, amazed once again by his sudden awareness of the niceties. He'd never given a fig about where she went before, and she found his behavior as puzzling as it was touching. Perhaps the marquess's influence isn't entirely detrimental, she decided with a fond smile, turning her attention to the rest of the mail.

Lord Seabrook was as good as his word, arriving shortly before the appointed hour. In a sudden fit of feminine vanity Elly donned her new walking dress of sapphire jaconet trimmed at the throat and tight sleeves with bunches of jonquil-colored velvet ribbons. A Lavinia hat of bright yellow straw and tied with blue ribbons completed the ensemble, and just for effect she carried a matching parasol of frilly yellow silk. She was pulling on her blue leather gloves as she walked into the drawing room when the sight of the marquess brought her up short.

"Snap," Lucien drawled, grinning at her stunned expression. "It would seem great minds think alike, Miss Denning; at least where fashion is concerned."

"So it would seem, my lord," Elly managed, gazing in amazement at his bright blue velvet jacket and yellow nankins. For a moment she considered dashing up to her rooms and changing; then her sense of humor stirred to life.

"Let us hope Henry does not take it into his head to wear his new blue jacket," she said, continuing into the room. "Else I fear we will create something of a stir when we walk down the street."

"Indeed, we should probably be taken up for breaching the peace," he agreed, hiding his surprise that Henry was to join them. He'd been hoping to get the little vixen off by herself in order to quiz her about the ghost, but apparently it would have to wait. He quickly adjusted his plans to fit the new circumstances.

A short time later they were tooling down the road towards Brighton in the marquess's black phaeton. The skies which had been heavy and threatening all morning suddenly lifted, and a broad shaft of golden sunlight shone down from the blue heavens illuminating the green countryside. Elly gazed at the verdant beauty all about her, and felt her throat tighten with an emotion she could not name.

" 'This sceptered isle . . . this precious stone set in the silver sea . . . this blessed plot, this earth, this realm, this England.' "

The soft voice at her side made Elly start, and she turned her head to find Lord Seabrook watching her, an enigmatic look on his dark face. "I . . . I beg your pardon, sir?" She stammered, her cheeks flushing with becoming color.

"Shakespeare," Lucien replied calmly, studying her a moment longer before turning his attention to the high-stepping pair of grays pulling the phaeton. "Judging from the expression on your face it seemed an apt quote."

"Very apt," she agreed weakly, somewhat discomfited to think he had read her mind so easily. Evidently there was more to the man than she had first supposed, she brooded, shooting him a speculative look from the corner of her eyes. She shook off the troubling thought and sent him a shy smile.

"Henry told me of your interest in Shakespeare," she said in what she hoped was a bright tone. "He mentioned you even have a garden, which he is looking forward to seeing."

"So I do, but I hope that you will come and see it as well, Miss Denning," Lucien answered, anxious to take advantage of the opening she had provided. He didn't know what the devil had made him quote that particular passage from *Richard II*; the words just

115

seemed to burst from his lips at seeing the expression in her light blue eyes, but now he was glad that they had.

Not only had that provided him with the means of involving himself even further with the Dennings, but it had also answered the question that had been plaguing him. Miss Denning loved her country. He felt certain that, should the need arise, he could count upon her full cooperation. Or at least, as much cooperation as could reasonably be expected from a willful, stubborn minx, he added with a wry smile.

The rest of the afternoon passed pleasantly as Lucien acted as guide, dutifully pointing out the sights he thought would be of interest to his guests. He showed an eager Henry the small Palladian-styled house where the Botanical Society held their monthly meetings, and drove a fascinated Elly down the famed Royal Crescent where several fashionable homes had recently been built.

"That is Lady Ablethorpe's residence when she is in town," he said, indicating a white brick townhouse with his whip. "I believe you are acquainted with her granddaughter, Lady Miranda?"

"Oh, yes. Miranda and I are dear friends," she answered, smiling at the thought of the sweet-natured blonde. "In fact, I had a letter from her only this morning."

"Indeed? And how is her ladyship?" he asked, more out of politeness than any real sense of curiosity. "She is well, I trust?"

"Lady Miranda is quite well, but I fear the same can not be said of her grandmother." Elly then related the distressing news of Lady Ablethorpe's injury. "Of course this means they must remove to Brighton for the rest of the Season," she concluded, doing her best to look sad, "and although I am sorry for her sake, I must admit it will be good to see Miranda again."

"Yes, I am sure it must be quite lonely for you at Seagate," he said, adroitly turning the conversation to his advantage. "It is rather isolated, is it not?"

"No, not really," Elly replied absently, recalling the other news contained in Miranda's letter. She wondered if she should ask Seabrook about the matter and then concluded it was really none of her affair. Besides, she admitted to herself, it was such a pleasant afternoon that she didn't wish to spoil things by instigating a brawl with him.

"You do not find it so?" Lucien's dark eyebrows arched in dismay. He was hoping the isolation of the house would have dampened some of her ardor for the place, but evidently he had underestimated her.

"Good heavens, no," she said with a light laugh, turning her thoughts to the present. "You forget, my lord, that Henry and I are used to going months on end with scarce a glimpse of another person! After that, Seagate seems as crowded to us as a London marketplace; doesn't it, Henry?" She glanced over her shoulder for confirmation.

"Especially when one is trying to do one's work," he agreed with a grumble. "Seems like there's always someone poking about and disturbing one's papers."

"What do you mean?" Lucien asked curiously.

Henry shrugged his shoulders. "The maids moved some of my papers while I was at lunch," he said, his tone faintly accusing. "I wish you would talk to them, El, and tell them they aren't to disturb my things. It's demmed annoying."

"I shall, Henry," she soothed, taking care to hide a smile.

Lucien missed the smile, his lips thinning as he wondered if any of the footmen . . . or the maids for that matter . . . might be up to no good. According to the information Whitehall had gathered, the local smugglers were somehow involved in the

117

plot against Prinny, and it would not be unusual if one of the household staff had a friend amongst those gentlemen. He would have to discuss the matter with the Stanleys at the first opportunity. He was wondering how to go about it when he felt a tentative touch on his arm, and he glanced down in surprise to see Miss Denning smiling at him.

"Pray pay Henry no mind," she said gently, pitching her voice so that her brother could not hear. "He is forever misplacing things and then laying the blame on others. The staff you have helped select is quite without fault, I assure you."

He relaxed slightly, although he still intended conferring with the butler and housekeeper. "That is good to hear, Miss Denning," he said, his brown eyes sparkling as he smiled at her. "I would not have you thinking I have engaged a gang of cutpurses and ruffians simply to spite you."

"Such a thought never crossed my mind, my lord!" she informed him with a haughty sniff, and then spoiled the effect by adding, "At least, not after I saw how hard they are willing to work."

The conversation then turned to Seagate, and by the time they paused for tea at a local inn, Lucien was feeling more glum than ever. Rather than complaining about the squalor and ruin, Miss Denning seemed to look upon it all as a challenge, her hazy blue eyes dancing as she talked about the progress she was making in setting the house to rights.

Devil take it, how am I to drive them from a home she apparently adores? he wondered, taking a deep sip of the ale the proprietor had brought him.

"Naturally, I am hoping to have started the work on the south wing before Lady Miranda arrives," Elly continued, blithely unaware of the marquess's dark thoughts. "She has indicated that she would love to tour the house, and—"

"You have been in the south wing?" Lucien sat up

118

so quickly some of the ale sloshed out of his tankard.

"Of course." She stared at him in puzzlement. "It is in the most need of repair, after all, and naturally I wished to see the damage myself."

Lucien bit back an angry curse. Part of a wall had collapsed in the wing, exposing one of the tunnels, and he shuddered to think what would happen if she were to stumble on it. "You have no business tramping about that wing, Miss Denning," he told her in his most forbidding tones, his jaw clenching with the effort of control. "It is much too dangerous, and I must insist that for your own safety you stay out of it."

Elly's good will vanished at the arrogant demand. She set her glass of lemonade down with a thump, her brows meeting in a ferocious scowl. "How many times must I remind you that Seagate is no longer your concern?" she said hotly, her chin coming up with pride. "It is *our* home now, and if you think I will allow you to dictate—"

"That is quite enough, Elly." Henry's cool voice interrupted her furious tirade. "Lord Seabrook is right; the south wing *is* dangerous, and you are not to set foot in it until it has been fully repaired."

"But, Henry—"

"That is enough." He sounded so much like their late father that Elly immediately fell silent, gaping at her brother as if he had suddenly sprouted a second head. When he saw she meant to give no argument he allowed himself a small smile.

"There is still some time yet before we need to return to the house," he said in the same firm tones. "Do you still wish to stop at the lending library? I believe you said they had a book you were wanting?"

"Yes, they are holding a volume of Coleridge's poems for me," she replied stiffly, hating the notion she would be forced to endure so much as another moment in the marquess's company. Nothing would have given her greater pleasure than to demand to be taken home at once, but she had no notion of when she would next be in town and the library had made it plain they would not hold the book forever. Besides, she thought mutinously, given Henry's new-found propensities she would consider herself lucky if he did not take to locking her in her rooms.

"Then that is where we shall go next," he declared with a solemn nod, ignoring her angry glare with such cool self-possession that she longed to box his ears.

After leaving the inn Lord Seabrook drove them to the small establishment on North Street where Henry further enraged her by insisting he and the marquess accompany her inside. While Henry was busy leafing through the gazettes that had just come down from London, Elly went off to investigate the stacks, deciding to pick up some additional volumes while she was there. She was trying to choose between a book of poetry and a copy of Mrs. Radcliffe's work when she became aware Lord Seabrook had joined her and was peeking over her shoulder.

"Ah, Mrs. Radcliffe," he drawled, his lips curving in a pleased smile. "I might have known you would like her."

Elly snapped the slender book closed and returned it to the shelves. "I am sure I do not know what you mean, my lord," she said coldly, making no effort to hide the enmity in her voice. She and her brother were once again at odds, and as before, the blame fell solely on the marquess's broad shoulders.

"Why, I mean those silly Gothics you ladies seem to crave," Lucien said, determined to drag her into conversation. He still had a few more questions he needed to ask, and seeing her studying the novel had given the perfect opportunity.

"I do not crave them!" Elly denied, despite her

120

vow not to speak to him.

"Then why did you pick it up?"

"Because I had heard some of Lady Miranda's friends discussing it, and I wanted to see what all the fuss was about," she answered truthfully. "I have already told you, I do not hold with all that silly nonsense!"

"So you did." He inclined his head mockingly. "But I would have thought all of that would have changed."

"Why?"

The defiant question surprised Lucien, and it was a few seconds before he answered. "Why, because of where you are living, of course," he said, picking his words carefully. He remembered Mrs. Stanley had told him she'd not said a word about the ghost, but he'd figured that was because she didn't wish to alarm the servants. Surely she isn't going to pretend nothing untoward has happened, he thought, his eyes narrowing with annoyance.

Elly's hands clenched as she considered his insolent reply. There was no way she would confess to this arrogant coxcomb that she had seen Seagate's ghost, she decided proudly. One could tell by his self-satisfied smirk that he was only waiting for such an admission so that he could laugh at her. Well, let him wait, she thought fiercely; Hades would freeze over before she would ever admit to such a thing. She took a deep breath to steady her temper, and then gave him a cool, uncaring smile.

"You are referring, I take it, to the ghost of Old Jenks?" she asked in the well-modulated tones of a lady discussing the weather.

"As a matter of fact, I am," Lucien was cautious lest he say too much and thereby betray himself. "You and Henry have been in the house for several days, and I was wondering if you had . . . er . . . met him as yet."

"To quote you, my lord, 'Alas, no,'" she replied with a sweet, condescending smile. "It is as I have always thought; such things are no more than superstitious moonshine."

"Do you mean you haven't seen or heard anything?" Lucien was so outraged as to forget his caution.

She shrugged her shoulders indifferently and turned to pick through the remaining stacks of books. "Just the usual noises one would associate with an old house," she said, plucking out a book on Pope's later works from the shelves and studying it with feigned interest. "Creaking boards, the wind blowing down chimneys, the rustle and squealing of mice; nothing so very terrifying."

Squealing mice! Lucien was incensed. How dare she compare his ghost to the sounds made by vermin! He had thought his performance was most convincing. "If mice have infested the house then you had best look sharp," he said stiffly, deciding it was best to end the conversation before she grew suspicious. "You would not believe the damage such rodents can do."

"Mrs. Stanley has already spoken of having the rat catcher in," Elly said, making her way to the front of the shop where Henry was waiting with visible impatience, "but I myself would prefer a cat. I shall have to discuss it with Henry."

Lucien made no reply, and they returned home in considerably lower spirits than when they'd set out. While Elly was busy plotting how to avenge herself, Lucien was planning his next performance. He'd thought he was doing the gentlemanly thing in giving Miss Denning a few days respite from the "ghost," but it seemed he had only wasted his time.

Less than a sennight remained of the time Alex had granted him, and he knew he would have to move swiftly if he hoped to achieve his objectives.

122

Now it was more than the prince's safety or the Dennings' freedom that was at stake, he admitted with a cold smile. This was between him and Miss Denning, and he was damned if he would allow the little minx to make a May game of him. After tonight he would make very sure that she no longer dismissed the ghost as "squealing mice."

The dream started as it always did. She was sitting in the darkness, listening in terror as roaring lions slowly surrounded the tent. She huddled in the corner, her legs tucked up against her chest; hoping that if she made herself small enough the huge beasts would leave. She could hear them on the other side of the flap, sniffing and growling as if debating whether or not to attack, and she reached instinctively for her mother's hand. It was cold, as cold as marble, and when she turned her head in confusion she saw her mother lying still and white, her lovely face covered with a shroud.

"Mama! No!" The scream burst from Elly's lips as she sat up in bed, her hands reaching for the mother who had been dead for over eight years. When her fingers met only empty air her eyes flew open, and she found herself staring into the midnight darkness of an April night. It took several seconds for her surroundings to register on her whirling senses, but finally she realized where she was, and she buried her face in her hands with a relieved moan.

It seemed so *real,* she thought, her slender body shaking as she struggled for control. Her heart was still pounding with remembered terror, and over the roaring in her ears she thought she could still hear the terrible sounds of the jungle.

"Leave . . ."

Her head jerked up at the low groan, and she glanced wildly about her. Oh God, not tonight, she thought, even as the sound came again.

"You have been warned; now you will pay."

Elly scrambled out of the old bed, fumbling for the taper she'd kept at the ready. This is absolutely it, she thought, angrily dashing the drying tears from her face. She'd already put up with quite enough this day, and she was hanged if she would allow some dratted ghost to plague her as well. When the candle was finally lit she swung around; determined to face the spirit—or whatever it was—and put an end to this nonsense once and for all.

"Now see here," she began heatedly, striding purposefully towards the fireplace, "I think I have had just about enough of your foolishness! I do not believe in ghosts, so you are wasting your time and mine. Go and haunt some other place!"

On the other side of the room Lucien pressed himself against the massive wardrobe, his dark eyes gleaming behind his phosphorescent mask. He watched silently as Miss Denning cautiously approached the fireplace, her single candle held high in her shaking hand. She is brave, I have to give her that, he conceded, feeling a sharp pang of guilt as he remembered the way she'd awakened calling out for her mother. He knew the woman to be long dead, and for an uncomfortable moment he wondered if Elly had been reliving her death. He angrily brushed the thought aside.

No, damn it, he would *not* feel sorry for the chit, he told himself savagely. He had his duty to do, and she was an obstacle to that duty. He'd given Twyford his word he would drive the Dennings out within a fortnight, and drive them out he would. He'd already set the stage; now all that remained was the performance. He drew his black velvet cape closer about him and stepped out into the center of the room.

Mrs. Magney watched from her safe shadows, her

indignation mounting with each passing second. Such goings-on would never have been tolerated in her day, and she was not about to put up with them now. That it was a Seabrook causing disruption surprised her not at all, although it did present her with something of a dilemma. In life she had taken a vow to serve the noble family, and she could not see that she was exempted from that vow merely because she was dead.

On the other hand, she told herself primly, I can hardly stand idly by and allow the fellow to do my new mistress a mischief. She had warned him off once before, but 'twould seem harsher methods were called for. Well, she had never been one to shirk her duty, and she readied herself to do what must be done.

"Do you hear me, you tiresome creature?" Elly demanded, crouching low and peering up the chimney of the marble fireplace. "I don't believe in spirits, and even if I did I should never allow one to bully me about as you are trying to do! I am very sorry you are dead, but I must insist you cease bothering me and go away."

There was no answer, and after a moment Elly decided she must have imagined the ghostly voice. She turned around, eager to return to her bed, when she caught a glimpse of something moving towards her. For a second she thought she was going to swoon as she saw what appeared to be a disembodied head moving soundlessly towards her. The features were human and yet not human, the dark eyes bottomless and the mouth agape as a horrible moan issued forth. She opened her own mouth but no sound emerged, sheer terror holding her in its toils as the specter glided towards her.

"Death," Lucien whispered in what he hoped was a suitably mournful wail. "Death to all . . ."

A sudden sound, like the mad fluttering of a bird's wings filled the night around him, and a gust of icy wind struck him full in the face. The air in front of him thickened and writhed, and out of the glowing mass emerged a shape that was clearly discernible. He gave a stunned gasp, confusion giving way to disbelief as he stumbled backwards towards the safety of the hidden tunnel.

Elly stood frozen, her shocked senses trying to absorb what was happening. The head had disappeared, and in its place was a glowing cloud of light and shadow that shrank and expanded with an odd rushing sound. A mighty tremor shook her, breaking her paralysis, and the scream that had been fighting for release burst from her throat seconds before she crumpled to the floor in a dead faint.

Chapter Nine

Across the darkened bedchamber Lucien gazed at the specter that seemed to have sprung straight from the worst of his childhood nightmares. The phantasm had interposed itself between him and Miss Denning, and when he took a hesitant step forward he was struck by another blast of sticky, chilled air. He moved back at once; his rational mind struggling to accept the terrifying reality confronting him. Even as he told himself there were no such things as ghosts, the swirling cloud took a shape that was sickeningly human.

It was the figure of a small woman, garbed in the clothing of a bygone era. As Lucien watched in stunned horror the woman moved towards him, shaking her finger at him in an admonishing manner. This proved too much even for a man of Lucien's exceptional bravery, and he turned towards the tunnel, his only thought escape. He dashed into the open passageway, catching the edge of his cape on a corner of the door. For a horrifying moment he thought the ghost had grabbed him, and he pulled himself free with a mighty tug.

The sound of tearing cloth made him pause, but not for anything could he reenter that room. He hurriedly secured the passage door, promising himself he would return later and retrieve the tangible proof of his visit. Once in the safety of the dimly-lit tunnel he regained some control over his badly-lacerated nerves. He still did not fully understand what he had seen, but he did know that whatever it was, it had been very, very real.

He was about to return to his own house when he suddenly remembered Miss Denning. The last he had seen of the recalcitrant bluestocking, she was collapsing in a swoon, and he knew he couldn't leave without making certain she was all right. The thought of encountering the ghost again made him shake, but he was too much of a gentleman to go off and leave a lady lying on the floor. He was re-opening the hidden door when the sounds of voices filtered through the thick walls, indicating help had already arrived.

A peek through the priest's hole confirmed this, and he waited until he saw her brother place her tenderly on the rumpled bed. Only then did he re-secure the door, his expression grim as he made his way out into the main part of the secret corridor. All along the way he kept remembering the ghostly encounter in the moon-lit bedchamber. Evidently Hamlet was right, he thought with a flash of gallows humor; there are more things between heaven and hell than could ever be imagined. All that remained now was deciding what the devil he was going to do about it.

". . . And mind you stay in bed, missy," Dr. Carlisle concluded, giving Elly's hand a condescending pat. "I am sure you will soon be back on your pins again."

"If you say so, Doctor," Elly returned, her fingers clutching the bedclothes as she fought the urge to throttle the plump physician Henry had insisted upon summoning. "Thank you for coming out at

128

such a late hour. It was very good of you."

"Not at all, my dear, not at all." Her other hand was treated to a pat. "It is a physician's lot, I fear, to be forever at the beck and call of his patients. Do not hesitate to send for me again should you suffer a relapse."

"I won't," Elly said, silently vowing it would be a cold day in Hades before she ever endured the odious man's company again. The only good thing she could think to say of him was that he was such a dolt, it had been easy convincing him her collapse had been caused by nothing more serious than "female complaints." She much doubted Henry would be fooled by such fustian, but for the moment all she cared about was that no one ever learn what had really made her swoon for the first time in her life.

"I have left a receipt with Mrs. Stanley," Dr. Carlisle said, rising to take his leave. "Also, I would like you to take beef broth and sherry at least two times a day for the next week; builds up the blood, don't you know."

"Yes, Doctor," Elly repeated, wishing sourly that he would just leave. Since awakening from her faint to find a distraught Henry bending over her, she hadn't had so much as a minute to herself, and she wanted nothing more than to be left in peace so that she could come to grips with her preternatural experience. Some of her feelings must have been evident on her face, for the doctor gave another chuckle as he retrieved his bag from her night table.

"Well, I daresay you must be wishing me at ⸺icho," he said, displaying the first flash of intelligence since bustling through her door. "I shall be on my way, then. Your poor brother must be fair worn with distraction by now."

"Yes, I am sure that must be the case," she replied, eagerly seizing on his words. "Pray tell him that I am fine, but that I am very tired. I-I shall see him tomorrow morning."

"A sensible suggestion," the doctor approved with a beaming smile. "Should you like some laudanum? I can leave it on the—"

"No!" Elly interrupted, then, fearing she may have given offense, tempered her words with a false smile. "That is to say, my housekeeper already has some, and I can always ring for her should I change my mind."

Dr. Carlisle allowed he thought this an excellent plan and finally departed, assuring her yet again that she had only to send for him and he would come rushing to her aid. The moment the door closed behind him Elly collapsed on her pillows, her expression troubled as she recalled the evening's events.

When she'd first awakened to the ghostly moans she had been more annoyed than frightened, for odd as it seemed, the ghost had become more of a nuisance than the source of any real fear. Even the disembodied head, disconcerting as it had been, hadn't *really* frightened her. It was only when she'd seen that . . . whatever it was . . . that she'd become so overcome with fear she had fainted. Even now the memory of it was enough to make her tremble, and she muttered a quick prayer she had learned at her mother's knee: " 'From ghoulies and ghosties and long-leggety beasties and things that go bump in the night, Good Lord, deliver us!' "

"Are you quite certain you ought to be up?" Henry asked as he helped himself to another rasher

130

of bacon. "Dr. Carlisle did say you was to spend the day in bed."

"Dr. Carlisle is a bothersome old woman," Elly muttered, her temper stirring at the mention of the pompous physician. She had not had much sleep the night before, and her disposition was far from sunny.

"That may as be," Henry answered, not bothering to dispute her summation of the doctor, "but I think he has the right of it where you are concerned. The world won't stop spinning if you take to your bed for one day, you know."

Henry's reproving tone brought a twinkle to Elly's soft blue eyes. "I know," she said, covering his hand with her own, "but kindly do not tell the servants as much. They think me quite indispensable, and it pleases my vanity that they should do so."

A reluctant smile played about Henry's lips. "Blast it all, El," he began, struggling for composure, "this is serious—"

"I am sure it is," she interrupted, flashing him an impish grin, "but no more scolding, I implore you. I am aware I am being foolish, but really, I'm feeling much more the thing this morning. Now, tell me what your plans are for today. Will you be working on your book?"

For a moment she thought he meant to continue their argument, but then he shrugged his shoulders. "Until luncheon," he said, turning his attention to his food. "This afternoon I thought to ride over to Lord Seabrook's and have a look at his garden. Would you like to go with me?"

Elly's eyes narrowed at the mention of the marquess. Seabrook, she thought, her brows lowering in a scowl. The man was becoming almost as big a pest as the ghost! Why didn't he return to his gaming and his ladybirds and leave them in peace?

131

"No, thank you, Henry," she said coolly. "I'm afraid I shan't have the time. Lady Miranda and the others will be arriving soon, and I want Seagate to be ready for them. Pray give his lordship my regards."

Henry looked thoughtful. "Lady Miranda . . . she's the pretty blonde you met at Aunt's party; ain't she?"

Elly gave a quick nod. She'd been so caught up in her own problems of late, that she'd completely forgotten her plans to foster a match between her brother and her friend. But now that Henry himself had raised the issue, she was anxious to make up for lost time.

"Indeed she is," she said, flashing him a bright smile. "And you will be happy to know she is every bit as intelligent as she is lovely. In fact, she is fascinated with botany."

Henry nodded as he chewed on his buttered scone. "Yes, she mentioned it at that dreary dinner party. Perhaps I should show her some of father's illustrations."

"That would be very kind of you," Elly approved with a bright smile. Henry was devilishly protective of their father's work, and the fact he would offer to share it with Miranda was a very good sign indeed. Perhaps, with a bit of luck, she might manage to pull this off after all, she thought, her spirits soaring.

Henry merely grunted in response, and they fell into an easy silence. While her brother devoted himself to his breakfast, Elly began planning how she would spend her day. Work on the south wing was progressing, and perhaps while Henry was out of the house she would venture over for a peek. She knew she'd promised to stay out of the area, but someone had to inspect what had been accomplished to date, and she could hardly bother Henry with something so trivial. She'd just pop in for a minute, perhaps offer a few suggestions, and then she would slip quietly away. She'd be as silent as a ghost; they wouldn't even know she was there. . . .

She shivered suddenly; memories of last night washing over her. She'd thought her first glimpse of the ghost was the most terrifying thing she could imagine, but even that paled in comparison to the horror of that swirling mist of light and noise. She shivered again, her hands creeping up to rub her arms. What in the name of heaven . . . or hell . . . had she seen?

Lucien stood at the window of his study, his back to his paper-strewn desk as he gazed out at the green countryside. How very ordinary it all seems in the sunlight, he thought, his dark eyes filled with shadows. Looking at the bright yellow daffodils bobbing in the soft breeze he found it almost impossible to believe the events of last night had actually happened. But they had, and he was not the sort of man to pretend something didn't exist simply because it was uncomfortable to face. His own stubborn nature aside he had his duty to think of, and he would allow nothing to stand in his way.

In his brief service with Whitehall he'd established the reputation for completing even the most dangerous of missions. Although he'd shrugged aside his superior's effusive praise he'd been privately proud of his success, and if he was brutally honest then he supposed he'd regarded himself as something of a hero. That was why he was so disgusted now; for his actions of last night had been anything *but* heroic.

He had run, he admitted with uncompromising integrity. He'd broken rank like the rawest recruit and fled, and he'd consider himself luckier than he deserved if he hadn't jeopardized the entire mission. He would have to notify his superiors at once, although God above knew what Alex would make of his ghostly tale. Still, the viscount's reaction would definitely be worth observing, he mused, his mouth twisting in a humorless smile.

His smile faded abruptly as he realized that this meant the Dennings would now doubtlessly be taken into custody. Under the harsh laws enacted by Parliament anyone who was deemed a threat to the Crown could be taken up, and the trivial matter of guilt or innocence was given little thought. Indeed, one of his school friends had been clapped into jail after penning a vicious but witty attack on the prince, and he had been so ashamed by the stain on his family honor that he had taken his own life. Despite having taken an oath to protect his country and his king, Lucien knew he could not allow a similar fate to befall Henry Denning . . . or his hell-cat of a sister.

Perhaps I could risk continuing the mission with the Dennings still in residence, he thought, considering the proposal he had once rejected as unfeasible. It was dangerous, yes, but if they were very careful and very quiet, there was every chance they could succeed. The ancient walls were several feet thick, and with just a few precautions they could . . .

A knock on the door shattered his thoughts, and Bryant, his butler, stepped into the room. "A Mr. Henry Denning to see you, my lord," he intoned in his most precise tones. "Are you at home?"

"Certainly, Bryant," Lucien replied, thrusting his dark thoughts from his mind. He'd forgotten his invitation to show Denning about. "Pray send him in."

While Bryant withdrew to fetch his guest Lucien hurriedly hid his papers in the safe, and he'd no sooner secreted them than Henry came striding into the room.

"Now it is I who have caught you with your nose to the grindstone," he teased, stepping forward to offer Lucien his hand. "Haven't come at an inconvenient time, have I?"

"Not at all," Lucien replied swiftly, giving Henry a quick smile. "Just some matters pertaining to the estate. Dull as dust, really, but it is something you had best become accustomed to if you mean to set up at Seagate."

"I suppose." Henry shrugged off the subtle hint, his sharp blue eyes resting on Lucien's drawn features. "I say, my lord, I hope you will forgive me for being overly-familiar, but arc you all right? You're almost as pale-faced and hollowed-eyed as m'sister."

Lucien's ears pricked up at once. "Is she ill?" he asked anxiously, making no attempt to mask his concern. He'd been worried about her since rising that morning, and was only waiting for the opportunity to enquire after her.

"A female disorder, if that fool of a doctor is to be believed," Henry replied, his usual reticence forgotten. "All I know is I found her lying unconscious on the floor of her room."

"When?" Lucien demanded, although he already knew the answer.

"Last night," Henry said, and then launched into a clipped description of past night's events. "She kept saying it was just another nightmare," he concluded, his handsome face clouded with worry, "but this time I insisted a doctor be summoned. I

135

told you she had the fever, did I not?"

"Yes," Lucien said with a nod, recalling what the younger man had said. "She was quite ill, if I remember correctly."

"She almost died," Henry said grimly. "When the fever was at its worst she had the most terrible nightmares, especially about our mother, and there were times when I feared for her sanity. I thought she was recovered, but this is the second time in less than a week that she has wakened the household with her screams."

Lucien bit back a self-deprecatory oath at the image of Miss Denning sitting up in bed, her hands outstretched for her mother. He shouldn't have bothered her, he decided savagely. It was his fault she had fainted, if it hadn't been for him she — His thought broke off abruptly as a sudden possibility struck him.

Had that . . . that thing been Miss Denning's mother? he wondered, his face paling with renewed horror. Had she somehow come from beyond the veil to protect her beloved daughter?

"My lord?" Henry was frowning at Lucien. "What is it? You look as if you've seen a ghost!"

Lucien managed, somehow, not to laugh at Denning's wildly appropriate remark. "What did your mother look like?" he asked instead, his tone imperious. "Was she a small woman?"

"Mama?" Henry stared at the marquess, wondering if the whole world had gone quietly mad about him. "No, she was actually quite tall for a woman, and dashed pretty, too. I recall my father saying she could have had her pick of any man in her salad days."

A plump face with thick brows and prodigiously ugly features popped into Lucien's mind, and his shoulders slumped in relief. Whoever that creature

136

had been in life, thank God she was not Miss Denning's mama. He glanced up to find his visitor gaping at him as if he were an escapee from a madhouse, and he fastened an insincere smile to his face.

"How goes the writing?" he asked, struggling to recall the details of Denning's book. "Will you be including that chapter on herbal remedies of the Africans?"

"I thought to, as they were of particular interest to both my father and myself," Henry answered, although without the usual passion he displayed for his work. "Elinore suggested I also add something of my journey across the Orange River, but I am not so certain."

The topic saw them safely over the next several minutes, and by the time they reached the gardens Henry seemed to have recovered his spirits. Lucien dutifully showed him each plant in the Shakespeare garden, explaining in which play the plant had been mentioned. They were making their way towards the small greenhouse where Lucien's mother had grown orchids when Henry said, "My lord, may I ask you something?"

"Certainly, Denning," Lucien answered, thinking the young scholar meant to quiz him about plants.

"Do you believe in ghosts?"

Lucien stopped in mid-stride, then whirled around to confront Henry. "What did you say?" he demanded, his face paling with shock.

Henry grew red at the marquess's stunned expression. "I am sure you must think me all about in the head," he muttered, frankly embarrassed, "but I assure you there are very sound reasons for my question."

Lucien quickly composed his features, hiding his interest behind a show of polite indifference. "Indeed?" he drawled coolly, a dark eyebrow lifting in query. "And pray, what might those reasons be?"

Henry shifted restlessly, his eyes not quite meeting his host's. "There is something about Seagate," he began, struggling to explain that which not even he fully understood; "an air, if you will, that has troubled me from the moment I arrived. At first I put it down to fancy, for as Elinore says, the place is straight from a Minervian novel, but now . . ."

"Now?" Lucien pressed, when Henry's voice trailed to a halt. Perhaps the lad had also seen that dreadful apparition, he thought, his heart pounding with excitement. He would have to probe very carefully, and learn if what Denning had seen in any way matched his own experience of the creature. Of course, there was no way he could admit to his own encounter without explaining how he had come to be in the house, but he was still determined to learn what he could.

"Now I am not so certain," Henry said bluntly, deciding to make a clean breast of it. "I have never seen anything, mind, but many has been the time I have felt as if something . . . some*one* was watching me. I will be doing something perfectly ordinary when I suddenly have the strongest sensation that I am no longer alone. I glance up from whatever it is I am doing and look about, but—"

"But you are alone," Lucien concluded, recalling experiencing the very same thing in the darkened tunnel.

"Exactly so, nor is that the half of it. My things are always being moved about; books, papers, that sort of thing. Naturally I thought 'twas the servants, but when I questioned them they all denied it, and demmed if I don't believe 'em."

"What do you think might be responsible for this

138

. . . er . . . phenomenon?" Lucien asked, fascinated.

Henry drew a deep breath. "I think the place is haunted," he said, his blue eyes meeting Lucien's dark gaze. "And what is more, I think the unholy thing is after my sister."

Shock piled upon shock would have sent a lesser man reeling, but Lucien was made of sterner stuff. He merely nodded, his expression grim as he pressed for greater detail. Henry was only too happy to oblige him, providing a concise, almost scientific recitation of events, ending with Elly's collapse the past night.

"You do not know my sister, Seabrook, else you would never believe that moonshine about 'female complaints'," he concluded with a derisive sneer. "Dr. Carlisle was idiot enough to be gulled, but I know El was hiding something."

"And you think that something was a visit from a ghost?" Lucien enquired, his mind one step ahead of his guest. "Why would she not say something, for heaven's sake?"

A wide grin split Henry's face. "I think you *do* know El well enough to guess the answer to that," he drawled, his expression wry.

An answering smile lit Lucien's dark eyes. "Sheer perversity, I should say," he said with reluctant admiration. "To say nothing of her obvious reluctance to appear as anything less than the most intellectual of bluestockings. The little baggage! And to think she denied ever seeing anything when I teased her on the matter!"

"You knew about the ghost?" Henry was obviously shocked.

Lucien silently cursed his incautious tongue, but before he could think of a reply Henry said, "But of course, I'd forgotten Seagate was once your

139

family's property. Naturally you would know all about the ghost." He gave Lucien a bitter smile. "Don't suppose you'd care to renew your offer for the place, would you?"

Lucien froze. He'd all but abandoned all hope of ever acquiring Seagate, but if Denning was experiencing a change of heart . . . "I have always been honest about my hopes for eventually reuniting the two properties," he said, his tone carefully even. "It was always my mother's most fondest wish, and naturally nothing would give me greater pleasure. Why? Are you considering selling after all?"

Henry thrust an impatient hand through his dark hair. "Damned if I know," he muttered in exasperation. "I like the place well enough, and God knows El would raise a devil of a dust if I was to sell out, but I must admit I have been considering doing just that. I won't have my sister menaced."

"Yes, I can see that you will not," Lucien said thoughtfully, already planning his next visitation. He had been considering abandoning his ghostly exertions, but now he could see he would have to rethink the matter.

"I mean it," Henry said, his determination increasing at Seabrook's obvious approval. "One more episode like last night, and I shall give Seagate to you at the original price you offered!"

After Henry had ridden off to visit Seabrook Elly scurried over to inspect the south wing. The workmen she had engaged had evidently been well worth their hire, and she was pleasantly surprised by the changes they had wrought. A new roof now kept out the wind and rain, and several rotting floorboards she'd noted on her earlier tour had been replaced. She was examining a newly-mortared wall when someone called out her name, and she

140

glanced up to see Mrs. Stanley bustling towards her.

"Here you are, miss," the older woman exclaimed in gently chiding tones. "Why, we have been searching everywhere for you this past quarter hour! I was beginning to fear Mrs. Magney had carried you off."

Elly wondered who the mysterious Mrs. Magney might be, but before she could demand an explanation Mrs. Stanley added, "You have visitors, miss. Lady Miranda Ablethorpe and a Miss Jessica Kingsley are in the drawing room asking if they might see you."

The news of her friends arrival brought a flush of pleasure to Elly's cheeks. "Miranda and Jessica are here?" she asked, scrambling to her feet and wiping her hands on the skirts of her gown. "Pray tell them I shall join them immediately."

"Very good, Miss Denning," the housekeeper said, although she made no move to carry out her mistress's instructions.

"Is there anything else, Mrs. Stanley?" Elly asked, noting the older woman's behavior.

"Well, miss," Mrs. Stanley cleared her throat nervously, "I've ordered tea to be served to your guests, so I am sure there will be more than enough time if you wish to change into something more . . . comfortable." Here she directed a pointed look at her mistress's dusty gown of flowered cambric.

Elly took the hint at once and hurried to her rooms to change into a fresh gown of yellow ruffled silk. That done she dashed down to the parlor, embracing her friends with tearful delight.

"It is so good to see you both again!" she cried, giving Miranda another hug. "I have missed you so

141

much! But where is Lydia? I do hope she is not ill?"

"No, a message from her solicitor arrived just as we were leaving, and she had to cry off," Miranda explained, her blue eyes resting on Elly's face with concern. "But what of you? I thought to find you blooming with health, and here you are drooping like a wilted rose. Does the sea air not agree with you?"

The younger girl's sharpness surprised Elly. "Oh no! That is . . . I find it quite delightful," she said, covering her perturbation with a hasty smile. "It is just I have been so busy with the house that I have scarce had a moment's rest. You would not believe the condition this place was in when Henry and I arrived."

"Mmm." Jessica's sharp green eyes narrowed thoughtfully. "If you say so, dear Elinore, although I do not think it is just the strain of hard work that has brought shadows to your eyes."

There was an awkward silence, which Miranda covered with her gentle grace. "Speaking of your brother, your butler informed us he was not at home. We are sorry to have missed him."

Elly turned to her with a feeling of profound gratitude. "Yes, he has ridden over to Lord Seabrook's," she said with a bright smile. "His lordship has a Shakespearean garden, which he has been promising to show Henry."

"A Shakespearean garden? Lord Seabrook?" Jessica gave a merry laugh. "My heavens, I would have thought the marquess much too interested in his ladybirds to bother with such intellectual pursuits."

Elly, who had once uttered these same sentiments, felt a sudden flash of irritation at her friend. "On the contrary, I have always found his

142

lordship to be most intelligent," she said, her voice cool. "Only yesterday he quoted a particularly effective passage from *Richard II*."

Rather than taking offense at the set down Jessica looked amused. "Did he?" she drawled, her mouth curving in a wicked smile. "He must have learned it, then, in order to impress the ladies."

"Now, Jessica, you mustn't tease Elinore," Miranda shook her head at the other woman before turning an apologetic look on Elly. "You must forgive her, my dear, I fear she is still vexed with the marquess for his failure to support a vote to end hostilities with America."

"And I shall remain so until he does what is only right," Jessica returned with a nod. "Napoleon is the enemy here, and it is foolish beyond all permission to squander our resources and our soldiers fighting over something so silly as trade, and furthermore . . ."

Her tirade continued unabated, and the topic gradually expanded to encompass the way the war was being conducted. Jessica had some definite notions on that score, as did Miranda, and they were soon enjoying a spirited discussion about the merits of various generals. Elly, who had been avidly studying the gazettes, added her own opinions, and the next hour passed swiftly. They were just about to ring for a fresh pot of tea when a piercing scream, followed by the sound of broken crockery, split the silence of the afternoon. They dashed to the door, and just as they opened it one of the maids went streaking past them, the ribbons of her cap streaming after her.

"I had best see what is wrong," Elly apologized, her brows gathering in a worried frown. "Pray excuse me." And she hurried from the room to the back kitchens.

The maid was sitting at the servants' table while Mrs. Stanley hovered over her, patting her shoulder and murmuring reassurances. When she saw Elly standing in the doorway, she abandoned the girl to one of the older maids and moved forward to greet her.

"I am sorry if the silly chit disturbed you," she said, looking decidedly harassed. "You just get back to your guests now, and—"

"Nonsense, Mrs. Stanley," Elly interrupted, annoyed that she should be shooed away like an irresponsible schoolgirl. "I want know what is wrong with . . . er . . . Susan," she managed to remember the young girl's name, "and why she screamed like that. Is she all right?"

For a moment she thought the housekeeper wasn't going to answer; then the woman gave a weary sigh. "She's fine, miss. And as for why she screeched, well, Mrs. Magney moved the linens about when she was folding them, and it startled her."

This was the second time in a little more than an hour that she had heard the name, and this time Elly was determined to get to the bottom of the mystery. "And who might this Mrs. Magney be?" she demanded, fixing the housekeeper with a stern look. "I can not recall seeing her name on any of the account ledgers. Is she a laundress, perhaps?" She thought of the folded linen.

"Er . . . no . . . miss, not precisely." The housekeeper's eyes darted nervously about as she refused to meet Elly's unwavering gaze.

"Then what, precisely, is she?" Elly would not be distracted.

Mrs. Stanley hesitated, then raised both her shoulders in a shrug of defeat. Her dark eyes met Elly's. "She's a ghost, miss."

144

Chapter Ten

Elly stared at the housekeeper in speechless dismay. "A *ghost?*" she managed at last.

Mrs. Stanley gave a brisk nod. "Yes, miss. She was the housekeeper here when the first George was brought over to be our king, and when she died I reckon you could say she just sort of stayed on. She's usually no bother to the servants, but young girls these days are so skittish."

Skittish. Elly almost burst into hysterical laughter. She supposed one who had never been confronted by that horror from the nether world might think in such terms, but if one had actually experienced it . . . She gave the older woman a sharp look. "Have you ever seen her?" she demanded, the apparition from last night uppermost in her mind.

"Oh no, miss. No one ever *sees* Mrs. Magney." Now that she'd finally admitted the ghost's existence, Mrs. Stanley was anxious to discuss her. "She's very proper about such things, and wouldn't dream of making a spectacle of herself. 'Tis just that she likes things just so, and she'll not hesitate to put them right again. Although," her dark brows gathered in a sudden frown, "I can't recall the last time she was moving things about during the day. Spirits prefer the dark, or so I have always been told."

"So they do," Elly replied weakly, feeling rather as if she were in the middle of a bizarre dream. A month ago she wouldn't have even imagined having such a conversation; now it all seemed oddly commonplace. She shook her head ruefully and shot Mrs. Stanley a whimsical smile. "First Old Jenks and now Mrs. Magney; is that the lot of them, or has Seagate any other ghostly residents I have yet to encounter?"

Much to her dismay the housekeeper took the question seriously. "Well," she began, laying a finger on her lip, "there is the Gray Lady, who is said to haunt the cliffs, and the old monk in the west chamber; although he's not been seen since I was a girl. And then—"

"That is quite sufficient, Mrs. Stanley, thank you," Elly said quickly, holding up both her hands in supplication. "I am beginning to feel as if I am running some sort of ghostly inn! How can you be so calm?"

"Don't suppose there's much we can do about it," Mrs. Stanley answered with stolid practicality. "And in a way it's kind of comforting like to know Mrs. Magney is keeping watch over the house and all of us in it."

"What about Old Jenks?" Elly charged with a grumble as she recalled her sleepless nights. "You'd hardly call *him* a comforting presence."

Mrs. Stanley belatedly remembered Lord Seabrook's blunt instructions, and made haste to correct her dereliction. "But that's different, miss, him being a darker spirit and all. Why, if he was to appear in front of me I'd die of fright on the spot!"

"Pray don't do that, Mrs. Stanley," Elly implored with a flash of black humor. "You'd only become a ghost and heaven knows we already have enough of them as it is."

"Oh, but Miss Denning, I—"

"If you are certain Susan will be all right, I will return to my guests," Elly said coolly, deciding to

146

end the preposterous conversation. "Turn her work over to one of the other maids and see that she rests. Oh, and pray have a fresh pot of tea brought to the drawing room. I was about to ring for some when Mrs. Magney made her displeasure known."

After pausing to give a kind word to the sniffling maid Elly returned to the drawing room where Miranda and Jessica were eagerly awaiting her. The moment she entered they pounced upon her, demanding an explanation for the excitement.

"Everything is fine," she answered with a reassuring smile as she took her seat beside the others. "One of the maids saw something that frightened her, that is all."

"What? Do you mean to say all this hue and cry was raised because of a mouse?" Jessica shook her head in gentle disgust. "No wonder men refuse to take our aspirations seriously when we women insist upon swooning over the least little thing!"

Elly lifted her cup to her lips, wishing the delicate china contained something a great deal stronger than tepid tea. "It wasn't a mouse that frightened her," she muttered, taking a long gulp of tea.

"Oh? Then what was it, a lion?" Jessica demanded with a laugh.

"A ghost."

The moment the words slipped from her lips Elly could have cheerfully bitten off her tongue. Both guests were staring at her as if she had taken leave of her senses, but having uttered the words, there was no way to recall them without looking even more foolish than she already appeared. She sat quietly and waited until they recovered their wits.

"A ghost? Do you mean to say Seagate is *really* haunted?" Miranda seemed genuinely intrigued, while Jessica was openly skeptical.

"That's even bigger nonsense than swooning at the sight of a mouse," she said, giving Elly a disapproving look. "Mice, at least, are real, while ghosts are nothing more than fancy and moonshine."

"I thought that very way when I first came to Seagate," Elly agreed, not taking umbrage at her friend's acerbic remarks. "But after my first night here I changed my tune quick enough."

"Elinore! Do you mean to say you've seen the ghost?" Miranda exclaimed, exchanging startled looks with Jessica.

In a rush Elly related the eerie events that had transpired since she and Henry arrived at the ancient house. She held nothing back, relieved to finally share the terrible burden she had been carrying for so long. When she finished speaking her friends were regarding her with wide, solemn eyes.

"Oh, poor Elinore!" Miranda gave Elly's hand a comforting squeeze. "How perfectly horrible for you! The first ghost you described sounds beyond terrifying, but that second one . . . However could you endure such horror?"

"I swooned," Elly admitted, a feeling of contentment filling her. She was wrong not to have confided in someone before this, she realized with a flash of hindsight. Keeping the matter to herself had only given the horror power over her; she saw that now.

"Well, I don't blame you," Jessica admitted with a delicate shudder. "I daresay I would have done the very same thing. But you say you don't think this second apparition was the smuggler?"

Before Elly could elaborate the maid came in with a new tray, and they spoke of other things until she had left again. "No," Elly said the moment the door closed behind the servant. "I am almost certain of it. Whenever the ghost appeared before he was always moaning and rattling his chains as one would expect a ghost to do, but that . . . whatever it was . . . did no such thing."

"How did the first ghost react to the presence of

the second?" Miranda asked coolly, as calm as if they were discussing the day's weather. "Did he flee?"

Elly was quiet as she struggled to remember the precise events of the past night, but it was all a hopeless jumble in her mind. "I do not know," she admitted at last, her brows gathering in a thoughtful frown. "I was awakened by a bad dream, and then I heard the ghost and rose to investigate. After that . . ." She shrugged eloquently.

"And all these visitations were in your room? You've never seen the ghost anywhere else?" Miranda pressed gently. At Elly's denial she gave a decisive nod of her head. "Well then, it would seem the first step would be to get you out of that room."

That had also occurred to Elly, but her pride had rebelled at the thought of being forced from her room by anything—even a spirit. She mentioned this to the others and was roundly denounced for her efforts.

"Don't be so stiff-necked, Elinore," Jessica said, not unkindly. "There is a time to stand and fight, and a time to retreat; one has only to study Wellington's tactics on the peninsula to know that. Besides, it will be interesting to see if the ghost follows you."

"And what if it does? There are only so many rooms in this house, you know."

"If it does, then we will have to think of something else," Jessica answered as if addressing a dull-witted child. "In the meantime, what can it hurt?"

That made sense to Elly, and she gave both women her solemn word she would vacate her bedchamber at once. They continued discussing the ghostly phenomenon until Miranda reluctantly admitted it was past time they were leaving. "We have already been gone far longer than we intended," she said, giving Elly a worried look. "Will you be all right, do you think? You are certainly more than welcome to stay with us if you—"

"No," Elly interrupted, giving the pretty blonde an impulsive hug. "I shall be fine, I promise you. Besides, I refuse to give that wretched ghost the satisfaction of knowing he has driven me from Seagate! My room is one thing, but my home is quite another."

"Just be careful," Miranda implored, her blue eyes solemn. "I shall be worrying about you all night. Promise me you will keep a prayer book at your side for protection."

"To say nothing of a good stout stick," Jessica added with a teasing smile that was meant to reassure Elly. "Prayer is well and good, but a whack with a stick may prove to be an even more effective means of protection. *Argumentum baculinum*; 'nothing persuades like force.' "

"I promise to keep both at hand," Elly said with a smile. "I only ask that you not tell another soul about all of this. I would not have people take me for a Bedlamite . . . or a hysterical female," she added, thinking of the marquess's probable reaction. She'd rather face a dozen ghosts than endure his teasing.

After her friends departed Elly went up to her rooms and began packing a few precious belongings to last her over the next several days. On a whim she opened her jewelry box, and picked up the set of ruby ear-rings that had belonged to her mother. The perfectly-matched stones were among her most prized possessions, and holding them brought her a sense of comfort. She stared at them for a moment. Then, acting on another whim, she decided to don them.

She set the ear-rings down and began fumbling with the set of seed pearls she had worn with her yellow gown. The first stud came out easily enough, but the second proved far less cooperative. She had just removed the wretched thing when it slipped through her fingers, falling on to the floor and then bouncing merrily across the carpet.

Muttering imprecations beneath her breath she gave chase; crawling on her hands and knees until she located the culprit beside the massive wardrobe that took up most of the north wall. She was about to rise when something caught her eye, a piece of black fabric that looked to be growing out of the wall some six inches from the bottom. What on earth, she thought, leaning closer for a better look.

It was a piece of velvet, she realized, fingering the soft material with a puzzled frown. New velvet, too, for she reasoned that had it been there for any length of time it would surely have become discolored by the dust. She tugged on the piece of fabric tentatively, and then with greater strength, until it came free. She set it aside after a cursory examination, but moved closer to the wall to see if she could determine what had caught it.

The seam, almost invisible to the human eye puzzled her at first, for she could not imagine what it might be. But as she followed the line in the wainscotting she realized it ran almost the total height of the wall, and in that moment she knew precisely what it was. She had never seen such a thing in real life, but she'd read just enough Gothics to recognize a secret door when she saw one.

She sat on the floor for several seconds, her mind in a whirl as she stared at the hidden door. Its presence answered a dozen questions, then raised a hundred more, and she wondered what she was going to do. She was no nearer to solving this dilemma when the door to her room opened and her maid, Mary, came scurrying in.

"Your brother has returned, miss, and he is asking that you join him and Lord Seabrook in the . . ."

151

Her voice broke off as she saw her young mistress sitting on the floor. "Oh, miss! You've gone and fainted again!" she cried, rushing forward with a look of distress on her face.

"What?" Elly blinked up at her, only then realizing she was still on the floor. "Oh, no. Not at all," she said, rising somewhat awkwardly to her feet. "I was merely retrieving my ear-ring."

"Are you certain, miss?" Mary asked, slipping a supportive arm about Elly and guiding her to a chair. "You're as pale as death, if you don't mind my saying so, and you've got the queerest look on your face."

"Indigestion," Elly said, laying claim to the first malady she could think of. "I will be fine in a moment."

"If you say so." Mary looked far from convinced. "But I still say you should climb right back into that bed, and the devil with your brother and Lord Seabrook."

Henry! Elly jerked to her feet, paling to think of what his reaction would be if he were to learn she had collapsed again. She'd be lucky if he didn't bundle her off to Bath like an invalid. "No. Truly, Mary, I am fine," she said, rapidly regaining her composure. "I told you, I was but retrieving an ear-ring I had dropped. See?" She unclenched her hand to reveal the pearl stud nestled in her palm.

Mary gave a loud sniff, but offered no further comment; and Elly hurried from the room before the woman could think of any arguments to stop her.

"Now remember," Lucien cautioned Henry with a menacing scowl, "not a word to your sister about your decision to sell Seagate if anything else happens. If she suspects such a thing she'd not say a single word even if the ghost were to carry her off!"

"I know," Henry agreed, his blue eyes somber. "She adores Seagate, and I think she would do anything to keep it. I only hope it will not prove necessary to sell it after all. She would be dreadfully angry."

"Better angry than dead," Lucien replied bluntly, ignoring a stab of remorse. It is for the best, he told himself, employing the same argument he'd used on Denning during their brief ride to Seagate. With his objective almost at hand, he was damned if he would allow an attack of conscience to keep him from his duty. And it wasn't as if he were evicting them, he reminded himself piously. The price he was offering was well above what the place was worth, and it would allow them to live in comfort for many years to come.

While they waited for Miss Denning to join them, Lucien paced the drawing room, silently reviewing his strategy. He'd already convinced Henry the best bet of getting Elinore to talk was for him to get her off by herself. All that remained now was deciding how—short of torture—he would accomplish this. It would mean walking the razor's edge, letting enough slip so as to entice her into admitting what he needed to hear but without revealing anything which might inadvertently lead her to the truth.

He was still mulling over various conversational gambits when she finally appeared, all smiles and pretty apologies for having kept them waiting. He moved gracefully to her side, capturing her hand in his and carrying it to his lips.

"Miss Denning, I am sorry to hear you are feeling unwell," he murmured, taking note of the visible signs of strain about her smoky-blue eyes with another stab of remorse.

"Thank you, my lord," Elly returned, too distracted by her recent discovery to notice his sharp-eyed scrutiny. "But I am feeling much more the thing."

Lucien retained her hand in his, chafing the chilled skin with a concern that was not wholly faked. "You'll forgive me if I take leave to doubt you, ma'am," he said, his expression stern, "but you hardly look the picture of perfect health."

His words finally penetrated Elly's troubled thoughts, and she flashed him a ferocious scowl. "Ever the gentleman, I see," she snapped waspishly, snatching her hand free and stalking over to join Henry in front of the fire.

Her show of spirit relieved Lucien, for he had found her listlessness as alarming as her wan features. He waited a few moments and then strolled over to take a chair beside her. "My apologies if I have given offense," he said with his most persuasive smile. "But after listening to your brother voice his concerns over your health, I fear I allowed my worry to overcome my manners. Do say I am forgiven."

Elly would have much preferred telling him to climb out of the butter boat and take himself home, but such defiance would have required more energy than she possessed. Telling herself she need only endure his company for a few minutes at the most, she gave him a strained smile. "Naturally you are forgiven, my lord," she said, her voice devoid of all animation. "And I pray you will forgive my sharp tongue. As Henry has already told you, I am not at all myself this afternoon."

"Still not feeling up to snuff, eh, El?" Henry asked, a pointed glare from Lord Seabrook recalling him to his duty. "Do you know what you need? A walk on the beach, just the thing to put the roses back in your cheeks."

Elly was about to reply that the last thing she either needed or desired was a walk on the beach, when it occurred to her that she had just been presented with the perfect means of escape. She quickly assumed a look of pleasure. "I do believe you are right, Henry," she said brightly, rising to her feet. "A walk sounds utterly delightful. If you gentlemen will excuse me, I—"

"I believe I will accompany you," Lucien interjected, also rising to his feet. "The path down to the beach is somewhat treacherous, and I would not wish you to fall."

Elly, who had so far avoided the beach for that very reason was helpless to do other than glare at Seabrook. With his tawny hair brushed back from his forehead and in his elegant jacket of green serge and his buckskin breeches, he looked very much the country gentleman at his ease, but that image was destroyed by the firm set of his square jaw and the implacable gleam in his velvet brown eyes. Elly knew she had one of two choices; endure his company here or endure it on the wave-washed beach. She swallowed a sigh and inclined her head graciously.

"Very well, then, if you will give me a moment I will go and change into something a little more suitable."

"Mind you also bring your cloak with you," Lucien called after her. "The wind off the sea is certain to be sharp."

Some twenty minutes later a disgruntled Elly was picking her way across the slippery rocks, Lord Seabrook's strong hand solicitously cupping her elbow. When they had walked a little way he flicked her a wry grin.

"Do you mean to maintain a dignified silence for the entirety of our walk, Miss Denning, or will you finally give your temper full rein and tell me what you really think of me?"

Elly was so shocked by the teasing words that she jerked to a stop, her eyes wide as she stared up into his handsome face. "I beg your pardon, sir?" she said, wondering if she had heard aright.

"You heard me." He continued grinning at her dumbfounded expression. " 'Tis obvious you are less than pleased with my company, and I would much rather you admit as much than stalk at my side like some damned statue come to life."

Elly's cheeks grew warm. "I do apologize if you find my conversation less than stimulating," she said, anger chasing away her burdensome thoughts. "But may I remind you it was *you* who insisted upon accompanying me. You are more than free to leave if you wish."

To her surprise he threw back his head and laughed, the rich sound rolling across the gray and white waves. "Good, that is better," he said, his eyes sparkling with approval. "I much prefer honest dislike to simpering indifference. If you are mad at me, for God's sake, say so."

"I am furious with you," she admitted, although for some inexplicable reason she was smiling. "It is bad enough to have Henry hovering over me like a mother hen with but one chick; I refuse to put up with you coddling me as well."

Her analogy made him smile again. "Henry is your brother," he said in a surprisingly gentle voice. "His concern for your health is understandable. And as for me . . ."

"Yes?" She tilted her head to one side, her smile provocative as she gazed up at him.

"As for me, I regard myself as your friend, and I, too, have been concerned about you."

The sincerity in his deep voice made Elly's heart skip a beat, and she glanced away. "I don't know what tales Henry has been spinning for you," she said, unable to meet his probing gaze, "but there is really nothing wrong with me. I have just been . . . tired, that is all."

"What about the nightmares?" Lucien pressed,

156

noting the slight inflection she had given the word "tired." "Henry says you have been having them off and on since coming to Seagate."

Elly pulled a face. "Henry seems to have been saying a great deal," she muttered.

"He is your brother, and—"

"And it is only natural he worry, I know. But that does not mean I enjoy being the object under discussion."

Lucien smiled briefly, then gave her a somber look. "What is wrong, Elly?"

It was the first time he had ever used her first name, but it sounded oddly right on his lips. She met his dark gaze for a timeless moment, and in the end it was she who looked away. "I don't know what is wrong," she admitted, deciding that was as much truth as she could trust herself to speak. "I've never been plagued by bad dreams before . . . except when I had the fever; now it seems that is all I ever have. Even when I'm awake—"

"Even when you're awake . . . what?"

For a moment Elly considered admitting the truth. She'd told Miranda and Jessica about the ghost, and they had believed her at once; perhaps he would do the same. But even as the hopeful thought formed she rejected it. She and the earl might be at peace now, but she doubted their truce would last. She was not about to confess anything that he might well use against her at some future date.

"Nothing," she said at last, turning to gaze out at the wind-whipped waves. "I was just being silly."

Lucien could have cursed with frustration. He could sense she was close to admitting the truth, but he also knew that if he pushed her too hard, too fast, she would retreat behind a wall of hostility. Still, he had to say something . . . .

"What do you think of the beach?" he asked suddenly, the smile he turned on her innocent of all

157

guile. "Lovely, is it not?"

"Very lovely," Elly echoed, amazed he had accepted her assurances so easily. She had thought him to be the sort of man who would stop at nothing once he had set his mind to something.

"You know, do you not, that this is the beach where Old Jenks died?" he pressed, pleased to see he had her at a disadvantage.

Elly gave a nervous start, wondering why he should mention the ghost now. "Er . . . yes, I believe Mrs. Stanley may have mentioned it," she said, unconsciously pulling her cloak closer about her. "He . . . he was killed, she said."

"Did she tell you how he was killed?"

"Well, no, but—"

"On William's orders he was wrapped in fishing nets so that he couldn't move, and then left lying on the beach to wait for the tide to come in. They say he lay there for hours, pleading that his life be spared, but his shipmates were too afraid of your uncle to let him go. They simply watched and waited until the sea slowly covered him. . . ."

Elly was unable to control the shiver that shook her slender frame. She could picture the doomed man's expression; see the terror in his eyes as he felt the cold, merciless waves washing over him. Poor soul, she thought with a flash of pity, no wonder he is haunting the house.

"You've seen him, haven't you?"

The calm acceptance in his voice brought Elly whirling around to face him. She studied him closely, looking for any sign he might be mocking her. Honesty and compassion shone in his deep brown eyes, but there was something else there as well. A hardness, a remote, watchful waiting, and the admission on her lips became a denial.

"Don't be silly, my lord," she said, her laugh sounding oddly hollow as she turned back to gaze at

158

the sea. "I have told you, I do not believe in ghosts."

Lucien's hands balled into tight fists at her reply. *Curse* her stubborn pride, he thought, fighting to control his impatience. How could any one female be so bloody obstinate? He wanted to shake the truth from her, but he knew better than to try. Not only was it certain to fail, but there was also the risk it would rouse her suspicions as well. Until she decided of her own accord to admit she had seen the ghost, there wasn't a damned thing he could do. The admission filled him with bitter fury.

"It is getting cold, Miss Denning," he said, his voice clipped as he reached out to clasp her upper arm. "Come, it is time we were heading back." And he led her up the path, as stiff and silent as the statue he had once named her.

Chapter Eleven

After escorting Elly back to Seagate Lucien returned to his own home to prepare for the evening's performance. Repeating the grimmer aspects of the old story had given him an idea, and he wondered if there would be enough time to slip down to the beach before making his appearance. A few pieces of seaweed draped strategically about the room ought to do the trick, he thought, smiling as he entered his study. Perhaps he might even leave a puddle of water on the floor, as the *coup de grâce*.

"About time you got back, Seabrook."

The quiet voice from the shadows brought Lucien whirling around, his heart leaping in to his throat. His first thought was that the horror from last night had somehow followed him home, and the sight of Twyford sprawled negligently on the red leather chair made his shoulders slump with relief.

"Alex, thank God 'tis you," he said, flashing the other man an abashed smile. "You startled me."

"So I see," Alex's expression was even more remote than usual as he studied Lucien. "Don't suppose you would care to explain why you're so damned skittish; would you?"

"No, I would not," Lucien replied. "But tell me what brings you to Brighton? There is no impediment, I trust?"

Alex gave him a long look and then slowly shook

160

his head. "No, things are going as planned," he said, his gray eyes never leaving Lucien's face. "What of you? The Dennings are still firmly entrenched, I note."

"Aye, but not for long," Lucien responded, and then gave a highly-censored account of his efforts to drive the Dennings from Seagate, leaving out any mention of his own ghostly encounters.

"Denning told me he will sell out if even one more thing happens," he concluded, hoping the other man accepted his condensed report without comment. "Perhaps I ought to have concentrated my efforts on him instead."

"Perhaps," Alex agreed coolly. "Although a man will often react more strongly when it is his family who is being threatened, rather than himself. From what you have said, Mr. Denning and his sister are quite close."

"Yes, quite close," Lucien echoed, remembering the concern in the younger man's voice.

"Good." Alex permitted himself a small nod. "But as it happens, the Dennings are not my concern at the moment. Does the name Jack McKenzie have any meaning to you?"

Lucien searched his memory a long while before answering. "A local boy with good connections," he said slowly, his mind conjuring up the image of a handsome, guileless face.

"Very good connections," Alex affirmed. "He is a member of the prince's own regiment, and unless I am much mistaken, the link in the chain we have been seeking."

The cold certainty in Alex's voice convinced Lucien that shocked protestation would be useless, and his initial disbelief was replaced by a burning fury. "Traitorous bastard!" he muttered, his dark eyes flashing with contempt. "I hope that he hangs!"

"I am sure he shall," Alex replied confidently, "but

for the moment our primary concern must be gaining the evidence to prove what we already know. McKenzie's mother was once one of the queen's ladies-in-waiting, and Her Highness is still quite devoted to the family. We shall have to tread carefully, Seabrook, very carefully."

"What do you want me to do?"

"I've received word from a *gentleman* of my acquaintance, that the lieutenant will be meeting his French contact at The Quail in Hove. I thought you might wish to stop by for a drink and see what you can learn. I would attend to the matter myself, but I need to go to the pavilion and meet with Major Phillips. Of course, if you have other plans I shall understand completely."

Lucien thought of his plans to return to Seagate. He'd told himself there was no other choice, but relief coursed through him at the unexpected reprieve. "When would you like me to leave?"

Following the marquess's departure Elly and Henry spent a quiet evening; each lost in disturbing thoughts. While Henry brooded over the best way of protecting his sister, she wrestled with the dilemma of what to tell him about the secret door. Now that the initial shock had worn off, her usually sensible mind was hard at work, and the vague suspicion someone was making a May game of her was now a hard, cold certainty. She also had a very good idea as to just who that someone might be.

It was this realization which ultimately convinced her to say nothing. Not only would such an announcement mean admitting to the ghost's existence, it would also mean explaining to Henry why she had lied about the matter. Since the only explanation she could give would be certain to offend him, she felt it wisest to hold her tongue. But that didn't mean she

162

intended doing nothing about her discovery; the following morning she set out for Brighton and Lady Miranda's.

She found her three friends assembled in the library, and without pausing for the civilities, she poured out all the details of her shocking find.

"Seabrook!" Miranda exclaimed when she had finished. "Elinore, are you certain?"

"Positive," she replied adamantly, her eyes bright with the force of her fury. "It is the only explanation that makes any sense. He has wanted Seagate from the start, and it was he who first told me of the ghost. Who else could it be?"

"Well, I think it is infamous!" Lydia declared with unaccustomed heat. "Of all the despicable, cowardly things to do . . . frightening someone from their home merely because he wants it for himself! I have a good mind to write my Uncle Ratcliffe. He is a member of the marquess's club, and I know he and the other members would never countenance such behavior!"

"Actually," a mischievous grin stole across Jessica's gaminesque features, "I find the whole thing vastly amusing! Only imagine the fastidious marquess skulking about dressed as a ghost; it is too funny by half. The only thing that would make it even more delicious would be if he had that stiff-rumped Twyford with him. Which reminds me, Elinore, where does the hidden door lead?"

"Jessica!" It was obvious neither Miranda nor Lydia appreciated their friend's unwonted levity.

"Well, it seems a logical question to me," the lively brunette was thoroughly unrepentant. "It could lead to a tunnel of sorts, or better yet, a secret chamber with a mouldering corpse chained to the wall. . . ."

"Jessica!"

"Actually," Elly said, smiling as she rose to Jessica's defense, "I believe it is skeletons one usually

163

finds chained to walls. But as it happens, I haven't had time to do any exploring. I only discovered it yesterday afternoon."

"Thank heaven for that," Miranda muttered feelingly, rubbing her arms as she cast a nervous look about her. "You must promise me you won't go anywhere near that terrible door!"

"At least not without us there to help you," Jessica added with another grin.

"What now?" Lydia ignored Jessica's comment with obvious forbearance. "I assume you do not intend to let matters stand as they are?"

"Of course not!" Jessica retorted, frowning at Lydia. "I daresay Elinore has already devised a clever plan for dealing with his lordship. Haven't you?" She gave Elly an expectant look.

Once again Elly was grateful for her friends' casual acceptance of the unacceptable. "Indeed I have," she replied, thinking of all the hours she had spent lying on her bed and working out the details. "But I will require your assistance."

"Anything," Lydia promised earnestly.

"Anything legal," Miranda added, her eyes flashing to Jessica.

Elly sat back in her chair, a smile every bit as wicked as Jessica's playing about her lips. "Would any of you know where I might find a fishing net?" she enquired calmly.

Alex had already eaten and was waiting when Lucien stumbled down to breakfast. One look at his guest's grim face and Lucien waved the hovering footman from the room. "What is it?" he asked, pouring some steaming coffee from the silver pot on the table.

"I have been going over your preliminary report," Alex answered in his guarded fashion. "What do you mean you doubt McKenzie is our man? Major Phillips and I are both convinced of it."

"Oh, I've no doubt the lieutenant is involved," Lucien clarified, digging hungrily into his eggs and ham. "I just take leave to doubt he is the leader. He is such a rank amateur he had no idea I was even following him."

"Perhaps. But then, if he *had* noticed, it would not have been he who was the amateur."

Lucien grinned at Twyford's bluntness. "He did make some attempts to alluded observation," he said calmly, "but as I say, they were amateurish at best. One would think a man plotting to kidnap a prince would have been less open when meeting an enemy agent."

"What about you?" Alex frowned with sudden concern. "How did you explain your presence at The Quail? Unless it is one of your usual haunts?"

"Hardly. But in the event anyone should take the trouble to ask, I let it be known that my supply of brandy was running shockingly low. A rather disreputable-looking captain then assured me he would be able to rectify my deficiency."

Twyford relaxed in his chair, tracing the rim of his cup with the tip of a long finger. "Then you think McKenzie is nothing more than a pawn?" he asked, returning to his original line of questioning.

Lucien nodded. "As I said in my report, there were several references to a mysterious 'him,' as well as a veiled mention of 'the party.' Seagate was also alluded to, but only in connection with the bay. It seems they're still planning to use the beach to stage the operation."

"Did they not seem in the least concerned they might be observed?" Alex asked, frowning. "That seems odd."

"Not really. It will be a moonless night, and one would have to be looking out the window at precisely the right moment in order to see anything. Also, I think we may assume that McKenzie and his associates will be making as little noise as possible."

"Maybe, but I would be a great deal happier if the Dennings were not involved," Alex said, his eyes meeting Lucien's in a level stare. "Your time is almost up."

"I know." Lucien answered, setting his fork down and returning Alex's gaze. "You have my word, Twyford, that I shall do everything physically possible to keep my promise to you."

Alex remained silent, and for a moment Lucien thought he meant to disagree. Then, inexplicably, he was smiling. "Make that *metaphysically* possible, Seabrook, and I shall be content," he said, the ice in his eyes dissolving to a soft gray. "But regardless of the outcome, I fear I must renege on my word to you. I want the Dennings out of there tomorrow."

Lucien protested, angry. "But, my lord —"

"No." Alex shook his head. "I am afraid there is no other choice. One way or another, this is your last performance."

Acquiring a net proved to be as simple as purchasing one from a bemused fisherman and arranging its delivery to the house. Rigging it, however, was another matter, and it occupied the better part of Elly's afternoon. When she was satisfied with its placement she went down to the library to take tea with Henry. The sight of the marquess sprawled on the settee banished her complacency, and it was all she could do to greet him with anything resembling civility.

"Lord Seabrook, how delightful to see you *again,*" she said, her teeth clenched in a parody of her warm smile as she held out a hand to him.

"Miss Denning," Lucien said, rolling to his feet as

he rose to face her. "Will you allow me to compliment you on your improved looks, or will that place me in your black books again?"

If nothing else, Elly had to admire his gall. Looking at his pleasant smile and friendly expression, she thought one would be forgiven for being taken in by his charm. Had she not known him for a complete villain she might even have been flattered by his attentions, but as it was she found herself swallowing an angry setdown.

"Come, my lord, what lady could possibly find fault with so charming a compliment?" she murmured, fluttering her lashes for all she was worth. "I vow, you will turn my poor head!"

Lucien frowned at her fulsome reply. What the devil is she up to now? he wondered, his suspicions thoroughly aroused. But with her brother looking on and beaming his approval, there was nothing he could do save play along. Later, however, he vowed to get her off by herself and determine just what sort of rig she was up to. Now that Twyford had stepped up the pressure, the last thing he needed was Elinore making mischief.

"And how was your morning, ma'am?" he asked suavely, guiding her to the tea table. "Henry told me you had gone into town."

"Yes, to the lending library," she answered, reluctantly assuming her duties as hostess. "That reminds me, Henry, I have obtained a copy of Mr. Marchvale's Canadian exploration for you. I thought you might enjoy it." The book had actually come from Miranda's personal library, a fact she distorted for the marquess's benefit out of sheer perversity.

"I say, El, that was good of you," Henry replied with a grateful smile. His sister had slept the whole night without so much as a peep, and he was beginning to hope the worst was behind them. "Did you find any books for yourself?"

167

"A few." Elly handed Lucien his cup with a smile as odiously sweet as the beverage it contained. "I have some of Mrs. Radcliffe's work, my lord, should you wish to borrow them."

Lucien choked, stunned by her words as much as by the sugar-thickened tea. He hastily set the cup down and flashed her an angry scowl. "What on earth makes you think I should wish to borrow such drivel?" he demanded, his eyes narrowing.

She blinked her eyes at him in a picture of feminine innocence. "Why, no reason at all, sir," she murmured dulcetly. "Only that it seems you are quite fond of tales of horror and the like. Have you told Henry of our resident ghost?"

"What do you mean?" Lucien asked warily. What was the minx up to now?

"You really ought to turn your hand to penning such tales, Lord Seabrook, you are so talented in telling them. Why, you almost had me believing in them."

"You've been telling m'sister ghost stories, my lord?" Henry asked, turning a disapproving look on his friend.

"I mentioned the ghost, certainly," Lucien answered.

"Nonsense, my lord, you told me a wonderfully gruesome story about poor Old Jenks wrapped in nets and left to die on our very beach," Elly maintained stoutly. "Were I not such an intellectual I daresay I should have been swooning with horror."

"I did not mean to frighten you," Lucien murmured politely, his eyes keenly observing Elinore as he tried to make out her game.

"Didn't you?" Her thick lashes were brought into play once more before she turned to her brother. "Speaking of books, Henry, you must tell us how yours is progressing. Did you finish that last chapter?"

Her brother allowed himself to be diverted, and began expounding on his work. Lucien listened politely, his mind on other matters, namely, what the failure of his plans would mean for the Dennings.

While elaborating on the work he had completed that morning Henry suddenly stopped talking, his blue eyes widening with excitement. "That's it!" he exclaimed, his napkin falling to the floor as he leapt to his feet. "That's what I've forgotten!" And he fled from the room without so much as a backward glance.

There was an awkward silence in the wake of his departure as Elly and Lucien exchanged wary looks. She was the first to break it, her expression rueful as she raised her teacup to her lips. "I hope you have concluded your business with Henry, my lord," she said, favoring him with her first genuine smile since entering the library. "I fear that is the last we shall be seeing of him this day."

"What makes you think it is merely business that brings me here?" he challenged provocatively. "I could have other reasons."

Elly blushed at the assessing look that accompanied his drawled words. "Oh, my lord, I make no doubt!" she replied tartly, cursing herself for the betraying color that spread across her cheeks.

Lucien noted the intriguing blush, but it was her words that caught and held his interest. "And what do you mean by that?"

Elly was silent as she considered the best way of handling his question. She could either simper and play coy, or let him know that she was fully aware of his nefarious intentions. In the end she chose the middle ground, deciding to let him know that she was not quite the simpleton he seemed to take her for.

"It means that you always seem to know precisely what you are about, my lord," she returned, meeting his gaze with a defiant tilt of her chin. "I do not believe there is anything you do that is not carefully thought out in advance."

"You make me sound rather cold-blooded, ma'am," he murmured. "But such is not the case, I assure you."

"Again, sir, that is something I do not doubt for a moment," she riposted, finding reluctant pleasure in their verbal fencing. "What I *do* doubt, however, are your motives. You will forgive me for pointing out that there are times when they seem a trifle murky at best."

Lucien's lazy smile thinned. "Careful, madam," he warned in a soft voice. "Questioning a man's motives can be almost as dangerous as questioning his honor."

Elly considered that for a moment. "And would you call me to account, my lord?"

"If need be."

"Then I shall have to mind what I say, shan't I?" she retorted, her gray-blue eyes dancing with laughter. "I should hate to be placed in the awkward position of naming my seconds!"

Lucien smiled at her audacious reply. He might have known his little bluestocking would give as good as she got, he thought, leaning back in his chair to study her through half-lowered eyes. "A duel is not how I would choose to settle a point of honor with you, Elinore," he murmured, his voice rife with masculine promise. "Although make no doubt I would have my revenge on you."

Elly thought about that for a moment. "I am sure you would, my lord," she said, thinking of her tiresome ghost. "Just mind you recall what Molière had to say on the matter; *'A woman always has her revenge ready.'* "

"A threat, Miss Denning?" he asked, his mouth lifting in a mocking smile.

170

Elly shook her head. "A promise, Lord Seabrook," she answered sweetly. "A promise."

It was approaching midnight, and the dimly-lit passageway was filled with shadows and menace as Lucien stood in front of the secret door. After some thought he decided to use the entryway nearest the wardrobe, remembering how close she had already come to discovery of the entrance by the fireplace. The familiar mask covered his face, and the glowing costume covered him from head to foot. One of the maids had caught sight of him as he crept from his room, and if the high-pitched shriek she uttered was any indication, then his costume was most effective. Draping seaweed about him was truly an inspired idea, he thought, arranging one of the wet, green strands clinging to his arm.

He recalled what had happened the last time he had paid one of his nocturnal visits. He'd neither felt nor seen any evidence of the creature since entering the tunnel, and he hoped his luck would hold. A second encounter would surely test his sanity.

Putting all such thoughts from his mind he stepped up to the peep hole, his shoulders relaxing as he spied Miss Denning huddled beneath the bedcovers. He'd learned from Mrs. Stanley that she had spent last night in one of the other chambers, and he was grateful that she had not elected to do so tonight. Not only did this room have the best access via the hidden passageway, but it also spared him the necessity of searching for her. How obliging of her to make it so easy for me, he mused, triggering the hidden mechanism and stepping into the darkened room.

Elly lay stiffly on her bed, the covers pulled up to her chin as she strained to catch any sound. She'd retired over an hour ago, but so far she had yet to hear so much as a single moan; a circumstance which left her feeling both relieved and somewhat anxious. She was almost positive Seabrook was behind the recent events, but she wasn't completely convinced. It was the small, but very real, possibility she could be mistaken which left her trembling with uncertainty.

What if I am wrong? she thought, turning fretfully on her side and tucking her hand beneath her cheek. What if there are such things as ghosts?

Certainly there could be a rational . . . a *human* explanation for much of what she had experienced, but that still did not explain that last apparition. What if —

"Leave. . . ." The ghostly whisper filled the night air, chilling Elly's blood even as the breath she had been unconsciously holding was gently expelled. It was her erstwhile smuggler, she decided with relief, and not that other terror. The voice came from near the wardrobe, and she turned carefully in the bed so that the far side of the room was within her field of vision.

At first she saw only the thickened shadows and thought she was imagining things, and then the tall, glowing shape emerged out of the darkness. Even though she had been expecting it, the sight temporarily unnerved her, and a small gasp escaped from her parted lips. She watched as the object glided closer, and closer still, making no sound as it drew nearer to the bed. Her hand fumbled for the end of the rope which she had hidden beneath her pillow, and she grasped it in a sweating palm.

"It is too late," the apparition said, pointing a finger at her as if in accusation. "Now you will die." It moved until it was almost directly between the wardrobe and the bed, its back to the secret door.

Elly wrapped the rope more tightly about her fist. "That is what you think," she said, and gave the

172

rope a sharp tug, releasing the suspended net so that it fell upon her intruder, knocking him to the ground.

The moment she was certain her trap had worked, Elly scrambled from beneath the covers, pulling on her robe even as she was shouting for Henry. She paused long enough to light a candle, and then turned towards the foot of her bed where her prey lay fighting the heavy net that ensnared him. When it was obvious he couldn't escape she knelt beside him, reaching through the weave to grasp the cloth mask covering his head. Despite his struggles she was able to pull it free, and frowned down at the scowling features of the marquess with a grim sense of satisfaction.

"You beast! I *knew* it was you!"

Chapter Twelve

Lucien glared up at his pretty captor, hot anger chasing out the last vestiges of the terror he'd felt when the net had dropped on him. He'd fought wildly at first, only ceasing his furious struggles as he realized the trap holding him was a physical one. He'd continued fighting to escape, of course, but all to no avail. The little minx had him right and tight.

"Kindly let me up," he demanded tersely.

Her eyebrows arched in amusement at his imperious tone. "Oh, I think not, my lord," she replied dulcetly. "You have a great deal of explaining to do, and I can not wait for you to begin. I am sure it will prove most," she turned the phosphorescent mask towards the light, "illuminating."

"Damn it, Elly, I insist you—"

The door to her room was thrown open and Henry dashed in, his hair and clothing in wild disarray. "Are you all right?" he demanded anxiously as he rushed to her side. "You weren't having another night—" He broke off in mid-sentence, his eyes widening as he pointed a quivering finger at Lucien. "What in Hades is *that?*"

Elly shot him a smug look as she rose gracefully to her feet. "Oh come, Henry," she drawled, triumph making her all but giddy, "never say you don't recognize your dear friend, the marquess."

Henry crowded closer, his jaw dropping as he stared at the patrician features visible through the strands of rope. "Seabrook?" he gasped incredulously. "What the devil are you doing in my sister's bedchamber?"

Realizing how the situation must appear, a mocking glow lit Lucien's eyes. "Denning, this is not as it looks," he said dryly. "Now help me out of this blasted net, man. I give you my word as a gentleman that I won't try to escape."

Henry looked indecisive for a moment and then shrugged his shoulders. "Very well, Seabrook," he said, ignoring Elly's indignant cries as he knelt beside him. "But I warn you, this had best be very, very good."

"Smugglers?" Henry and Elly exchanged confused looks as Lucien finished speaking. "Do you mean to say you have carried out this ridiculous farce because you wanted to spy on a group of common thieves?" Elly added, glowering at him with frank suspicion.

"Hardly common thieves, Miss Denning," Lucien informed her coolly, his expression guarded. They were sitting in the library, and he'd debated long and hard what to tell his captors before deciding on the truth ... or at least a carefully laundered version of the truth. There was no mention of the prince or the plot against him in the clipped story he had reluctantly related to the Dennings.

"I still do not see why you felt the need for such theatrics," Henry said, echoing his sister's doubts. "I'm a loyal Englishman, even if I have been out of the country for several years, and I'd have been more than happy to help you capture these traitors. Smuggling brandy and silks is one thing, but weapons . . ." He shook his head firmly. "I would never allow such a thing."

"The decision was not mine to make," Lucien replied, grateful that Henry, at least, seemed to accept his tale. "You must realize that I have told you this in the strictest confidence, and only then because I had no other choice."

"Of course, of course," Henry agreed, waving his hand impatiently, "and I can assure you that neither m'sister or I are tattlers. Your secrets are safe with us. But I—"

"They are not *my* secrets," Lucien corrected, his expression stern. "They are England's secrets. Lives are at stake, that is why it is imperative that I have not only your silence, but your cooperation as well."

Elly frowned at his words. She wasn't all that certain she believed his improbable tale of spies and smugglers, but she was willing to concede the need for secrecy if he was telling them the truth. Blind cooperation, however, was another matter.

"What sort of cooperation?" she asked, folding her arms across her chest in a suspicious gesture.

"It is rather late," Lucien informed her coolly. "I think it might be better if we waited for a more agreeable hour."

"Ha!" Elly gave a derisive snort. "I am sure you do, but I—"

"No, Elinore," Henry interrupted, using her full name in order to communicate his displeasure with her, "his lordship is right. This is neither the time nor the place for lengthy discussions."

"But, Henry—"

"You have kept your word as a gentleman and not attempted to leave." Henry ignored her, his attention fully focused on Seabrook. "May I assume

176

I may rely on that same sense of honor to bring you back tomorrow?"

"You may."

"Excellent." Henry nodded. "Then we shall expect you here at noon."

"Henry!" Elly leapt to her feet, her eyes bright with indignation. "You can not mean to let him waltz out of here without so much as a by-your-leave! How do you know we can trust him?"

"If I didn't trust him," came the maddeningly calm reply, "I should have called him out for being in your bedchamber."

Elly's eyes widened at this pronouncement; somehow that aspect of this bizarre situation had completely eluded her. She didn't know which she found more shocking, the notion that she may have been inadvertently compromised by Seabrook or the realization that Henry was aware of it and was prepared to act. Suddenly, delaying the inevitable confrontation seemed a very good idea to her.

"Very well, then," she said, rising to her feet and drawing the lapels of her robe about her throat. "If you will excuse me, I shall retire. I trust I shan't be disturbed again?" She was unable to resist a final dig at Seabrook.

"You have my word on it," he assured her, his dark eyes flashing with anger.

"Thank you, I am vastly reassured." And with that parting shot she sailed out of the room, her chin held high in the air.

After leaving the library she went directly to her bedchamber, noting with a disappointed pang that the secret door had been closed. She considered trying to find the means to open it, but reluctantly decided against doing so. Now that she knew of its existence there would be plenty of time for exploring.

Perhaps I shall invite Lady Miranda and the others to help, she thought, removing her robe and climbing back beneath the covers. Miranda might be reluctant, but she was certain Jessica would be willing. And I shall insist that Seabrook give me a complete tour, she decided, settling on her back and closing her eyes. It was the least the wretch could do considering the misery he had put her through.

She was drifting off to sleep, mentally tallying the marquess's sins against her when she remembered the second "ghost." Seabrook had reluctantly admitted to everything, save that. And if he wasn't the ghost, then who or what had it been? The thought kept her awake long into the night.

Lucien also spent a sleepless night, wrestling with the dilemma of how he should proceed. He knew Alex would doubtlessly insist upon immediately placing the Dennings under arrest, but he was certain there was no need for such action. He was just nodding off to sleep when a solution suddenly presented itself to him, a solution so perfect he wondered why he hadn't thought of it before.

Despite his lack of sleep he rose early the next morning. After consulting with his staff he set out for Seagate, using the brief ride to gather his thoughts. Henry, he was certain, would eagerly agree to his scheme, leaving Elly as the only impediment. Upon careful reflection he hit upon just the plan. His mouth curved in a smile of wicked pleasure. Besting her would be a rare treat, and he found himself quite looking forward to it.

He found them already in the library, and without wasting any time he carefully laid out his plan, making it obvious that they had no choice but to agree. When he had finished he crossed his

178

arms over his chest, studying them down the length of his nose.

"Well?" he challenged, fixing his eyes on Elly's face. "Do you have anything to say?"

"A great deal, actually," she returned, bristling at his high-handed treatment. "Although I doubt it will do me much good. You seem to have an answer for everything; except, perhaps, how we will explain taking up residence in your house. It is bound to cause comment, you know."

She had instinctively struck at the weakest part of his grand scheme. "I am aware of that, Miss Denning," he replied, deliberately speaking as arrogantly as possible. "But it is a risk we shall simply have to take."

Elly considered informing him that the risk of damage to the reputations of herself and her brother was far greater than any he might run when a sudden thought occurred to her. "You say you want Henry and me to leave because you feel we would jeopardize your mission; is that not so?" she asked, organizing her thoughts with lightning speed.

He gave a quick nod, thinking with amusement that he could all but hear the gears spinning in her pretty head. "It is," he said coldly, lifting his chin another inch. "I've already explained that we know the arms will be shipped out sometime this month, and that the smugglers will be using your beach. As Seagate has the best view, it is imperative that we have free access to the house day or night. That is why I need you and Henry to leave. Not only is your presence a hindrance to us, but there is also a degree of danger for you."

Elly ignored the last part of his statement, deciding he had only said it for effect. "Yes, I can see why you would have need of the house," she said slowly, "and as Henry said, we are more than willing to cooperate with our government. However," she added before he could speak, "that doesn't mean I think it is necessary for us to vacate. It seems to me there is another possibility you have yet to consider."

"Indeed?" he enquired with a lift of his eyebrows. "And pray, what might that be?"

"You can move in with us."

He blinked at her in mock astonishment. "I beg your pardon?"

"El, of course, it is the perfect solution!" Henry exclaimed, beaming his approval. "This place has more rooms than a rabbit warren; ought to be no problem at all putting him up. And this way, I shan't have to leave my books."

"But I have plenty of books at my home," Lucien protested, having already anticipated this particular argument. "Hundreds, in fact, and I am sure I could arrange for you to visit the library at the pavilion as well."

This inducement gave Henry pause, but in the end he rejected it. "No, I think El is right. If we were to put up with you it would cause no end of unpleasant speculation. And not only that. If our home is under watch as you have intimated, such an action would be certain to alert the smugglers. It would be better if you came here."

Lucien opened his mouth as if he meant to protest; then he let out a heavy sigh. "I can't convince you to remove to my house?" he asked, addressing his comments to Henry.

"Only if there is no other way," Henry replied firmly.

"And you will do exactly as I say?" Lucien pressed, eager to drive home his advantage before Elly tumbled to the truth. "You will stay out of the south wing, and not interfere with me in any way?"

"You have my word on it," Henry promised, relieved things had been so easily rectified. If he hurried, there was every chance he could complete his last chapter by luncheon.

"What about you?" Lucien's eyes flicked to Elly. "Will you also agree not to interfere with me?"

"Certainly," she replied, a clarion call sounding a distant warning. She could scarce believe the marquess had given in so easily, for if she knew anything about him it was that he was almost as stubborn as she. Her eyes narrowed on his face. Just what the devil is going on here? she wondered, her suspicion mounting.

Lucien saw that suspicion in her misty blue eyes and said, "Then we are agreed. You may remain here unless it proves too dangerous, and I shall continue to come and go through the hidden passageway. Upon reflection I do not think it necessary for me to actually take up residence, so long as I am not disturbed." Here another pointed look was cast in Elly's direction.

She ignored him with a loud sniff, still unable to shake off the niggling doubt that she had just been outmaneuvered. "You may rest assured, sir, that I have no intention of interfering with your noble duty," she informed him, recognizing the clever threat behind his words. If she and Henry did not toe the mark, he would either move in on them bag and baggage, or, worse yet, have them incarcerated in his own home. As that was a fate she was determined to avoid at all costs, she saw no other recourse but to pretend to play along . . . for the moment, at least.

"Thank you," he inclined his head mockingly. Now that he had more or less won the Dennings' cooperation, all that remained was convincing Alex to agree to his plans. He only hoped the viscount would prove half so amenable.

"What do you mean you've told the Dennings everything?" Alex demanded, his gray eyes flashing with silver fire. "Have you taken complete leave of your senses?"

"Come to them, more like," Lucien replied, thinking Twyford had taken his news far better than he'd dared hope. "Much as it pains me to admit it, I fear Miss Denning is right. Removing them from Seagate would be certain to attract attention, and I think we are both agreed that is something which is best avoided."

Alex glared at him a moment longer. "Perhaps," he grumbled, his tanned fingers drumming out an impatient tattoo on the polished surface of Lucien's desk, "but I still don't like it."

"Nor do I, but there is little we can do about it. This way at least I can continue coming and going as I please with no fear of discovery. And of course, having them still in residence will provide us with the perfect facade. Our friends will never suspect us of using Seagate with them living there."

Alex gave him a thoughtful look. "There is that," he agreed, although his expression was still troubled. "But what of the Dennings? Can you trust them to hold their tongues?"

Lucien gave a reassuring nod. "Denning is a gentleman, and even though his sister is a nagging, independent shrew, she is far from being a prattling fool. She has given me her word to say nothing, and I would stake my life on her keeping that word."

"That may be, but it's not *your* life which is at stake."

"Damn it, Alex, if you think for one moment I would deliberately risk His Highness's life—"

Alex raised his hand soothingly. "Calm yourself, Seabrook. I was but making a simple observation. I agree with you that there is little we can do but accept the situation. It will mean making a few adjustments; still, it's nothing I can't handle. Now what of you? Still pursuing your theory regarding Lieutenant McKenzie?"

Lucien gave another nod. "As I said, this whole plan smacks of daring and intellect; traits which McKenzie most definitely lacks. He has to be taking his orders from someone, and I am determined to discover that someone's identity."

"How?"

"Deductive reasoning. Whoever this other traitor is, he must be someone who is familiar enough with the tides hereabouts to know the beach at Seagate offers the safest landing. That would seem to indicate a local man . . . a childhood friend of McKenzie's, perhaps. Also, he must be of sufficient rank to be granted access to the prince. I have only to make a list of such men and then eliminate them one by one; whoever is left is our man."

Alex's lips curved in a rare smile. "Very logical of you, Seabrook, I must say," he murmured approvingly. "Now, if you would, I should like you to answer one small question, and then I shall return to London and leave you to your deducing."

There was something in his friend's voice which made Lucien stiffen with wariness. "What is it?"

Alex's smile became a full-fledged grin. "How the hell did the little shrew manage to drop a net on you?"

183

Despite her promise to Seabrook, Elly told her friends of the marquess's secret identity; reasoning that since they already knew so much, there was no harm in telling them the rest. As she had expected, the ladies each took the news in a unique way.

"Do you mean to say that Seabrook has had access to your bedchamber?" Miranda asked, her brows meeting in a pretty frown. "Oh dear. That could be . . . awkward."

"I do not see why," Elly responded, albeit with a slight blush. "We are the only ones who know, and I trust I may rely upon your discretion. Besides, his lordship was a perfect gentleman."

"Perfect gentlemen, Elinore, do not creep into a lady's bedchamber dressed as a ghost," Miranda pointed out with a shake of her head. "It is not seemly. Still, I suppose there was little else he could do, and as it was in the line of duty, that makes it all right."

"Well, I, for one, am not the least bit surprised to hear Seabrook is a spy," Jessica complained, anxious to change the subject. "The man has always been depressingly noble, for all he is a rake. I suppose this means that pompous Twyford is one as well, since the pair of them are as close as two inkleweavers."

"His lordship did not say," Elly replied, grateful for Jessica's unexpected tact. "He only said that he had been keeping a close watch on the smugglers in the hope of catching them."

"Well, I certainly hope he succeeds!" Miranda declared, her tone surprisingly heated as she abandoned the matter of propriety. "To think these traitors are selling weapons to be used against our brave soldiers, perhaps even against my own father; why, it is not to be borne! We must do something!"

"But what?" Lydia asked, the cool voice of reason as always. "Elinore has already given Seabrook her word not to interfere, and in any case I do not see that there is much we can do. Perhaps the wisest course would be to do as the marquess suggested and stay out of his way."

"Don't be such a gudgeon, Lydia," Jessica retorted impatiently. "Surely you do not mean to imply that because Seabrook is a man we poor females should do naught but stand to one side and meekly wring our hands? I would not have thought you so poor spirited!"

"I am implying no such thing." Lydia did not seem offended by her friend's cutting accusation. "What I am saying is that his lordship is the professional, and that we would be well advised to consider his words. This is not a game, Jessica, it is real life, and lives could well be lost if we act imprudently. Do you really want that on your conscience? Do any of you?" She cast a questioning look about the parlor.

The other three ladies pinked in shame, their eyes downcast as they shuffled their feet. Elly was the first to break the silence, her expression admiring as she studied the other woman. "You are right," she said softly, "but so is Miranda. We are Englishwomen, after all, and we owe the same loyalty to our country as would any man. I am not saying we should act imprudently, but I am saying we should act. It is our duty."

Lydia considered this and then gave a slow nod. "Very well," she said at last. "Have you a plan?"

A tap on the door prevented Elly from admitting that she did not, and the maid entered the room with a curtsey.

"Beg your pardon, Miss Denning, but Mr. Claredon, the squire's son is here, and he asks please if he could have a word with ye."

Elly was tempted to say no, recalling the auburn-haired man's overly-familiar ways with a certain amount of repugnance, but she could not in all good breeding do so. She turned to her friends with an apologetic smile. "I am afraid I shall have to admit him," she said. "It is obvious I am at home."

"That is all right," Miranda answered, understanding the need for doing one's duty. "I know Marcus quite well, and if we wish to be rid of him we have only to start discussing intellectual matters. He is really the slowest top imaginable."

The others agreed, and a few minutes later Marcus Claredon was conducted into the parlor by the pretty maid. When he saw the four women he stopped in the doorway, raising his quizzing glass to his eye as he gazed about him. "What a stunning assemblage of beauty!" he cried, stepping forward to execute a deep bow. "I feel the envy of every man in England!"

"Mr. Claredon . . ." Elly rose to offer him her hand, more than a little disgusted by his obvious compliment. "I believe you already know Lady Miranda Ablethorpe, allow me then to introduce you to my other friends Miss Jessica Kingsley, and Miss Lydia Averleigh. Ladies, Mr. Marcus Claredon of Ashurst Hall."

Each lady murmured an icy "How do you do?" to the interloper, but if he detected any noticeable lack of welcome in their voices, he did not show it. After bowing and flirting with each one in turn, he settled onto the striped side chair, his emerald-green eyes bright with curiosity as he glanced about the room.

186

"My compliments to you for your Herculean efforts, ma'am," he said to Elly. "The place looks a dashed sight better than it did the last time I clapped eyes on it."

"You have been to Seagate before, sir?" Elly asked, not willing to encourage him any more than was polite. She'd begun to think her earlier assessment of him had been a trifle harsh; now she decided she'd been right all along. The man was shockingly forward.

Claredon nodded briskly. "My esteemed father and your late cousin were old friends," he said. "And although I did not exactly run tame here, I do recall visiting it on rare occasions. I recall the only thing the place had to recommend it was its ruins and its beach. Which brings to mind the reason I have descended upon you like a blight."

"You wish to walk on our beach?" Elly asked, brightening at the thought they could be so easily shed of the rascal.

"In my best Hessians?" He gave her a look of horror. "I should say not! Actually, I am here at the behest of my father. I believe I mentioned he was an admirer of your father?" When Elly nodded reluctantly he continued. "Well, when I mentioned I'd encountered you and your brother in the town he could not wait to make your acquaintance."

"I am sorry we have yet to visit." Elly felt it only polite to apologize. "But it has taken us longer than we expected to settle in, and now that Henry is working on his book — "

He interrupted with a wave of his hand. "Please, no explanations are necessary. I understand completely. If the mountain won't come to Mohammed, and all that. But I am under strictest orders to invite you and your brother to our home

187

on the evening of the thirty-first. Father is having a dinner party, and nothing would please him more than if you were to attend. Naturally, you ladies are also invited," he added with a quick smile for the others.

"I am not sure we can accept," Elly began hesitantly, not at all certain she and Henry ought to be tearing about the countryside when there was so much going on. "Henry is not one for the social scene, and I—"

"Please," he pressed, his expression so eager that she actually felt a twinge of guilt. "As I said, father would be ever so grateful; especially as the prince will be there and has expressed a desire to meet your brother."

"The prince will be attending?" Miranda was clearly shocked. "But I thought he never left the pavilion!"

"He and father have known each other a donkey's age," Claredon said with a careless laugh. "And of course, the old boy is quite enamored of my mama. He usually honors us with his noble presence at least once every few years. Do say you will do likewise."

Given such a pretty supplication, Elly did not see how she could refuse. Besides, she might never have another chance to see a real prince, and she acknowledged her vulgar eagerness to do so with a rueful sigh. "Very well, Mr. Claredon." She smiled. "Henry and I would be honored to attend."

"Wonderful!" He leapt to his feet, grasping her hand and carrying it to his lips before Elly could think to protest. "And may I hope, ladies that you will also be there? The prince would probably be delighted to be treated to four such lovely presences."

"I shall have to secure my grandmother's agreement first," Miranda prevaricated, "but I am sure there should be no problem."

"Then I shall tell father at once." To their great relief it appeared he was making as if to go. "My mother will be mailing the invitations of the morrow, so you should soon be receiving them. Now, if you will excuse me, I really must be off. An old friend is waiting for me in Hove. Until the thirty-first, ladies." And he departed after another sweeping bow.

"Well, that was easy," Jessica said before the door had scarcely closed behind him. "But really, Miranda, was it necessary to accept his dreary invitation? You must know how it will be. The food will be so rich as to be inedible, and the rooms so hot as to invite mass swooning!"

"We shall manage," Miranda said with a reproving look. "The prince, for all his faults, could prove to be an invaluable patron for Hen — for Elinore's brother. It will not hurt us to endure the prince's company for one evening."

Jessica pulled an impish face. "But what of our plans to help trap the smugglers?" she wanted to know. "We can scarce do that at some boring society party!"

"Perhaps not," Miranda agreed, "but nonetheless we shall try."

"Thank you," Elly said, touched by her friends devotion. "You have no idea how much I appreciate your noble sacrifice."

"You should," the irrepressible Jessica inserted with a merry laugh. "Catching smugglers shall prove to be child's play compared to an evening watching Prinny flirt like a caper merchant! Now, we have dawdled long enough; I must insist upon hearing your plan. Has it anything to do with fishing nets?"

Elly's eyes twinkled at the hopeful note in the other woman's voice. "No, I am afraid not."

Jessica gave another loud sigh. "Pity, it proved so efficacious with Lord Seabrook I was hoping we might use it again. Ah well, maybe next time."

Chapter Thirteen

Something was wrong. Lucien stood in front of the window in his study, his eyebrows meeting in a straight line as he stared out at the lush garden. It was nothing he could put his finger on, but a feeling deep in his belly warned him things were not all they should be. With the trap baited and waiting, there could be no margin for error, and he sensed that somewhere, somehow, he had missed something of vital importance. But what? He turned away from the window with an impatient oath, crossing the room to resume his agitated pacing.

The three days since the encounter in the library had been hectic ones, filled with hard work and frustration as he complied his list of suspects. Operating on the theory that the plot to kidnap the prince required a certain degree of maturity he concentrated his search on men his own age and older; eliminating those with any known connections to the smugglers as too obvious. He'd also kept a wary eye on Elly, but she'd resumed her friendship with Lady Miranda and spent most of her days in Brighton. At least that was what Henry had told him the last two times he'd called at Seagate to find her gone.

The memory of those two visits brought an irritated scowl to his face. He *missed* her, damn it, although why he should miss that obstreperous she-devil he knew not. She'd been a thorn in his side since their first meeting; before then, if one counted the adroit way she had blocked his early attempts to buy Seagate. She thwarted him at every turn, and he could not say that he held her in any degree of affection. Attraction, perhaps, he conceded grudgingly, and even a certain amount of admiration and respect, but she had never elicited in him the gentler emotions he associated with the fairer sex. He wanted to shake her more often than he wanted to kiss her, and even then he—

"I beg your pardon, my lord." The nervous voice of his secretary penetrated the chaotic tangle of his thoughts, and he turned to see the younger man hovering uncertainly in the doorway.

"What is it, Richard?" he snapped, making no attempt to mask his irritation at the disruption.

"M-my apologies if I have disturbed your privacy," Richard Stanfield stammered, his cheeks flushing with embarrassment. "I did knock, but there was no answer and—"

"It is all right," Lucien interrupted wearily, annoyed with himself for taking out his black moods on his staff. The lad was a distant relation of his and had always given him exemplary service. It was not Stanfield's fault some blue-eyed witch was driving him to distraction. Fixing a much more pleasant expression on his face he repeated his question.

"This arrived for you in this morning's post," his secretary responded, stepping forward to offer Lucien a cream-colored card. "I know 'tis your policy to refuse such invitations, but I thought you might wish to look at this first."

"I do not see why," Lucien responded, giving the embossed card a cursory glance. "I scarce know the

192

Claredons, and in any case I can think of no worse torture than spending an evening with my boring neighbors. Send the usual regrets." He made to hand the card back, and was surprised when the younger man did not take it.

"I-I think you might wish to reconsider," Richard said, clearing his throat with obvious trepidation. " 'Tis rumored His Highness will be attending, and—"

"The prince will be there?" Lucien exclaimed, his brown eyes widening in astonishment.

Richard nodded eagerly. "Yes, my lord. I happened to encounter Miss Denning while I was taking my morning constitutional, and when I mentioned the invitation to her, she said she and her brother had also been invited and would be attending as they wished to meet the prince. He and Squire Claredon are old friends, you know," he added in a confiding tone.

"No, I did not," Lucien answered, giving the invitation a closer examination. Devil take it, he brooded angrily, if the prince was attending, then that meant he would have no other choice but to follow suit. With so much going on, they could hardly allow His Highness to go racketing about the countryside without some kind of added protection.

"I think you are right, Richard; this is one invitation I dare not refuse," he said, handing him the invitation with a tight smile. "Please write the Claredon's and inform them that I shall be attending."

"Very good, Lord Seabrook," Richard responded with a relieved sigh. "Will you be requiring anything else?"

Lucien shook his head. "No, that will be all, thank you," he murmured, his thoughts already

193

turning to the day's work. "Oh, you might inform Cook there will be no need to bother with dinner; I shall be away from the house for the rest of the day."

"Will you be at Seagate, my lord?" Richard asked, his curiosity temporarily overcoming his awe of his employer. Rumor in the servants hall was that the marquess was enamored of Miss Denning and would soon be making her an offer.

Lucien's brown eyes narrowed fractionally. "Indeed I shall be, Richard, indeed I shall."

"I don't know about this, Elinore, perhaps it would be best if we waited until Miranda and Lydia have arrived," Jessica suggested, chafing her arms with chilled hands as she cast an apprehensive glance about her. "Secret tunnels can be quite dangerous, you know."

"You're the one who wanted to know where the door led," Elly reminded her, running sensitive fingers along the underside of the oak mantelpiece. She'd been unable to open the door near the wardrobe despite all her efforts, and was about to admit defeat when she remembered the disembodied voice emanating from the fireplace. Reasoning that meant there was another entrance to her room, she began her search, resolved that she wouldn't stop until she discovered it.

"It is quite rude to toss one's words back in one's face," Jessica retorted with an indignant grumble. "And as it happens, I was only funning. I *hate* closed, dark places, and a secret tunnel is certain to have bo—"

"I found it!" Elly's joyful exclamation halted Jessica in mid-tirade.

"What?" Jessica abandoned her protests and

crowded closer, peeking curiously over Elly's shoulder.

"This." Elly caressed one of the acorns that had been carved into the light golden wood. "It gives a little when I touch it. Perhaps if I press a little harder . . ." And she proceeded to do just that, watching in amazement and delight as a section of wall to the right of the fireplace swung open on a hiss of sound.

They exchanged startled looks and then Elly was snatching up the brace of candles she'd purloined from the dining room. She advanced purposefully towards the open door, pausing to send Jessica a challenging look. "Well? Are you coming or not?"

Jessica hesitated for only a moment, and then stalked over to the table and picked up a second brace of candles. "Oh, very well," she said, using a burning taper to light first Elly's candles and then her own. "But I am warning you, if that door swings shuts and closes us in there, I vow I shall haunt you through all of eternity!"

Elly sent her a saucy grin. "Don't be silly, Miss Kingsley, you know full well there are no such things as ghosts."

After entering the tunnel Lucien decided to examine a passage he hadn't checked in years. He'd explored it as a boy, and later had thought his remembrance of it as immense due to a child's perspective. Glancing about him now, however, he was relieved to see his memory had not played him false. The passageway was huge; at least ten feet high, and easily wide enough for a coach to pass through without touching the sides. What was even better was that it connected with the main road, just as legend had always maintained, and he knew

195

it would be easy for him and his men to arrange an ambush if the need presented itself.

He was making his way back to the passage he usually used when the sound of a footfall in the corridor just behind him reached his ears. He froze at once, fearing a repeat of his last memorable encounter in these twisting corridors. Then good sense came to his rescue, and he realized with relief that the sound he'd heard had been made by human feet. He glanced at the torch flickering in his hand and gave a weary sigh, knowing there was nothing else to be done. Pulling a pistol from his pocket, he pressed himself against the corridor wall, blowing out the flame and plunging the tunnel into Stygian blackness as he waited for his mysterious pursuers to catch up with him.

"Just a little farther," Elly promised, urging Jessica along with a none-too-gentle prod. "I only want to see how far this passage goes; then we shall turn back."

"That's what you said when we found the last passage," Jessica complained, her nose wrinkling at the smell of dust and decay that hung heavily in the air. "Our candles are burned almost halfway down, and if we don't hurry they shall go out long before we find our way back."

Elly gave her candles a startled glance, noting to her dismay that Jessica hadn't exaggerated the danger. She'd been so caught up in the thrill of exploration she hadn't given their light source a single thought; a rather serious oversight considering their location. "You are right, Jessica," she said, giving her friend a contrite smile. "We shall turn around at once. And just to be safe, perhaps it might be a good idea if we extinguished your candles now? We

196

can light them from mine when they start burning low."

Jessica grimaced at the thought of losing the meager protection offered by her half-gutted candles. "Why do we have to extinguish mine?" she asked, even as she was complying with Elly's suggestion.

Without the light provided by the second brace, the shadows filling the corridor seemed to take on menacing proportions, writhing and dancing on the damp stones as the young women carefully began retracing their steps. Elly thought of the amorphous, glowing ghost that had materialized in her room that night, and prayed it did not appear again. The thought of encountering that horror in the narrow confines of the secret tunnel made her heart race with fear, and she unconsciously increased her pace.

"Slow down!" Jessica implored, doing her best to keep up with Elly. "There is no need to rush off pell-mell; we will have plenty of time to reach the door before our candles—" Her protest ended in a loud shriek as one of the shadows detached itself from the wall and leapt in front of them.

"Halt! Surrender or I will fire!"

Elly stopped short, her scream echoing Jessica's as she fought the instinct not to drop the candles and run for her life. When the faceless shadow moved into the faint light, she was grateful for her control.

"Seabrook! What are you doing here? You almost frightened us to death!"

Lucien stepped towards the two ladies who were huddled together and were glaring at him with accusing eyes. "What am *I* doing here?" he echoed incredulously, his coiled reflexes giving way to white-hot fury. "What the devil are *you* doing here?

197

You're damned lucky I didn't shoot the pair of you!"

"And you're equally as lucky you didn't frighten me into dropping our only source of light, else we would have been in a very pretty pickle indeed!" Elly shot back, recovering her wits as well as her temper. "How dare you pop out at us like that!"

Lucien could only gape at her in disbelief. "You're a madwoman," he said at last, his voice shaking with conviction. "You're a menace who ought to be clapped into Bedlam for the public safety! And as for you," here he cast a furious glare at Jessica, "I might have known you would be in the thick of this! Twyford told me you were a trouble-making bluestocking, and he was right!"

That brought Jessica's chin up, and she elbowed her way past Elly to confront Lucien. "Ha! What do I care what either you or that pompous prig might think of me?" she challenged, her hazel eyes gleaming with pride. "Just because the two of you are agents of the crown does not give you the right—"

"Jessica," Elly interrupted hastily, casting Seabrook a worried look. "I do not think you should be mentioning—"

"How do you know about Alex and me?" Lucien's outraged bellow ricocheted off the tunnel's curved ceiling. He gave Elly a look of murderous fury. "Why, you little shrew, you told her, didn't you? And after you gave me your word never to tell anyone!"

"Now, see here, Seabrook," Jessica was quick to take up the cudgels in Elly's defense, "you have no right to take that tone with Elinore. She only told Lady Miranda, Lydia, and me about this silly rig you're running, so there is no need to carry on as if she has committed treason or some such thing!"

198

Lucien's temper cooled to icy coldness. "Ah, but that is precisely what she has done," he replied, his voice menacingly soft. "And this time I am afraid I can not let it go unremarked." He pocketed his pistol and then reached out to take the brass candelabrum from Elly's fingers. "I think it is time we were returning to more hospitable climes. Ladies," he stepped to one side with a mocking bow, "after you."

Fifteen minutes later they were back in the library, listening as Lucien rang a peal over their heads. "Of all the cork-brained half-witted schemes I have ever heard in my life, this is without doubt the most ridiculous!" he stormed, pacing up and down in front of them like an outraged papa. "What of your promise not to interfere with my work, hmm? I suppose that meant as little to you as your promise to keep my identity a secret?"

"I wasn't interfering, I was helping," Elly corrected, her feeling of contriteness giving way to rising indignation. "And you needn't rage at poor Henry, he had naught to do with any of this."

"Didn't he?" Lucien thrust an angry hand through his tawny hair. "He is your brother, and it is his responsibility to make sure you don't run into trouble. Although he doesn't seem to be doing a very good job of it," he added in a sneering tone.

Elly leapt to her feet, only to be pulled back down by a surprisingly somber Henry. "No, Elly, his lordship is right," he said, his handsome face set in grim lines. "I have done a very poor job of protecting you, and I am only grateful you have not been made to suffer overly much for my laxity."

Elly melted at once, laying a loving hand on his cheek. "You have not been lax," she denied fiercely, blinking back sudden tears. "You have been a wonderful brother to me!"

"Perhaps." His dark blue eyes were thoughtful as he met her gaze. "Is that why you have always seen fit to treat me like a dull-witted boy who could not be trusted to pull on his own shoes?"

Her hand dropped to her lap in shock. "Henry, I-I . . ." Her voice trailed off as she realized that was indeed how she often treated him.

Lucien gave her a sharp look, then turned to Jessica. "I will trust the good sense in which you take such pride to keep you from mentioning a word of this to anyone," he said coldly. "But should that prove insufficient, you might consider the weight of law that would be brought against you and the others. I trust you take my meaning?"

Jessica rose to her feet, her chin held at a defiant angle. "I take it quite clearly, my lord," she answered with cool self-possession. "Nor is there any need for your braying threats. As Elinore told you, we ladies also love our country, and we will do what we must to protect her. Good day," she said coolly, and quickly left the library.

There was a short, uncomfortable silence; then Elly rounded on Lucien. "How dare you threaten my friend!" she stormed, her fists clenching in anger. "This is my fault, not hers!"

"That, Miss Denning, is something of which I am all too aware," Lucien returned with deadly calm. "Unfortunately threatening you seems to have little if any effect. Perhaps I might enjoy more success with Miss Kingsley."

"You . . ." Words failed, and she could only glare at him in tight-lipped frustration. While she was attempting to come up with a suitably cutting retort, Seabrook turned to Henry, his expression closed and angry.

"I would like to speak with your sister," he said,

his tone clipped as he sought for control. "Alone, if you do not object."

Henry did object, actually, but in the end his common sense won out over his brotherly instincts. This was their war, he reasoned with a wry smile, and it was up to them to make the peace. "Very well," he said, rising to give both combatants a measuring look. "Just keep in mind that Elly is my sister, Seabrook, and much as I may sympathize, I really can not allow you to throttle her. Despite what you may think, I do care what happens to her." And he left, closing the door quietly behind him.

Once again a heavy silence filled the room, and once again it was Elly who broke it. Operating on the principle that it was easier to attack than to defend, she sent him a mocking smile. "There was no reason to send Henry packing, my lord," she informed him dulcetly. "I've no objections to his listening to you ring a peal over my head."

Lucien's lips tightened in annoyance, but he managed to check his temper. "Then you admit I've good cause to be angry?" he challenged, folding his arms across his chest as he settled back in his chair.

"Not at all. It is just I don't give a fig who knows that you are hipped with me."

The flippant remark brought him snapping to attention, his booted feet hitting the carpeted floor with a thud. "Hipped!" he roared, his brown eyes flashing with fury. *"Hipped!* My God, don't you have any idea of the trouble you've caused me? You have endangered everything I've worked for, and I'll be damned if—" He broke off at the sight of the triumphant smirk curving her soft mouth.

"Clever, madam," he conceded with a reluctant laugh, "very clever, indeed. You make me lose my temper in order to distract me. Unfortunately for you, I am now wise to that particular ruse."

Elly pulled a face, annoyed at how easily he had seen through one of her more successful ploys. "Familiarity breeds more than contempt," she muttered, acknowledging his accusation without a twinge of remorse. "It also breeds predictability."

She looked so disgruntled, Lucien could not help but smile. "Believe me, Miss Denning, predictable is hardly an adjective that could ever be applied to you," he told her, the last of his anger fading. "You are continually astonishing me."

"As you are me," she returned, aware that he no longer seemed so angry with her. It was as if a truce had been called between them, a truce she realized she wasn't eager to break. She was silent a long moment, then gave a gusty sigh.

"I'm sorry I went into the tunnel," she said, her playful demeanor vanishing. "I shouldn't have done it."

The stark apology stunned Lucien. He was so accustomed to her fierce defiance that he wasn't all that certain he trusted her sudden capitulation. One glance into eyes of smoky blue quickly disabused of him of this notion, and the smile he sent her was genuine. "No," he agreed softly. "You shouldn't have."

"It is just the thought of a secret tunnel was irresistible," she continued as if he hadn't spoken. "I've always been intolerably curious, you may ask Henry, and I was determined to go exploring."

"And you knew it would annoy the devil out of me," Lucien drawled, watching the play of thoughts across her expressive face. He remembered he had once thought her plain, and mentally shook his head that he could have been so foolish.

"There was that," Elly admitted with an impish

grin. "And again, the very notion was irresistible. You are rather top-lofty, my lord, and the chance to take you down a peg is beyond my powers to resist."

"As is the tantalizing prospect of putting you firmly in your place," Lucien riposted silkily. "But I take issue to being labeled top-lofty. It was concern for your safety, and not arrogance, which led me to forbidding you access to the tunnels."

Elly blinked at this. "You never forbid me to go into the tunnel," she protested, frowning as she recalled their many conversations.

"You gave me your word to stay out of my way," he reminded her, not taken in by her protestations. "You must have known that would include keeping out of the tunnels as well."

She could not honestly dispute this, and so she decided to ignore him. "Is the whole house filled with passageways and secret chambers?" she asked instead. "Jessica and I saw several tunnels branching off, but we didn't explore them."

"Thank God for that," Lucien muttered feelingly, shuddering to think of what might have happened had they inadvertently tripped one of the passages hidden traps. "Those passages are dangerous; you've no idea how dangerous. You must promise me never to go near them again, regardless of the provocation."

"But —"

"Regardless," he emphasized, rising from his chair and crossing the room to stand in front of her. He reached down and pulled her to her feet, his strong hands cupping her shoulders as he gazed down into her startled blue eyes.

"Your word, Elly," he said softly, his warm breath feathering across her cheeks. "Give it to me."

She stared up into his face, noting, and not for the first time, the sheer perfection of his masculine features. His eyes were half-closed, burning into hers with an ebony fire that made her senses swim. A lock of sandy-brown hair had fallen across his forehead, and she brushed it back with a trembling finger.

"Why?" she asked huskily, her finger lingering to trace the high curve of his cheek. "After today how can you have any faith in me or my word?"

"Damned if I know," he admitted, his heart pounding with excitement. Her gentle touch was having a decided effect upon him, and it took all his considerable willpower not to touch her in return. Only the knowledge that now was neither the time nor the place stayed his hand, although he made no attempt to evade the soft brush of her fingertips against his skin.

"Well, that was honest," Elly said, smiling at his blunt admission. She was aware her actions were in danger of placing her beyond the pale, and regretfully allowed her hand to drop to her side. It was the first time she had ever conducted herself so wantonly, and she was shocked to discover she rather enjoyed the sensation. Before her stunned mind could dissect this startling revelation, Lucien began speaking again.

"I meant it. There are times when I may have felt like beating you, but I have never doubted either your honesty or your integrity."

"And I daresay this morning was one of those times," she quipped, deeply touched by his faith in her. A faith she was honest enough to admit she didn't always deserve.

"That's true enough," he agreed ruefully. He was already missing the touch of her hand, but he was glad she had had the good sense to stop. "As I said, you never cease to astonish me."

"As you have astonished me on more than one occasion," she riposted, feeling a sudden light-heartedness. "And to think I once dismissed you as a vain, posturing dandy!"

"Dandy!" He glowered at her for a moment and then grinned. "You're doing it again."

"Doing what?" She sounded suspiciously innocent.

"Using anger to distract me. You still haven't given me your word to stay out of the tunnels, you know."

"I haven't? How remiss of me. Very well, I promise to stay well away from your precious tunnels . . . for now."

His shoulders slumped with relief. "Thank you, Elly, I —"

"But," she interrupted, lifting a slender finger in warning, "I shall expect a full explanation once this business with the smugglers is settled. You've a great deal to answer for, my lord, and don't think for one moment that I shall let you wiggle out of it. Is that quite clear?"

"Quite clear, ma'am." Lucien was smiling with pure pleasure. He liked the notion that once this ugly business was behind them he would still have cause to call on her. He liked it quite a lot.

Chapter Fourteen

The next few days passed swiftly if uneventfully for Elly. Now that her "ghost" was no longer plaguing her, she was able to devote herself to more mundane matters as seeing to the house and establishing herself with her neighbors. Much to her amazement they seemed most eager to accept her and Henry, a situation she found highly gratifying until Miranda explained the reason behind the universal acceptance.

"You must be joking!" she exclaimed, staring at the younger woman in dismay. "These people can not believe the marquess is enamored of me!"

"Why not?" Miranda responded with an amused laugh. "It's a perfectly logical conclusion when you think of it. Seabrook has been dancing attendance upon you since the moment of your arrival, and not a day goes by but that he's not up at Seagate on one pretext or another. What else are they to think but that he's fallen victim to the parson's mousetrap?"

"But with *me?*" Elly demanded, more mystified than ever. "I could understand it if I were a titled beauty like you, or even a great heiress like Lydia. But as it is . . ." She shook her head, amazed that people should be so gullible.

"Country folk don't place the same store in appearance as do London folk," Miranda soothed, knowing better than to placate her friend with false flattery. "And as for the matter of inheritance, there *is*

Seagate. Perhaps they think he's wooing you so that he might persuade Henry to sell it to him."

This made sense to Elly, although she was still discomfited by the notion that she and Lucien should be the object of common gossip. The thought he might have heard these rumors horrified her, and she gave Miranda a troubled look. "You don't think he knows, do you?"

"Who? Seabrook? I should think it odd if he did not!" Miranda answered, and laughed again. "He is far too wise in the ways of the *ton* to know that a gentleman can not be so singular in his attentions as he has been without inviting such speculation."

"But it's not true!"

"Of course it's not, and when the villagers see that, they'll turn their wagging tongues elsewhere. Prinny will be arriving tomorrow, and he is always good for a bit of gossip. Don't worry, Elinore, it will all turn out in the end."

This conversation was much in Elly's mind the following afternoon as she sat sifting through the invitations that had arrived in the morning's post. Her neighbors were falling all over themselves to make her and Henry welcome, and she could not help but wonder if they would be half so generous once it became obvious Seabrook had no real interest in her. Probably not, she decided, her lips curving in a rueful smile. In fact, she and Henry would doubtlessly become *personae non gratae* when the truth was finally known.

"Such a little cat smile, Elinore. What new mischief are you plotting?" The drawled words scattered her thoughts, and she glanced up to find Seabrook lounging negligently against the doorframe.

"That would be telling, my lord," she said, quickly masking the uneasiness his unexpected appearance caused her. The possibility he knew of the gossip was too lowering to be borne, but she did not know how

207

to ease his mind without making it sound as if she were harboring hopes.

"That is what I feared," Lucien responded, smiling as he pushed himself away from the door and sauntered towards her. When he reached her desk he leaned over and plucked a card from the heap of invitations piled upon it.

"What have we here? An invitation to Lady Gipperson's next soirée?" he said, his lips curving in amusement as he studied the card with mock interest. "I shouldn't accept if I were you. The lady is a dashed boor."

Elly's anxiety vanished in a flash as she snatched the card back. "As the invitation was for Henry and me, I am sure you need not concern yourself," she told him with an annoyed scowl. "And for your information, I have already decided we shall attend."

"You'll regret it," he warned, dark eyes dancing with unaccustomed mischief. "Her ladyship's tables are usually as bereft of decent food as her conversation is empty of wit. You and your learned brother will most surely starve."

Elly's lips twitched, but she refused to smile. She didn't know why Seabrook was flirting with her . . . as he surely was . . . but she did know it was time to put an end to it. "If you have come to see Henry, I'm afraid you've just missed him," she said, determined to maintain her distance. "He's gone into Brighton to attend a meeting of the Royal Botanical Society."

"I know, I passed him on my way here."

The confession set her back apace, and she blinked up at him in astonishment. "Then why are you here?" she demanded bluntly.

The suspicion in her voice made Lucien smile, although, in truth, he had no idea why the devil he had come. One moment he had been tooling his grays towards Brighton, and in the next he had found himself pulling up in front of Seagate's massive portico.

There was no way he could ever admit such a thing, of course, and he hid his confusion behind a teasing facade.

"Perhaps I just wanted the pleasure of your company," he said, sending her a look known to make even the most experienced of flirts sigh with longing.

"Gammon, sir, I am not so green as to be taken in by such fustian," Elly returned with relish. "As I have already noted, you are a man who never acts without good cause, and if you do not tell me the truth, then I will have to insist that you leave. You must know it is not proper for me to receive you when Henry is from the house."

He wondered what she would say if he told her he had just spoken the truth. "I wanted to check one of the access tunnels," he said instead, thinking quickly. "The door is jammed from the passage, and I will need to trigger it from this side."

Elly's eyes lit with pleasure. "May I come?" she asked, her suspicions forgotten in her excitement. "I know I promised not to interfere with your work, but surely there can be no harm in watching . . . can there?"

Lucien could think of a dozen different reasons why he should refuse her request, but none of them seemed to matter in the face of the excitement shining in her light blue eyes. Knowing he would doubtlessly regret his decision, he held out his hand to her.

"Very well," he conceded, drawing her to her feet. "But I warn you, if I ever learn you've made use of what I am about to show you, I vow I shall shake you within an inch of your life."

Ten minutes later they were in the south wing, and Elly watched in delight as a tapestry-covered wall parted to reveal the tunnel's opening. "No wonder you wanted to keep me out of here," she exclaimed, peering over Lucien's shoulder into the darkened tunnel. "This is marvelous!"

"Somehow I knew you would feel that way," he drawled, flashing her a wicked grin. "This is just the sort of thing to appeal to a female with your Gothic imagination."

Elly pretended to take offense. "Ha! You dress like a ghost strayed from a Minervian novel, and then dare accuse *me* of such a thing? You are too forward by half!"

"It is part of my charm," he returned, feeling a lightness he hadn't known in years. He knew he should close up the passage and leave before adding to the store of gossip being bandied about by his curious neighbors, but he was suddenly loath to return to his old, responsible ways. Acting on impulse for the second time that day, he turned and picked up the brace of candles sitting on a nearby table.

"Well? What are you waiting for?" he asked, holding his free hand out to her. "You know you shan't rest until you have seen everything. This way, at least, I'll know you'll be able to find your way out again."

Elly was too excited at the prospect of another go at the tunnel to object to his hint she wasn't to be trusted. She eagerly accepted his hand, ducking her head as she followed him into the secret passage.

He spent the next half hour taking her on a carefully conducted tour. He showed her just enough of the main tunnel to satisfy her curiosity, even as he kept her well away from the passages leading to the sea and the main road. He even showed her one of the large, inner chambers; deriving a great deal of pleasure from her obvious astonishment.

"Why, it's almost like another house," she gasped, gazing up at the arched ceiling in amazement. "And to think this was here all this time, and my cousin never even knew of it!"

"You will forgive me for pointing out that your cousin was hardly the most astute of persons," Lucien said, surreptitiously guiding her back to the entrance.

"I much doubt if he would have noticed the Coliseum were it right beneath his nose."

"You're only saying that because he refused to sell Seagate to you. If he had, I daresay you would now be describing him as the very model of intelligence and good sense," she accused, feeling oddly comfortable with him walking at her side.

"True, but then if he had, we wouldn't be having this discussion, would we?"

The thought struck Elly so sharply that she stumbled. He was right, she realized with a surge of conflicting emotion. Had it not been for Seagate, they might never have met. The realization filled her with such desolation that she forced herself to give a credible laugh.

"Another crime to lay on poor Cousin's doorstep, I see," she said, refusing to look at him. "Not only did he deprive you of your ancestral home, but he has brought me down on your head as well. I quite wonder that you don't call him out, my lord."

"And so I should, were it not for the fact he is already dead," Lucien said, sensing her sudden uneasiness. He wondered what might have triggered it, and gave a sidelong glance about the darkened corridor. It was empty of anything save ordinary shadows, and he was relieved that he didn't feel the same disquiet he always noted in the spirit's presence.

That he had finally accepted the ghost's existence still amazed him, but without giving the matter a great deal of thought he realized that was precisely what he had done. Life was filled with things which had no rational explanation, and the nether world was evidently one of them. Not that he intended sharing this momentous observation with Elly, of course, he thought with a slight smile. He was well aware of her thoughts on the matter, and wasn't about to admit to anything which might lower his estimation in her eyes.

211

Once he was convinced he'd satisfied her curiosity, Lucien guided her back to the parlor. Although discretion dictated he take his leave, he found himself accepting her invitation to join her for tea. With matters rapidly approaching culmination, this might be their last peaceful afternoon for many days to come, and he wanted to spend it with her.

Besides, he rationalized with a smug sense of righteousness, the gossip about them could only aid his cause. Thinking of the talk being bandied about town, he sent her a wicked grin. "It is just as well you have so many servants about," he teased, raising his cup to his lips. "For should the tattlemongers learn of my visit, I fear we may be forced into posting the banns at once."

The cup and saucer in Elly's hand rattled precariously as she shot him a stunned look. "Do you mean you know of the gossip?" she asked, her cheeks flushing in dismay. Her earlier fears that he might suspect her of fostering such speculation returned full force, and it was all she could do not to cringe in embarrassment.

"Certainly I am aware of it," he said comfortably. "And I must say it has proven most provident. Talk I am on the catch for you has given me the perfect excuse to come and go with impunity." He shrugged his shoulders and sent her a rueful smile. "I wonder why I did not think of it myself."

Elly smiled at his wry admission, but a moment later she was frowning. "But why would a group of smugglers pay any mind to society gossip?" she asked in confusion. "I should think they'd be far more concerned with talk of brandy shipments and such."

Lucien cursed himself for forgetting her quick mind. "Ah, but the lower orders are often fascinated by the antics of their betters," he returned adroitly. "They like nothing more than to watch us making cakes of ourselves."

"Oh." It seemed an odd explanation to Elly, but she supposed he knew more about the smugglers than did she. Still, the thought of a group of dirty, desperate men sitting about a crude table earnestly discussing the latest *on-dits* made her smile. She would have to share the image with Jessica, she decided with a flash of whimsey. Her friend would doubtlessly find it highly amusing.

"I meant to ask, but will you and Henry be driving to the squire's alone, or will Lady Miranda and the others be joining you?" he asked, hoping to divert her.

"We will be travelling together. Lady Ablethorpe is still unwell, and we thought it might be more circumspect to arrive *en masse*," Elly answered, smiling tentatively as she handed him his plate of cookies and buttered bread. For a wild moment she wondered if he was hinting for an invitation to join them, and was annoyed at the way her heart raced with hopeful anticipation.

"That's good," Lucien nodded approvingly. He'd have to make sure one of his own men rode with them as a footman . . . just in case.

"I suppose you will be arriving in solitary splendor?" Elly prodded, silently cursing the effect he had on her senses. She hated the odd, out-of-control way he made her feel, and for a moment she longed for their earlier animosity. Things were much easier when we loathed each other, she thought with an aggrieved scowl.

"Probably," he answered with a casual shrug. "Not that I am looking forward to it. In fact, I am dreading it. If it wasn't for the prince I doubt I should attend at all, but it does not do to slight His Royal Highness. May I hope you will save me a dance so that I will have some reward for my pains?"

"I hadn't thought there would be dancing at a dinner party, but naturally I should be happy to save you a set," Elly replied, trying not to be

213

too pleased by his request.

"Thank you," Lucien drawled, although in truth the thought of sharing a dance with Elly was sweetly tempting. He'd been aching to hold her in his arms, even if it was only for a simple country quadrille.

They continued talking for another hour, enjoying each other's company in a way neither could ever have imagined. Finally it was time to go, and Lucien rose easily to his feet. "Now I really must leave before Henry returns and finds me here," he said, crossing over to where she sat and drawing her to her feet.

"Remember to save me that dance, hoyden," he instructed, his hands resting naturally on her shoulders. "And mind you behave yourself while you're at it. Brighton folk may not be up to your penchant for mischief."

The intimate timbre of his voice made Elly's heart race wildly. "I should hope I always conduct myself with propriety, my lord," she replied, her cheeks flushing with nervous excitement. This was the closest she had ever stood to a man, and it shocked her to realize she wished to be held even closer still.

Lucien smiled at her pert reply. "I doubt if you even know the meaning of the word," he murmured, his hands dropping to her narrow waist as he drew her firmly against him. "You are the biggest virago it has ever been my misfortune to encounter."

"And you, sir, are the greatest bully I have ever met," she returned, vividly aware of the strength in his powerful hands as they cupped her waist. He towered over her, and the heat radiating from his muscled body was having a decided effect upon her sensibilities. She knew she should step back, or at least demand that he end their quasi-embrace, but somehow the words would not come. The ability to speak seemed to have fled along with her common sense, and she was helpless to do other than gaze up at him with her heart in her eyes.

214

"Then 'twould seem we are well matched," he murmured huskily, reading the surrender in her azure-colored eyes. If her brother walked through the door they were as good as engaged, but, oddly, he didn't care. A man could do worse than find himself leg-shackled to such a charming spitfire, he decided complacently, his lips coming down on hers in a kiss of searing demand.

The feel of his mouth against her own shocked Elly, a shock that quickly escalated into delight as desire swept through her. "Lucien . . ." She whispered his name against his lips, her arms twining about his neck to hold him closer still. She could feel the urgent pounding of his heart against her own, and the sensation made her tremble with eagerness.

"Elly . . ." Lucien felt her response, and his senses raced with fierce pleasure. So much lay unresolved between them, but for the moment he was content to hold her, revelling in the knowledge that she shared the passion that was threatening to overwhelm his good judgement. His hands slid up her spine to cup the back of her head, holding her still as he parted her lips with an expert brush of his tongue.

The intimate kiss stunned Elly with its sensual mastery, and she returned it with shy desire. This was what she wanted, what she had secretly been longing for, and the knowledge filled her with a confusing jumble of emotion. But even as she was struggling to comprehend what her heart was telling her, Lucien was pushing her gently away, his chest rising and falling as he fought for control.

"You are a potent little bluestocking," he murmured huskily, his hand trembling as he brushed his thumb across her kiss-softened mouth. "You go to my head like the costliest brandy."

Elly's cheeks grew warm at his provocative words. She wasn't such an innocent she didn't know he had been just as affected by their kiss as had she, and she took fierce satisfaction in his wry admission. Drawing a deep breath for courage she lifted her hand to trace his dark eyebrows.

"The same might be said of you, my lord," she murmured, feeling greatly daring. "Had anyone told me even a week ago that I would allow you such liberties without boxing your ears, I should have thought him quite daft." Her eyes took on a decided sparkle. "It would seem you have the most lamentable effect upon my usually sound judgement, sir."

"As you do mine," Lucien agreed, unable to tear his eyes from the tempting curve of her lips. She looked so beautiful, so utterly feminine, that he found it impossible to remember he had once considered her plain. How foolish he had been to think he preferred simple prettiness to Elly's sweet fire, he mused, the edges of his mouth curling in a rueful smile.

At the sight of that smile Elly's good sense took another dangerous tumble. Only the knowledge that he had been the one to break their kiss prevented her from throwing herself shamelessly back into his arms and begging him to kiss her again. Deciding it was time she demonstrated equal control over her emotions, she took a careful step back, saying the first thing to pop into her head.

"Will you come here tomorrow?" she asked, then clapped a hand over her mouth, horrified she could have said anything so half-witted.

"Perhaps." Lucien was amused by her patent distress. "Will you be waiting for me?"

"Perhaps," she returned, mentally scrambling for some way out of this morass. She thought of the party tomorrow evening, and seized upon Marcus Claredon's image with desperation.

"Of course," she continued with studied insouciance, "a great deal may depend upon Mr. Claredon."

Lucien's smile vanished. "What about Claredon?"

"Well, when he was here the other day he did mention he might be stopping by again," she lied, feeling a slight stab of remorse for her blatant dishonesty. She usually eschewed such feminine ploys, but the situation was a desperate one, and she prayed she'd be forgiven for this one lapse.

"Claredon was here?" Lucien was surprised. Somehow he'd formed the impression that Elly had received her invitation by post.

"Certainly, and he was quick to praise all the changes I had made," she said, taking a smug pleasure in the fact. "He said I had improved Seagate beyond all measure. Unlike you, *he* was quite welcome here while my cousin was still alive."

The knowledge Claredon had been in Seagate alarmed Lucien. He had already eliminated the squire as a suspect, but he'd yet to do the same with the man's foppish son. He doubted Marcus was involved, and even if he was, his being at Seagate was likely a mere coincidence. Unless Claredon already knew of the secret passages, it was doubtful he would have stumbled upon them while visiting the old man. Still, it wouldn't hurt to find out. He gave Elly a measuring look.

"Did he mention the secret passages?" he asked, wondering if he should inspect the tunnels one final time.

Elly blinked at the question. "Of course not," she said, her brows gathering in a frown. "Why should he? I thought the wretched things were a secret to all but you and your noble family."

Lucien ignored her dig. "Did he ask for a tour, or was he at any time out of your sight?"

"Certainly not! As if I would grant him such liberties!" Elly replied, forgetting her earlier hints that the man was enamored of her. "He stopped by only long enough to issue his invitation, and then he was gone. Why? Do you suspect him of haunting us as well?"

She obviously meant this last as an insult, but he

217

ignored her taunting words. "Never mind why, just be sure to keep your distance," he said, fixing her with a forbidding frown. Until he could eliminate Marcus one way or another, he wanted Elly to have nothing to do with him. "The less you are with that fop, the better."

So he was jealous. Elly's mercurial emotions rose jubilantly. "That might be rather difficult, Lord Seabrook, considering the fact that he and his father will be our hosts tomorrow evening," she said with acid sweetness. "Unless you are hinting we cry off at the last moment?"

"My God, no!" Lucien exclaimed, thinking he could ill afford to tip his hand should Marcus be the traitor he was seeking.

So much for jealousy, Elly decided, feeling more confused now than when she had been in Lucien's arms responding wantonly to his kisses. She might have once dismissed his odd demand as mere masculine pique, but now that she knew him better she couldn't help but wonder if there might be something more to his insistence that she avoid Claredon. She remembered her teasing remark that Lucien was a man who never acted without cause, and a cold suspicion settled in the pit of her stomach.

"What is going on here?" she demanded, her eyes narrowing warily. "Why are you so curious about Mr. Claredon?"

"Perhaps I am jealous of him," Lucien said, anxious to be on his way. Elly's questions were getting decidedly uncomfortable, and in any case he needed to hasten his investigation of Marcus.

"Don't be an idiot!" she snapped, feeling more bewildered than ever. She didn't want to think he had been making up to her for some nefarious reason, yet what other possible explanation could there be? Unless, her heart began fluttering wildly, unless he did care for her . . .

"Ah, but I am an idiot," Lucien said, smiling at her waspish tone. She is a shrew without peer, he thought fondly, slipping his arms about her. He knew he had to go, but in the meanwhile he was unable to resist claiming his territory. "Now, mind you keep well out of that dandy's way, or I vow I shall call him out."

"What?" At first Elly was stunned with disbelief, and then she began struggling frantically. "Lucien, let me go at once! What are you talking about? You can not mean—"

"Later, my love." He pressed a hard kiss on her lips and set her apart. "I must be off. In the meanwhile, remember what I have told you. Stay away from Claredon."

"But Lucien, you simply can't make an announcement like that, and then just waltz out—" She stopped abruptly, realizing she was speaking to empty air. Lucien had vanished, leaving her torn between incredible fury, and incredible hope.

Chapter Fifteen

After an almost sleepless night, Elly spent the better part of the morning agonizing over her toilet. She drove poor Mary to distraction, trying on every gown in her wardrobe before announcing fretfully that she had nothing to wear. Such behavior was so unlike her customary indifference to clothing that the maid gave her a sharp look, asking bluntly if she required a purgative.

"For you are not yourself this morning, miss," she added, her tone aggrieved as she returned yet another rejected gown to the wardrobe. "Mayhap your system wants cleansing."

" 'Tis not my system that is at fault, Mary," Elly replied with a sigh, collapsing upon her bed to stare up at the plastered ceiling. She'd already committed its pattern to heart, having spent more nights than she cared to count studying its twining roses and dancing cherubs. At first it was the ghost who kept her awake, starting at every noise; so she supposed there was some sort of poetic justice that it was now his earthly counterpart who was depriving her of her sleep.

How dare the wretch kiss her so passionately and then take a French leave, she brooded, idly plucking at the ribbon on her dressing gown. The least he could have done was remain long enough to explain himself, so that she didn't lose yet another night's rest thinking impossible thoughts.

"If you say so, miss, but I still say you need purging," Mary continued, pressing her suggestion of a draught. "My mam had a dose of buckthorn every week, and she lived to be all of ninety! I could fetch some from Mrs. Stanley, if you'd like. She keeps a fresh supply in her herb chest."

The notion of taking the strong cathartic was enough to distract Elly from her troubling thoughts, and she gave the hovering maid a quick smile. "No, Mary, thank you. As I said, I am fine. Pick out any gown; I don't suppose it really signifies."

After she finished dressing she made her way down to the breakfast room, where she found Henry still lingering over his eggs and toast. At the sight of her wan face he set his cup aside with a worried frown.

"I say, El, are you feeling quite the thing? You're looking whey-faced as the devil."

"Thank you, Henry," she muttered, taking her seat with a grimace. "Between you and Mary, I quite wonder that I even ventured past my door, since I am obviously such an antidote. She suggested buckthorn as a remedy, what might you prescribe?"

"Certainly not buckthorn," Henry was momentarily distracted. "It's far too caustic, and its dosage difficult to calculate. Culver's root might work, or a dose of calomel if you are feeling bound, but I—"

"I was only funning, Henry," Elly interrupted with a sigh. She'd forgotten his rather pedantic turn of mind. "I promise you I am in the pink of health."

"Well, you don't look it," Henry was blunt in the manner of all brothers. "Didn't have another nightmare, did you?"

Elly gave a guilty start. "Of course not," she denied. "I just had a little difficulty in falling asleep, that is all."

"It is the party, I expect," Henry said with a wise

221

nod. "The prospect of meeting a royal is bound to make one nervous as a cat."

This seemed as good a reason as any to Elly, and she was quick to agree with him. They spent the remainder of their morning meal discussing the Claredons' dinner party, and Elly was pleased to hear him remark that he had already asked Miranda to stand up with him for a dance.

"I don't like turning a calf as a rule," he confided, "but I know you ladies set great store by such things. Lord Marleigh mentioned he meant to ask Lady Miranda to stand up with him as well, and I thought I'd best put in my application before that dandy laid claim to all of her sets."

"He couldn't do that; it would be as good as a declaration," she said absently, wondering if Lucien would keep his promise to dance with her.

"I'll never understand the gentry," Henry grumbled, shaking his head in disbelief. "Oddest courting customs I've ever seen. A man can have his way with a gel from the lower orders, and no one thinks a thing of it. Let him stand up with a society chit for more than two dances, and they're already posting the banns."

All this talk of courting and posting the banns struck Elly as highly significant, and she cast Henry a speculative glance from beneath her thick lashes. Perhaps, she thought hopefully, Lucien has already spoken to him, and he is feeling me out to see if I would consider a match. Picking up her teacup, she assumed a look of cool indifference.

"Speaking of dancing, I have also promised Lord Seabrook a dance," she said, her heart pounding with nervous excitement. "I hope you don't mind?"

"Mind? Why should I? I don't mean to stand up with him, you know." He was staring at her as if she'd run mad.

"I meant," she clarified with obvious patience,

222

"you might have preferred that he first ask you for permission before approaching me. That is usually the way it is done."

"Oh." He shrugged his shoulders. "Well, don't suppose I have any objection one way or another," he said, reaching for another slice of toast. "I've always thought him a capital fellow, and I don't mind if he stands up with you. That reminds me, I had a note from him this morning," Henry continued, digging into his pocket and extracting a folded piece of paper which he then handed to Elly. "Seems like he won't be stopping by this afternoon after all."

Elly snatched the missive from his hand, her lips thinning at the tersely written words. The note claimed "pressing business," and mentioned his hope to see them that night. A very proper note all in all, but it was hardly the sort of note she'd been secretly hoping for. She dropped the letter on the table.

"Doubtlessly his newest mistress was growing restive and he had to pop back up to London to smooth her feathers," she said with a sniff, her hands shaking as she picked up her teacup. "I shouldn't be surprised if we don't see him this evening."

"El! 'Tis no such thing!" Henry was properly shocked by her speech. "Seabrook ain't the type to go haring back to London just because of a lightskirt . . . not that *you* should even make mention of such a person," he added with a disapproving frown.

"Don't be a gudgeon, Henry," she snapped, fighting the urge to burst into angry tears. So it had all been a hum, she thought, her heart all but shattering from the pain. Had the kiss meant anything to him at all he would have been here by now, but apparently she had been right all along. The beast had been using her.

"I ain't a gudgeon!" Henry was highly incensed.

223

"Ladies ought not to talk about such creatures, and further more I —" He broke off as he noted her sudden pallor. "Elly? Are you all right?"

"No," she managed in a weak voice, rising shakily to her feet as she succumbed to the tears burning her eyes. "No, I am not all right." And she dashed from the room, ignoring his demands for an explanation.

Ashurst Hall was ablaze with lights as Elly and her party made their bows to their host and hostess. Miranda and the other ladies were greeted with every evidence of pleasure, while Elly's and Henry's welcome was far less warm. The squire merely shook their hands, declaring himself charmed to meet them before turning pointedly to the next person in the receiving line.

"Well, that was rather odd," Miranda observed as they made their way towards the stately drawing room. "I understood Marcus to say his father had specifically requested you attend, and yet he scarce seemed to know who you are."

"Is that so surprising?" Jessica asked with a laugh. "I think we are all agreed that Marcus is a paperskull, and after speaking with his father it would seem the apple hasn't fallen very far from the tree! The man is as lack-witted as can be."

"You mustn't be so unkind, Jessica," Lydia said, shaking her head in gentle disapproval. "The squire is our host, after all."

"Well, I agree with Miss Kingsley," Henry declared with surprising heat, casting a fulminating glare in the direction of the squire and his family. "That Marcus fellow is a dashed loose screw, insisting we come and then snubbing us as if we was a bunch of encroaching Cits! Bad breeding, I would call it."

"And what of you?" Miranda turned to Elly with a quizzical smile. "What would you call it?"

"Call what?" she asked, only half-attending to the conversation. She'd been searching the crowds since the moment of their arrival, but so far she hadn't caught so much as a glimpse of Lucien.

"Marcus Claredon's behavior, silly." Jessica gave another laugh. "What on earth ails you? You've been in a trance all evening, and we've scarce heard three words from you!"

Elly's face grew pink at her friend's teasing. "I am sorry, Jessica," she said stiffly, struggling for composure. "I hadn't realized I was being such poor company."

"Oh, rot!" Jessica gave her arm an affectionate squeeze. "You must know I was only twigging you! Although you *have* been rather distracted," she added, tilting her head to one side and regarding Elly with lively interest. "Is anything amiss?"

"No, nothing," Elly denied quickly. "I was only looking for the prince. Is he here yet, do you think?"

"Prinny? Not likely." Miranda answered with a shake of her head. "He is rather fond of grand entrances, and I doubt he will arrive until the last possible moment."

The talk soon turned to other topics, and while her brother and friends chatted companionably Elly was left alone with her thoughts. She wondered if the "pressing business" Lucien had alluded to would keep him from the party. Oh, she knew he'd said he dared not miss the party so as not to offend the prince, but what did that signify? He'd also said he'd visit her and Henry that afternoon, and only look at how he'd broken that promise. He was a rake, she decided with mounting indignation; a libertine who kissed her passionately one moment, and then ignored her very existence in the next. If she ever saw the wretch again she—

"You're scowling, Elly, so I can only surmise you are thinking of me," a low voice drawled in her ear seconds before a strong hand stole about her waist. She whirled around and found Lucien standing behind her, a pleased smile lifting the corners of his mouth. For one moment her joy at seeing him was in her eyes, and then she remembered she was angry with him.

"I am sure I don't know what you mean, my lord," she said with a dainty sniff, stepping pointedly away from him. "And for your information I wasn't scowling. I was . . . thinking."

"My mistake," Lucien replied, delighted by her proud anger. She'd never be so furious with him unless her feelings were deeply involved, he reasoned, taking comfort in the thought. Once this was behind them, he would have to do something about those feelings.

"Seabrook, nice to see you," Henry exclaimed, offering his hand with a pleased smile. "Wasn't sure you'd be here tonight. Were you able to get all that business out of the way?"

"Not all of it, unfortunately," Lucien answered, flicking a surreptitious glance in Marcus's direction. He'd spent the afternoon investigating the other man, and although he'd found nothing overtly incriminating he had uncovered enough to whet his interest. A letter detailing his suspicions was already on its way to Alex, and he'd had a discreet word with the prince's guard, advising them to be doubly alert. He'd have preferred the prince cancel his engagement, but the prince had adamantly refused, dismissing Lucien's fears with a wave of his fat hand.

"I know what you mean." Henry gave a wise nod. "A man's work is never done, and all that. This book I am penning is proving to be a dashed chore, and I shall be relieved once it is finished."

Lucien nodded politely, although his eyes never left Elly. It was obvious by the way she kept her back to him that she hadn't yet forgiven him, but there was little he could do about it now. After flirting with the other ladies he drifted away to mingle with the rest of the guests. But even while he was listening to their inane chatter, his attention never wavered from Marcus. He was aware of the other man's every move, and when Lieutenant McKenzie arrived his senses prickled with warning.

Despite that, he also kept a watchful eye on Elly, and it did not help his disposition to see his little bluestocking conducting herself like an accomplished coquette. She had a circle of men surrounding her, and he watched grim-faced as they vied for a place on her dance card. He remembered the promise of a dance he had won from her, and wondered angrily if she also remembered. Too bad if she had not, he decided with mounting possessiveness. He had no intention of letting her forget it.

For Elly's part the evening was a torture to be stoically endured. Except for that one outrageous remark Lucien hadn't paid her the slightest attention and, in fact, seemed to be going out of his way to avoid her. Worse, meeting the prince had been a profound disappointment, and she found it nigh impossible to believe the plump, affected creature she was introduced to had ever been known as "the first gentleman of Europe."

Dinner was equally as bad. She and Henry had been seated as far from the main table as was possible, and she had to watch as Lucien made up to the pretty blonde other guests obligingly identified as a titled lady whose sullied reputation rivalled her spectacular cleavage. The sight so depressed Elly that when one catty female pointed out that the stunning blonde was known to be a "particular friend" of Lucien's, she didn't respond other than accidentally upending the boat of Hollandaise sauce on the lady's gown.

227

Following dinner the company moved to the ballroom, where a small quartet was tuning their instruments. Elly was immediately surrounded by the gentlemen she had met before dinner, and her wounded vanity found solace in their flattering attentions. Once the dancing started, she was too busy to give Lucien much thought, until he appeared unexpectedly at her side just as the band was striking up a waltz.

"My dance, I think," he said, taking her in his arms and whisking her away from her indignant partner.

Elly stiffened in resentment, but with the whole neighborhood looking on there was little she could do. Not that she intended letting him get away with such outrageousness, of course. Her chin came up as she met his velvet-dark gaze.

"Neatly done, my lord," she said coolly, even as her heart was racing with a tangle of emotions. "I trust you are satisfied with yourself."

"For the moment," he agreed, his arms tightening about her slender waist. She was wearing a low-cut gown of icy-blue silk, and he thought she looked regal as a queen. Among the jewels he'd inherited from his father was a diamond and aquamarine necklace, and as his eyes lingered on the tempting curves of her breasts he imagined how she would look in it.

"Well, I am not so pleased with you," she returned huffily, trying her best to ignore the feel of his strong, hard body moving in perfect time with hers. "Kindly return me to Mr. Dashton at once!"

"What? And cause a scandal?" His eyebrows arched in mock horror. "Come, Miss Denning, only think of the damage to your reputation!" He gave her a warning squeeze before easing the pressure. "Now relax, hell-cat, and enjoy the music. You must

228

know I would never let you waltz with another man."

Elly thrilled to his possessive declaration . . . but only for a moment. "Ha! That is a likely story! You are just as bad as that oaf Marcus Claredon! The pair of you twist the truth to suit your own ends, and if you think for one moment that I—"

"What the devil are you talking about?"

"Don't play the innocent with me!" Elly was outraged by his harsh demand. "First you try to buy our house and when that doesn't work you haunt it, and then—"

"No," Lucien interrupted again, shaking his head impatiently as his mind raced with awareness. "Claredon. What did you mean about Claredon? When has he ever lied to you?"

"Well, tonight for one," Elly frowned up at him, confused by the expression in his face. "After insisting we attend, he didn't even bother introducing us to his father. And as for the squire, he acted like we were a tribe of Gypsies who had slipped in to make off with the silver. Henry was most insulted."

Lucien digested this. "But when he issued the invitation he claimed otherwise?"

"Indeed he did! He said his father was a particular admirer of my father, and he all but begged us to come. I wanted to refuse, but I thought it would be rude."

In an instant all the clues he and Alex had uncovered became transparently obvious to Lucien. "The bastard!" he snarled, his eyes narrowing with the force of his fury. "So *that's* how they mean to do it!"

"Lucien?" Elly stared up at him, aware something serious had happened. "What is it? What is wrong?"

"The prince," Lucien's eyes scanned the room, coming to rest on the Regent as he sat flirting with his elderly hostess. "I must speak with him at once."

"But Lucien—"

229

"I'm taking you to Henry," he said, his hand closing over hers as he dragged her off the floor. "You are to stay with him for the rest of the evening."

"Don't be ridiculous, I am promised for the next quadrille," Elly gasped in protest, tripping over the skirts of her gown as Lucien pulled her after him. "Lucien, stop this at once! I insist you tell me what is going on!"

He paid her no heed, but continued tugging her along as he sought out Henry. He found him on the far side of the room talking with Miranda, and thrust Elly into his arms. "Watch her," he instructed tersely. "And on no account are you to return to Seagate tonight. I will instruct your coachman to drive you to my house."

"But, my lord—"

Lucien turned away, ignoring Henry's weak protests; his mind already on his next move. They had always assumed the attempt would be made at the pavilion and had planned accordingly. Now it seemed other arrangements would have to be made.

"Just wait one moment!" Elly grabbed his sleeve, her face indignant as she tugged him to a halt. "If you think I will let you leave this time, you are mad! What the devil is going on?"

At the first touch of her hand on his sleeve he had whirled around, prepared to do battle; and for the length of a heartbeat they glared at one another like combatants. Lucien was the first to relax, his shoulders tensing as he sought for some way of explaining himself. "Elly, I wish I could tell you, but—"

"Has this anything to do with those wretched smugglers?" she interrupted, having already reached this conclusion. It was the only explanation she could think of, and it irked her to think he thought her some weak-willed miss to be protected from any danger.

He seized upon her querulous demand. "Yes, they

230

are making a run tonight, and I don't want you anywhere near that bay. If there is anyone certain to
throw a spanner in the works it is you."

"Well, thank you very much!" She bristled indignantly. "I would think you would want their work
disrupted! How else do you mean to stop them?"

"Oh, I'll stop them," he promised, his voice soft
with deadly determination. "You may count upon
that. Meanwhile, I don't want either you or Henry
to return home."

"But why?" She was genuinely mystified. Granted
she knew almost nothing about smugglers, but what
little she had heard so far had led her to believe they
were not particularly dangerous. Why should it matter one way or another whether she and Henry were
home?

"I mean it, Elly." Lucien's hands descended on her
shoulders to hold her against him. They were all
alone in the dimly-lit hallway, and he was unable to
resist touching her. He loved her, he admitted with
anguish, and knowing this might well be the last
time he would ever touch her was eating him alive.
How ironic that he should find love just as he was
embarking on the most dangerous mission of his
life, he mused, his strong hands flexing on her
shoulders.

"I want you safe," he said simply, his eyes burning
into hers. "Give me that much, Elly. Please."

His eloquent plea as well as the emotion smoul-
dering in his eyes was Elly's undoing. She reached up
a shaking hand to stroke his cheek. "I also want you
safe," she said, fighting tears. "Will you promise me
to take every care? If something were to happen to
you, I could not bear it."

He silenced her by laying his finger across her
lips. "No promises, my love," he said, his voice deep
with passion. "No guarantees. That is the way of my
world. But by all that is holy, I will do everything

231

within my power to return to you."

His answer told her more than she wanted to know, and it was all she could do not to scream out her anguish. She wanted to hold him tight and tell him of her love, to plead with him not to go. Instead she knocked his hand aside, her brows meeting in an irritated scowl. "Oh, very well, you wretch," she grumbled, fighting back tears. "Go and catch your silly smugglers. But if you get yourself killed, I shall never forgive you!"

Lucien gave a delighted laugh, his arms closing about her as he swept her up in a hard kiss. "I love you, Elly," he said, brushing another kiss against her mouth as he set her down again. "Now mind you do exactly as I told you, or I vow that if I *am* killed, I will haunt you through eternity!" And he dashed out to find the prince.

"My jacket?" His Royal Highness, Prince George blinked up at Lucien in confusion. "Don't be daft, my boy; the thing ain't at all in your style."

"I know that, sir," Lucien replied through clenched teeth, aware of how quickly time was slipping away from him. He'd already wasted valuable time contacting his men and sending out a variety of messages, and now it was time to arrange the final piece of the trap he had devised. "But it is as I have just explained. I am certain the attempt against you will be made tonight, so I wish to take your place in the royal coach. My own coach and men will see you safely home."

The Regent's watery blue eyes sparkled in amusement as he glanced down at his own corpulent form and then at Lucien. "Don't mean to discourage you, Seabrook, but do you really think those smugglers will take you for us? Unless they're as blind as m'pater, it simply won't wash."

Lucien said nothing at first, knowing his plan was not without flaws. Still, he did not see a viable alternative. The double they'd already put in place was at the pavilion, and there wasn't time to fetch him. He supposed he could have Marcus arrested under the Combination Acts, but that wasn't enough for him. He wanted him convicted of treason, and to do that he would need more proof. What better proof could there be than catching him red-handed in the act of kidnapping the prince himself?

"I know it is risky," he conceded, meeting the prince's gaze, "but I believe we can make it work. We won't make the switch until moments before you leave. It will be dark, and if I am in your coat and cape, there's no way they'll know the difference until it's too late."

"Ah, so you mean to relieve us of our cape as well," the prince said with a rich chuckle. "We shall doubtlessly catch our deaths riding about in our shirtsleeves. But," he raised a bejeweled hand, forstalling Lucien's protest, "it is the least we can do for England. 'Tis more than a cold you'll be courting, what?"

Lucien inclined his head, appreciating the Regent's unspoken understanding of what would happen should their plan fail. "Thank you, Your Highness," he said quietly. "Then I may count upon you to meet me in the royal drawing room at precisely midnight?"

"Or thereabouts." His Royal Highness gave a sweet smile. "Were I to be on the dot, dear boy, the blackguards would be sure to smell a rat."

In the end making the switch proved to be amazingly easy. After entertaining the guests with his version of a Scottish reel the prince winced, collapsing on a chair and claiming loudly that he had sprained his ankle. His coach was brought quickly about, and just as two of his most trusted men were leading him

233

out the door, he announced his urgent need of the necessary. The two guards helped him to the door, and he stepped inside, where an impatient Lucien was waiting.

He donned the prince's ornate green velvet coat and mink-lined cape, and was about to slip from the room when the prince laid a detaining hand on his arm.

"Yes, Your Highness?" He gave the Regent an expectant look.

"For luck," the prince said, handing him a gold fob adorned with a large ruby. "Besides, 'twas designed to go with the coat, and we should hate for anyone to see us so shabbily dressed."

Lucien attached the jewel to his coat. "Thank you Your Highness," he said, deeply moved by the prince's generosity. "I shall treasure it always."

"We hope so, my lord," Prince George answered solemnly. "We sincerely hope so."

At first all went as planned. The prince's usual escort fell in behind the ornate coach, and they set of with a great deal of noise and confusion. The two men in the coach with Lucien were, of course, privy to the deception, and he admired the relative calm with which they faced the coming confrontation Had he not taken the precaution of having his own men already positioned ahead and behind them there was every chance they would have been killed by the smugglers once the coach had been stopped

"You're sure they won't waylay us until we are past the Hove Road?" Sir Nigel Beaumont asked, casting anxious glances out the coach's glazed window " 'Tis dark as the hubs of hell out there."

"It's the most logical spot for an ambush," Lucien replied, checking his gun before slipping it into his coat pocket. "The road is bounded on both sides by heavy woods, and a whole army could secrete themselves there without being seen. Also, the road is quite narrow at that spot; making it impossible for a coach to turn around once it has been attacked. If I were going to take a coach like this, that is where I would choose."

The other man grunted his approval of Lucien's plan, and the three settled back to wait. Less than ten minutes later gunfire exploded around them, taking everyone by surprise. Lucien used two pistols he had arranged to be placed in the coach, but there were simply too many attackers. The guards were dispatched, wounded or dying, and then the coach was forced to halt. Lucien gave both men warning looks.

"Don't resist," he ordered, furious that his plan had gone so awry. He knew eight men at least had been shot, and he wasn't willing for anyone else to be harmed because of him. "Let them take me and then get word to Twyford. That is vital. Tell Alex—" He got no further as the door was opened and a hooded man thrust his head into the carriage.

"Stand and deliver!" he roared, pointing a weapon at Sir Nigel's chest.

"No need for so much lead, old boy," the other man, Lord Geoffrey Havermale, drawled in affected outrage. "Although if this is a common robbery, you've obviously no idea of the error you have committed. Do you know who we are?"

"Know who 'e is." The man stuck his gun against Lucien's stomach. "Try to stop me and I'll gut-shoot 'im."

"Don't make a move, you imbeciles!" Lucien exclaimed in a fair imitation of the prince's rich voice. "The man is a Luddite!"

"Don't you mind what I be." The masked man gave a crude laugh. "Just come with me and no one gets hurt."

Lucien protested as much as he thought safe, offering the man everything from a fortune to a duke-

235

dom before grudgingly complying with the demands of his kidnappers. As he climbed out of the coach, the sight of the wounded and dead lying on the ground filled him with fury, and he vowed that if it was the last thing he did on this earth he would see Marcus dead.

In a matter of minutes he was bound and gagged; a blindfold wrapped about his head. He was then dumped unceremoniously into a carriage, and driven away into the night. He could hear his captors jubilant and excited laughter, but he closed his mind to it, remembering instead the sweetness in Elly's voice as she had pleaded with him to take care. He allowed himself a brief moment to mourn for what now might never be, and then turned his full attentions to extracting himself from the mess he was in before it was too late.

Chapter Sixteen

At Lucien's elegant home Elly nervously paced his study, awaiting his return with anxiety and annoyance. It was well past two in the morning, and yet there'd been no word from him. Surely it couldn't take this long to capture a boatload of common smugglers, she thought, dashing a shaking hand across her eyes. Drat the man, where *was* he?

"You'll do yourself no good pacing about like this," Henry warned, his blue eyes worried as they rested on her strained face. "Now for heaven's sake, while you stop wearing a hole in the marquess's carpet? It'll all turn out in the end; you'll see."

Elly didn't share his blind optimism. Something was wrong; she sensed it as strongly as she had ever sensed anything, and yet what could she do? The promise Lucien had forced upon her bound her as tightly as the strongest chains, and there was naught she could do but wait for him, listening to the grandfather's clock chiming the quarter-hour and going quietly out of her mind.

"An odd evening, wasn't it?" Henry asked, hoping to distract her with chatter. "Must say I was disappointed in the prince; what a caper-witted fellow he turned out to be. Only imagine a man of his size doing a reel! No wonder he injured himself."

"It was a sight." She let herself be diverted, smiling as she remembered the heavyset prince whirling about the room like an overgrown toy.

"Reminded me of those dervishes we saw at that bazaar in Alexandria," Henry said with a laugh. "Remember, El? We went there with father, and—"

The door to the study was suddenly thrown open, and two men Elly remembered from the party came rushing inside. One look at their grim, set faces, and she felt her heart turn to ice. "What is it?" she asked, her voice unnaturally calm. "What's happened?"

The men seemed surprised to see them, a response they made no attempt to hide. "Miss Denning, Mr. Denning, what are you doing here?" Lord Havermale demanded, his suspicious eyes flicking from Henry to Elly.

"Lord Seabrook asked us to wait here," Elly said, fighting for control. "Is there some problem?"

Instead of answering, Havermale crossed the room to Lucien's desk, searching for the set of sealed instructions he'd been told to expect. "Well, I am afraid you will have to wait elsewhere," he said, not looking up. "Crown business; you'll have to leave."

"Has this anything to do with those smugglers Lord Seabrook is after?" Henry asked, stepping closer to Elly and draping a protective arm about her shoulders.

Havermale and Sir Nigel exchanged horrified looks. "You know about the smugglers?" Sir Nigel managed in a weak voice.

"Only that they have been using the bay at Seagate to move their cargo, and that the marquess was determined to smash their ring," Henry answered coolly, eyeing both men with the dignity worthy of a duke. "Now kindly tell us what is going on. Is Lord Seabrook all right?"

Again the two men exchanged looks, and this time

it was Sir Nigel who answered. "We don't know," he admitted, running a hand through his thinning hair. "He's disappeared."

Elly bit her lip, holding back a cry of anguish. Disappeared, she thought, clinging to the word with desperation. If Lucien was dead, surely they would have said as much. She took a deep breath to steady herself and then gave both men an assessing look. "What do you mean he has disappeared?" she asked, grateful for Henry's comforting presence at her side.

"We managed to keep the villains in sight for the first quarter-mile," Sir Nigel said, not caring that he was breaking his oath to Lucien. "They rounded a bend ahead of us, and when we got there they were gone. We kept on riding, thinking they were surely ahead of us, but there was no trace of them. It was almost as if they'd vanished into the night." He shook his head in wonder.

"Nonsense," Henry was scowling at him. "No one simply vanishes like that! There must have been another road, or else they—"

"The tunnels!" Elly cried, turning to Henry. "They must have gone into the tunnels!"

"What tunnels?" Havermale had found the letter, and after scanning its contents he slipped it into the pocket of his jacket.

"Seagate is riddled with tunnels and secret chambers, that was the reason Lucien was so determined to have it," Elly said, her mind racing. "There must be a tunnel that connects with the main road, and if the smugglers knew of it—"

"Then they would have used it," Sir Nigel concluded, his eyes glittering with rage. "Damn it all, if they have gone into a blasted Cretan maze then Seabrook is as good as dead. We'll never reach him in time!"

Elly ignored the searing pain that tore through her

239

at the man's incautious words. "Not necessarily," she said slowly, a daring plan forming rapidly in her mind. "I have an idea. . . ."

Lucien knew the moment they entered the tunnels. He could feel the difference in the air about him, hear the distorted sounds of the wheels in the passage. Rather than being alarmed by this development he was actually relieved. He knew these tunnels like most men knew their own homes, and if he could manage to slip away from his captors he knew he could easily find his way to safety. Unless, he thought grimly, Claredon's men were equally familiar with the twisting maze of corridors.

He was still working on a possible escape plan when the carriage suddenly rumbled to a halt. The door to the coach was thrown open and rough hands grabbed him, dragging him out and pushing him onto the ground.

"Here now, lads," he heard one of the men drawl, "is that any way to treat a future king of England? Gently, we don't want our cargo damaged."

The remark elicited much coarse laughter, and a booted foot connected brutally with Lucien's side. He ignored the pain and the laughter, finding his footing and pushing himself proudly to his feet. When he was standing, the blindfold covering his eyes was removed, and he glared into the eyes of one of his captors.

The man was filthy and unshaven, his black eyes glittering with malice as he towered over Lucien. The malice changed to confusion and then incredulity as he took in Lucien's appearance. "What the devil's goin' on here?" he demanded in dismay. "This ain't the prince!"

"O' course 'tis!" The man who had abducted Lu-

240

cien pushed himself forward. "I pulled 'im from the carriage meself! An' what o' that, eh?" He indicated the medal on the front of Lucien's coat. " 'Tis the order o' St. George!"

"It ain't the prince," the first man insisted, obviously shaken. "I seen him once in town, an' he's twice the weight of this one. Who are you, eh?" He sent Lucien staggering back with a jab of a grubby finger. "Answer me quick, else I'll slit your throat!"

Over the cloth still gagging him Lucien raised his eyebrows mockingly. There was no sign yet of Claredon, although he was certain that would soon change. He couldn't imagine so important a transaction taking place without the man. All he had to do was keep his eyes open and his wits about him.

The gag was roughly removed, and after working the stiffness from his jaw Lucien gave his captors a cool smile. "I am the marquess of Seabrook," he said, straightening his shoulders. "And you, gentlemen, may consider yourselves under arrest."

"I still think we ought to have waited for Twyford and the rest of the soldiers," Sir Nigel grumbled, clutching his pistol in a sweating hand as Elly led them down the main corridor. "We have no idea how many of the blackguards we may be facing."

"We can't afford to wait that long," Havermale said, tamping down his own nervousness. "Besides, we have the element of surprise on our side."

Elly ignored them, her heart in her throat as she retraced the route she and Lucien had taken only yesterday. She remembered his warnings of the tunnels' dangers, and prayed he'd only mentioned them to keep her from exploring on her own. That they hadn't triggered anything so far reassured her somewhat, although she wouldn't allow herself to relax.

241

This has to work, she thought, holding back tears. She wouldn't let Lucien die.

"You're sure we'll be able to find our way back out, Miss Denning?" Sir Nigel asked with another uncertain glance about him. Something about the dark, endless tunnels made him decidedly uneasy, and the feeling grew stronger as they moved deeper into the maze. It was almost as if they were being watched . . . followed, and the sensation was more terrifying than the possibility of encountering an army of armed smugglers.

"Yes, Sir Nigel. Lucien—Lord Seabrook—revealed several possible exits when he showed me the tunnel." Elly hesitated when she reached another of the many tunnels that intersected with the main passage. She remembered Lucien guiding her away from it, saying it held nothing of interest. She'd thought it odd at the time but . . .

"Go!" The voice whispering in her head made her start, and she glanced wildly around her. She was about to decide she'd imagined the whole thing when the voice sounded again, more urgently. *"This way, hurry. Hurry!"*

"We go this way," she said, tightening her grip on the torch in her hand. "It will take us to where they're holding him."

"Maybe you should go back, Elly," Henry suggested, laying a restraining hand on her shoulder. "This could be dangerous."

"I don't care." Elly shrugged his hand off, impatience eating at her. She didn't know if she had really heard that voice or not, but she wasn't about to ignore it. All that mattered was reaching Lucien.

"But—"

"Shhh!" Havermale silenced them with a wave of his hand. "I hear something!"

From the other end of the connecting tunnel

voices echoed oddly, the sound bouncing off the curved stone walls. "Don't be such an old woman, McKeef. How many times do I have to tell ye, there be no such things as ghosts! Now hush with your stories and keep a sharp eye out. Them Frenchies will be here soon as the tides ebb."

"But he's here, I tell ye!" The terror in McKeef's voice was clearly audible. "I can *feel* him! Me mum had the sight, and I has it too. Old Jenks'll steal our souls; that's what he'll do. Steal our souls and drag us into hell with him!"

"I wish that dolt would shut up," Sir Nigel whispered beneath his breath. "His partner may not believe him, but he's beginning to give me the jimmie-jams."

McKeef's partner administered another sharp warning, but it seemed to have little effect. As the voices faded away Elly could hear more dire warnings of what would befall them should Old Jenks get his evil hands on them. That was when the idea hit her.

"I believe you are right, Henry," she said, managing a demure smile as she turned to her brother. "Perhaps it would be best if I didn't go any farther."

"Eh?" Henry cast her a suspicious look. "What's going on here, El? Never known you to be so biddable . . . unless you was up to something," he added knowingly.

"Nonsense, Henry," she protested, in a fever to be gone. "It is just that I know Lucien wouldn't want me to place myself in any danger."

"Very wise of you, Miss Denning," Havermale approved. "This is no place for a lady; off with you now."

"Unfortunately, m'sister ain't a lady," Henry said bluntly, more convinced than ever that Elly was up to no good. "Now tell me what you're planning."

Elly glared at him, then relented with a sigh, knowing now was not the time for a show of defiance. "It seems to me that if McKeef is so afraid of Old Jenks, then perhaps the others might share his fear. That could give us the edge we need."

Henry's scowl vanished as comprehension dawned. "Do you mean . . . the ghost?"

"Precisely." She nodded. "Now listen carefully, this is what I have in mind. . . ."

As Lucien suspected, his announcement was greeted by a moment of stunned silence followed by disbelieving laughter. "Arrest!" the first man roared, obviously amused by Lucien's bravado. "I think you have mistook the situation, my fine lord. 'Tis you who are in *our* hands, and like to remain so 'til we decides what to do with you."

"You mean until Claredon decides what to do with me," Lucien said, playing his ace with ice-cold cunning. "Yes," he said at the other man's horrified look, "I know all about the bastard, just as I know you're awaiting the French ship *Le Coeur;* bound for Lyons, if I am not mistaken. Your little game is finished, and if you have an ounce of decency you'll surrender like men rather than be hunted down like dogs."

The sound of clapping drew Lucien's attention to the entryway, where he saw Marcus leaning against the curved wall. "Bravo, Lord Seabrook," he said, moving forward with a mocking smile. "How eloquently you express yourself! What a pity that your words must fall upon deaf ears."

"Marcus, I was wondering when you would slither into view," Lucien drawled, the hair on the back of his head prickling with warning. He couldn't explain it, precisely, but he knew he was suddenly not alone. He flexed his hands, testing the strength of the ropes

244

binding him. When they didn't give so much as an inch he decided to see if he could convince Marcus to undo them. He'd need both hands to fight his way to one of the tunnels. . . .

"Really, Seabrook, you wound me." Marcus looked offended. "That is hardly the proper way to greet one's host."

"And this is hardly the way to treat one's guest." Lucien was quick to make use of the opening Marcus had provided. He turned his back, displaying his bound hands, and then turned back to face his captor. "Are these ropes really necessary? Unless, of course, you fear I shall overpower you and your men?"

Marcus reacted just as Lucien had anticipated; his mocking smile becoming sulky. "Don't be a boor, Seabrook," he said indignantly. "You know as well as I that there is no escape for you."

"Then kindly untie my hands. The rope is cutting me."

Marcus hesitated only a moment before turning to one of his men. "Untie him at once."

The man looked at Lucien's powerful shoulders and muscular body. "But Mr. Claredon . . ."

"Just do it, you dolt!" Marcus snapped. "What can he do? We outnumber him ten to one!"

The man did as he was bid, although he grumbled about it beneath his breath. The moment his hands were freed, Lucien began glancing idly about him, studying the chamber with assessing eyes. "So these tunnels really do exist," he said indifferently, noting each possible escape route. "I thought they were only stories."

"Oh, they exist, all right," Marcus gloated. "I discovered them when I was a lad, and I've used them ever since. Unfortunately I never went beyond this cave and the passage that connects to the road. No need to. Now, I can see I shall never get another chance."

"Then you admit you have no choice but to surrender?" Lucien asked, tensing in readiness for his break. The men were intent on their conversation, and if he managed to keep them distracted there was a chance he could make it to the tunnel before they could stop him. All he needed was a small diversion. . . .

"Heavens no!" Marcus was laughing at him. "I mean, I may have to accept my French *ami*'s offer of an estate in the Caribbean. A reward for my services, you see. Not the way I would have preferred this charming little game to end, but I—"

"Death! Death to all!" A theatrical wail sounded from the left of the main chamber as a ghostly figure appeared in the shadows, arms outstretched. "Death!"

"The ghost!" Men who faced the dangers of their profession without so much as blinking an eye quailed in fright, backing away from the figure as it advanced towards them, wailing and waving its arms.

The ghost startled Lucien as well, but he was quick to take advantage of the other's fear. He brought his hands down on the neck of the man nearest him, darting towards the tunnel with no thought but escape in his mind. Claredon saw him and called out a warning, but before any of them could act, two of the other men came scrambling out of the tunnel.

"Run for it!" McKeef shouted, falling on the packed sand in his terror. " 'Tis Old Jenks come fer us!"

A second ghostly figure appeared, flapping its arms and sending up a chorus of wails to rival the other spirit's.

246

The smugglers were in a panic, bumping into each other and shouting like disorderly children. Lucien easily brought down a second smuggler with the back of his hand and was about to reach the safety of the tunnel when the sound of a gunshot stopped him in his tracks. He turned to see Marcus holding a pair of pistols in his hands.

"Idiots," he shouted, aiming one of the pistols at the first ghost to appear, "can't you see it is a trick? There are no such things as ghosts, and by God I'll prove it to you!" And he tightened his grip on the pistol, slowly drawing back the hammer.

"Elly! Look out!" The second ghost cried out a warning, and Lucien's eyes widened in horrified understanding.

"No!" He started forward, knowing even as he moved that he'd never reach the other man in time.

Mrs. Magney's lips tightened in annoyance. She'd put up with many a prank in her day, but enough was enough. She'd not allow such riffraff to dirty up her tidy house and threaten her mistress in the bargain! Gathering herself, she exploded out of the shadows, making her displeasure known in no uncertain terms.

The cold, sticky air stuck Lucien like a fist as the ghostly shape materialized in the air between Marcus and Elly. The sound of birds' wings filled the chamber with a mighty roar, drowning out Marcus's terrified scream. The ghost's face was set in a furious scowl, and she was waving her hands in a gesture Lucien would have found comical under any other circumstances. She was shooing them away.

Marcus screamed again, dropping the pistol as he

247

raised his hands to shield his eyes from the dreadful apparition. Lucien saw his chance and took it, pulling his own pistol from his pocket and firing a single bullet into Marcus's chest.

It was all over in a matter of minutes. Havermale and Sir Nigel emerged from the tunnel with their own weapons drawn, and with Henry's help easily subdued the remaining smugglers. Lucien dropped his pistol to the floor, stepping over a groaning Marcus as he rushed to Elly's side.

He scooped her up in his arms, anxiously examining her for any sign of injury. "Elly, my God, Elly! Are you hurt, my darling?"

Behind the glowing mask she had kept as a memento, Elly studied Lucien's face with a sort of dazed wonder. She reached out a trembling hand to touch his cheek. "You're all right," she whispered softly. "They didn't hurt you."

The touch of her hand broke the icy fear that had paralyzed Lucien, and his relief turned into fury. His hands descended to her shoulders. "You little minx!" he thundered, his fingers digging into the white cloth — a bedsheet, he realized with outrage. "Is this how you keep your word to me? You might have been killed!"

"So might you," she returned, albeit in a weak voice. "Lucien, did you see her? That must have been Mrs. Magney. She — "

Lucien yanked the mask from her, glowering down into her pale features as he gave his temper full rein. "I don't care if she's bloody Anne Boleyn!" he roared, dragging her to her feet. "If you ever disobey me like this again, I vow I shan't be responsible for my actions!"

His anger finally penetrated her dazed state, and she gave him an indignant look. "Well, what was I supposed to do, let them carry you off? I love you,

you ungrateful beast, and I wanted to save you! Now I am wondering why the devil I bothered."

Beneath his anger Lucien delighted in her cross declaration, but he was not about to let her off so easily. It was time she learned who was master here. "I love you, too, but don't think I shall let you carry on like this once we are married," he said decisively. "Once you are my wife, you will learn to obey me."

"Ha!" She struggled to free herself. "As if I would even consider marrying such an overbearing tyrant! I am an independent female, and I will never, ever *obey* any man!"

"You'll obey me, and like it, minx." He drew her against him for a bruising kiss. "Now get back to the house and wait for me."

Elly took a quick step back. "I won't marry you," she vowed recklessly, anger and elation warring within her.

Lucien cast her a confident grin as he turned away. "Yes you will," he said complacently. "Because if you don't, I'll put on my ghostly garb and carry you off. Now go. I have other business to attend to at the moment."

Elly lay on her bed, staring up at the ceiling with brooding eyes. Ten days, she thought, and there had been no word from Lucien. She knew he was in London preparing the case against Marcus, but how long could it take to write a simple message? Lord Havermale and Sir Nigel had taken the time to visit her last week when they'd returned briefly to Brighton, and even the prince, busy as he must be, had sent her a bouquet of flowers thanking her for her "spirited assistance." But from Lucien there'd been only an ominous silence.

Perhaps he was already regretting his impetuous

declaration, she decided, turning on her side and tucking her hand beneath her cheek. They barely knew each other, and doubtlessly it was only propinquity that had led him to believe he was in love with her. He was a marquess, and he would certainly look for someone whose birth and position equalled his. Someone like Miranda, although it looked as if she and Henry would make a match of it. He'd already written her father, and there was talk of a December marriage.

Odder still, she'd had a letter from Jessica that morning describing Twyford in glowing terms, even praising his stand on a recent vote in Parliament; a reversal in opinion that had Elly shaking her head in wonder. Well, at least *some* good has come out of all this, she thought sniffing back hurt tears. She supposed she would have to content herself with that.

She was so wrapped in her own dark thoughts that it took some time for the eerie sounds to penetrate. At first she put them down to the wind whistling down the chimney or even wishful thinking, but when they continued she raised her head from the pillow and began glancing about her. What on earth . . . ?

"Mrs. Magney?" She sat up in bed, drawing the sheets up to her chin as she searched the darkness for some sign of the ghost. "Is that you?"

When the glowing shape stepped out of the shadows her heart began bumping furiously, and she nervously wet her lips. She was about to call out for Henry when a familiar chuckle reached her ears. "Hoyden, did I not warn you what would happen if you disobeyed me?"

"Lucien!" Elly scrambled out from beneath the sheets, forgetting all sense of propriety as she rushed into his arms. He pulled her into a passionate embrace, but when he would have kissed

250

her she jerked back her head with a laugh.

"Oh, no you don't, you forward creature," she said, giving his mask a playful tug. "I may find Old Jenks a perfectly delightful fellow, but I fear my fiancé would take it amiss were he to find us like this."

"I would take it more than amiss, my love," Lucien responded, pulling the mask from his head and grinning down at her in delight. "In fact, if I ever do find you kissing another man he had best be a ghost, else he soon will be."

"Tyrant." She slipped her arms about him, lifting her face to his provocatively.

"Minx." He brushed his lips across her nose, then claimed her mouth in a deep, burning kiss.

Elly surrendered at once, her anger and earlier trepidation forgotten as she gave herself to the man she loved with all of her heart. His mouth was urgent against her own, and when his tongue sought entrance she granted it gladly.

"I love you, Elinore," Lucien groaned, sliding his lips down her neck to the tempting hollow of her throat. "I missed you so much! A dozen different times I wanted to say to hell with everything and come to you, but I could not. Do you forgive me?"

When he held her like this Elly would forgive him anything, a sentiment she was far too wise to utter. Instead she kissed him passionately, showing him with deeds what she could not express in words. When Lucien drew back a second time, his face was flushed with desire.

"I think, my sweet, that 'tis time we were sensible. Henry is waiting for us in his study. Hurry and dress so that we can join him."

"Henry?"

"Certainly, you don't think I would approach you without first obtaining his permission, do you?" He took masculine satisfaction in the languid light shimmering in her soft blue eyes. "Meanwhile we had best get out of your bedchamber before we are compromised beyond all hope of redemption."

"Henry heard from you and he never told me?" Elly demanded, annoyance diffusing the warm glow of love.

"At my request," Lucien clarified, kissing the pout from her lips. "This courtship of ours may have been highly unconventional from start to finish, but I mean to do this one thing right. Now hurry, the sooner we have your brother's blessing the sooner we can post the banns."

"I haven't said I'll marry you," Elly reminded him, although there was little doubt in her mind but that she would do just that. "How do I know you aren't making up to me just to get your hands on Seagate? You have already shown there is no end to the lengths you will go to to get what you want."

"Because I already have Seagate," he answered easily, pulling her back into his arms for another kiss. "Henry has promised to sell it to me the moment he and Lady Miranda are wed. They will be living in her London home for most of the year, and after having met our fearsome ghost, he seems most eager to be shed of the place."

The mention of the ghost brought a troubled frown to Elly's face. "Lucien . . . that night, here in my room, you . . . you saw her too, didn't you?"

Lucien nodded, knowing this was something they had to settle between them. "And have felt her many times before," he said, cupping her face with loving hands. "At first I refused to believe it, but now I am glad to have proof of the nether world."

"You are? Why?"

"Because it means there are some things that endure beyond death," he said simply, brushing a thumb against the bow of her lips. "And that means

252

I can look forward to loving you through all of eternity . . . and beyond."

His moving declaration brought tears to Elly's eyes. "As I will love you, my darling," she said, pressing her lips to the palm of his hand. "And I would be happy to be your bride."

They embraced again, revelling in the love and passion that would be theirs always. As she returned Lucien's burning kiss Elly sent a silent prayer winging heavenwards, thanking the fates for the love she had found. Lucien is right, she decided complacently; some things do endure beyond infinity. And how glad she was to find it so.

Mrs. Magney stood in the shadows, her arms folded across her ample belly as she watched the embracing couple. Well, it is about time, she thought with an approving nod. Any fool could see the two of them were meant for each other. Maybe now things would get back to normal. Good. She always liked things tidy in her house.

A Memorable Collection of Regency Romances

BY ANTHEA MALCOLM AND VALERIE KING

THE COUNTERFEIT HEART   (3425, $3.95/$4.95)
by Anthea Malcolm

Nicola Crawford was hardly surprised when her cousin's betrothed disappeared on some mysterious quest. Anyone engaged to such an unromantic, but handsome man was bound to run off sooner or later. Nicola could never entrust her heart to such a conventional, but so deucedly handsome man. . . .

THE COURTING OF PHILIPPA   (2714, $3.95/$4.95)
by Anthea Malcolm

Miss Philippa was a very successful author of romantic novels. Thus she was chagrined to be snubbed by the handsome writer Henry Ashton whose own books she admired. And when she learned he considered love stories completely beneath his notice, she vowed to teach him a thing or two about the subject of love. . . .

THE WIDOW'S GAMBIT   (2357, $3.50/$4.50)
by Anthea Malcolm

The eldest of the orphaned Neville sisters needed a chaperone for a London season. So the ever-resourceful Livia added several years to her age, invented a deceased husband, and became the respectable Widow Royce. She was certain she'd never regret abandoning her girlhood until she met dashing Nicholas Warwick. . . .

A DARING WAGER   (2558, $3.95/$4.95)
by Valerie King

Ellie Dearborne's penchant for gaming had finally led her to ruin. It seemed like such a lark, wagering her devious cousin George that she would obtain the snuffboxes of three of society's most dashing peers in one month's time. She could easily succeed, too, were it not for that exasperating Lord Ravenworth. . . .

THE WILLFUL WIDOW   (3323, $3.95/$4.95)
by Valerie King

The lovely young widow, Mrs. Henrietta Harte, was not all inclined to pursue the sort of romantic folly the persistent King Brandish had in mind. She had to concentrate on marrying off her penniless sisters and managing her spendthrift mama. Surely Mr. Brandish could fit in with her plans somehow . . .

THE ROMANCES OF LORDS AND LADIES
IN JANIS LADEN'S REGENCIES

BEWITCHING MINX (2532, $3.95)

From her first encounter with the Marquis of Penderleigh when he had mistaken her for a common trollop, Penelope had been incensed with the darkly handsome lord. Miss Penelope Larchmont was undoubtedly the most outspoken young lady Penderleigh had ever known, and the most tempting.

A NOBLE MISTRESS (2169, $3.95)

Moriah Landon had always been a singularly practical young lady. So when her father lost the family estate over a game of picquet, she paid the winner, the notorious Viscount Roane, a visit. And when he suggested the means of payment—that she become Roane's mistress—she agreed without a blink of her eyes.

SAPPHIRE TEMPTATION (3054, $3.95)

Lady Serena was commonly held to be an unusual young girl—outspoken when she should have been reticent, lively when she should have been demure. But there was one tradition she had not been allowed to break: a Wexley must marry a Gower. Richard Gower intended to teach his wife her duties—in every way.

SCOTTISH ROSE (2750, $3.95)

The Duke of Milburne returned to Milburne Hall trusting that the new governess, Miss Rose Beacham, had instilled the fear of God into his harum-scarum brood of siblings. But she romped with the children, refused to be cowed by his stern admonitions, and was so pretty that he had the devil of a time keeping his hands off her.

THE TIMELESS PASSION OF HISTORICAL ROMANCES

FOREVER AND BEYOND (3115, $4.95)
by Penelope Neri

Newly divorced and badly in need of a change, Kelly Michaels traveled to Arizona to forget her troubles and put her life in order again. But instead of letting go of her past, Kelly was haunted by visions of a raven-haired Indian warrior who drove her troubles away with long, lingering kisses and powerful embraces. Kelly knew this was no phantom, and he was calling her back to another time, to a place where they would find a chance to love again.

To the proud Commanche warrior White Wolf, it seemed that a hundred years had passed since the spirit of his wife had taken flight to another world. But now, the spirits had granted him the power to reclaim her from the world of tomorrow, and White Wolf vowed to hold her in his arms again, to bring her back to the place where their love would last forever.

TIGER ROSE (3116, $4.95)
by Sonya T. Pelton

Promised in wedlock to a British aristocrat, sheltered Daniella Rose Wingate accompanied the elegant stranger down the aisle, determined to forget the swashbuckling adventurer who had kissed her in the woodland grove and awakened her maidenly passions. The South Carolina beauty never imagined that underneath her bridegroom's wig and elegant clothing, Lord Steven Landaker was none other than her own piratical Sebastian—known as The Tiger! She vowed never to forgive the deception—until she found herself his captive on the high seas, lost in the passionate embrace of the golden-eyed captor and lover.

MONTANA MOONFIRE (3263, $4.95)
by Carol Finch

Chicago debutante had no choice: she had to marry the stuffy Hubert Carrington Frazier II, the mate her socially ambitious mother had chosen for her. Yet when the ceremony was about to begin, the suntanned, towering preacher swung her over his shoulder, dumped her in his wagon and headed West! She felt degraded by this ordeal, until the "preacher" silenced her protests with a scorching kiss.

Dru Sullivan owed his wealth and very life to his mining partner Caleb Flemming, so he could hardly refuse when the oldtimer asked him to rescue his citified daughter and bring her home to Montana. Dru dreaded having to cater to some prissy city miss—until he found himself completely alone with the violet-eyed beauty. One kiss convinced the rugged rancher not to deny Tori the wedding-night bliss that he was sure she would never forget!

Available wherever paperbacks are sold, or order direct from the Publisher. Send cover price plus 50¢ per copy for mailing and handling to Zebra Books, Dept. 3727, 475 Park Avenue South, New York, N.Y. 10016. Residents of New York and Tennessee must include sales tax. DO NOT SEND CASH. For a free Zebra/ Pinnacle catalog please write to the above address.